A
TASTE
of
BETRAYAL

A
TASTE
of
BETRAYAL

A Faith Clarke Mystery

Julie Bates

For my family who keep me grounded and encourage me to follow my dreams.

Praise for the Faith Clarke Mysteries

"An absorbing, fast-paced, and contemplative whodunit."—*Kirkus Reviews*

"[Cry of the Innocent] was an enjoyable read, the character of Faith was well drawn."—Jim's Books and Reading

"*Cry of the Innocent* is a very satisfying debut to a promising mystery series! I can't wait to read more about Faith Clarke's adventures! I recommend this novel for fans of *In the Midst of Shadows*, *Death of the Dance*, and *Cape Menace!*" — History from a Woman's Perspective

Chapter One

Spring 1775

A rock exploded through the front window, shattering the stillness of the night. Titus jumped from where he had been placing wood in the fireplace to warm the taproom before the tavern's guests came down later for breakfast. Shards of glass rained down inside covering the floor with diamond sharp fragments waiting to cut unwary flesh. A chilly draft rushed in brushing icy fingers down his exposed skin, raising goosebumps that traveled over his body, reminding him of the capriciousness of spring. Titus cursed softly when his candle went out, leaving him in the shadowy darkness where every sound was magnified, whether he wished it or not.

Outside, the wind roared as it had throughout the night, a mighty ocean of sound that swept through town and wreaked havoc on objects too fragile to withstand its wrath. It had kept waking him, reminding him of a nightmarish hurricane he had endured as a child. Never fond of storms, sleep eluded him even when resting beside his wife Olivia in their rooms above the outdoor kitchen behind the tavern. He smiled remembering how lovely she looked with her ebony curls spread out against the pillow. She would not have objected had he chosen to waken her with a kiss and drown out the storm with passion, but he knew how hard she worked every day in the kitchen below them. Rather than disturb her from the rest she needed, he had risen and dressed in the darkness, and hoped work would distract him from the nightmares that had plagued him through the night.

The restless spring weather masked the approach of the rock thrower. It also made it difficult to see if the perpetrator lingered outside. The gaping hole revealed darkness and nothing else. Titus edged toward the broken window, using the interior shadows to hide his approach. Fortunately, his dark skin made him hard to see, which meant the assailant hadn't realized a witness was about.

Opening the front door of the tavern cautiously he stepped out onto the porch for a better look around. A loose board squeaked underneath his foot, causing him to freeze momentarily before he identified the noise. Nothing seemed to be stirring except the wind. The sun had yet to emerge over the horizon. Faint light glimmered intermittently from the gibbous moon, soon obliterated by dark clouds that continued to race across the sky. In the distance, someone was singing a ditty that involved bringing a friend a glass before another roar of wind drowned him out. From the sounds of things, the fellow had had way too many of the latter. It was no night for anyone to be out.

Titus peered into the restless night looking for movement beyond that stirred by the temperamental air. The air stilled suddenly as if drawn in check by an unseen hand, providing a brief tableau of a landscape peopled more by spirits than the living. Titus shivered, grateful when the wind resumed. Down toward the Capitol Building, the light posts flickered like fireflies, made restless by the unrelenting wind. It was too early for the normal traffic of trade to be about. Folks who were up were just beginning their day or given the fading sounds of the singer, just ending it. Then there were those who chose this time for stealth.

As his eyes adjusted to the predawn darkness, he sidestepped the benches on either side of the narrow porch before he slipped down the steps and into the front yard. As the one man who worked regularly at the tavern, Titus felt responsible for keeping the women and children safe. In his left hand, a fireplace poker hung, in case he needed to defend himself. Titus knew better than to carry a gun. He had been free less than a year and intended to stay that way. Even defending himself with a firearm could cause panic in the

2

town. Having been enslaved most of his life had taught him the importance of caution. He hated the double standard as much as anyone but saw no point in hanging to prove it.

The night swallowed his quarry, all sound obscured by the rising roar of the wind as it swept through town, pushing leaves and twigs through the street in a riotous dance. Walking through the gates and around the side revealed nothing new. The horses in the barn were quiet. Had there been a stranger about, they would have been snorting and stomping. A yearling calf recently traded to the tavern to settle debt mooed plaintively, undoubtedly hoping for breakfast.

"Joshua will be out soon to feed you," he promised softly.

Reassured by the quiet, Titus turned to go back in. He still had tasks to accomplish before Mistress Clarke rose to help open the tavern for business. The window needed repair before the guests sleeping upstairs rose. Thankfully, the breaking glass hadn't disturbed anyone. Off in the distance, a rooster crowed, sending Solomon, the overly dominant bantam out of the enclosure where his hens slept to answer the challenge. Titus stepped back in, carefully latching the door. Behind him, the floorboards creaked, warning him he was no longer alone. Titus whirled about, poker ready.

Faith Clarke stood in the entrance of the main room, barefoot with a huge wool shawl wrapped around her shift. Hair fell about her shoulders in wild confusion, a state mirrored by the wideness of her eyes. "What happened? I heard a crash."

"Stay back, some idiot threw a rock through the window," Titus said as he held up his hands to warn her away. "You'll get cut by all this broken glass. It was probably some liquored up fool. I've already looked about; whoever did it is long gone." Titus hoped that was all it was. He walked over to the hearth and set down the poker, taking a stick broom in its place to sweep up the shards scattered on the floor.

Faith shivered as chilly gusts blew in through the broken pane; chilling her ankles and making the hair rise on exposed flesh. Grabbing the tinderbox by the mantle, she set about lighting a fire. She stared at the shattered front window of her tavern in dismay as Titus tidied the mess. Light from the growing flames glimmered off the jagged edges making them look like bestial teeth. Faith glared at the damage. Glass was expensive. It could be some time before it was possible to order another pane.

"I'll cover the hole with a board, Miss Faith. You best return to bed. I'll keep an eye out in case they return."

"The night watch needs summoning. They're supposed to keep an eye out for fires and hooligans." Faith said grimly. "It's nearly dawn, and we must prepare for our guests upstairs. I'm amazed someone hasn't come down to check on all that noise."

"I'm not," Titus responded. "Given all that's been going on, most folk would rather get about their business than get mixed up in anything that could cause trouble."

Faith grimaced. He had a point. The mood in town had turned tense. Patrick Henry's defiant cry of "Give me Liberty or Give me Death," in Richmond a few weeks ago had roused the populace, leaving everyone a little more on edge.

Faith acknowledged the truth of his words with a nod. "Go get the watch. I'll get dressed and begin our preparations for the day. Olivia is probably already up. It wouldn't hurt to check on her before you go."

Titus finished sweeping the glass into a pile. "Yes, ma'am." His tone made it clear he was unhappy leaving Faith alone. He knew all too well what happened when angry men drowned their common sense with cheap liquor. Titus' immense size tended to quell most men tempted toward violence in the tavern. He doubted anyone would be foolish enough to bother his wife. Olivia's kitchen was full of sharp knives and metal tools that she knew how to use. Her cool nerve had rattled him a time or two.

"I will be fine," Faith replied with more conviction than she felt. While she might wish otherwise, she was well aware of the rising emotions throughout the American Colonies. Within the walls of her establishment, she listened to the increasingly volatile rhetoric as she noted that the number of British troops in town seemed more visible. So far, the clashes had been small, but she knew that was not likely to last.

4

Faith Clarke, owner of Clarke Tavern, felt tension jab between her shoulder blades like a knife. Her friends at the *Virginia Gazette*, Will and Georgia, kept her informed of news within the colonies. Will frequently came in to deliver the latest edition of the newspaper and drink a tankard while he watched Faith work. She liked Will, but he was indentured to Georgia Clements for four more years, so he was not free to have a relationship with anyone, although it didn't keep him from supporting the Patriot cause. On rare occasions, Jeremy Butler, Washington's spy, came into the tavern or dropped by the kitchen to visit Titus and Olivia. Faith let Titus serve him while she pretended to ignore the Irishman, which amused him.

Faith returned to her room to dress. After pulling on long stockings and shoes, she hurriedly fastened her stays, before adding additional layers of petticoat and apron. She yelped as a pin jabbed her finger while fastening her bodice. After hurriedly finger combing her hair, she twisted and pinned it in place, before covering it and sailing out to relieve Titus.

He had used the time to sweep up shards of glass from the floor. His sherry brown eyes met hers before he spoke. "Do you want me to call Joshua to join you before I go?"

Faith shook her head. "Let your son get his sleep." The York's thirteen-year-old son had recovered from his abduction the previous year, but Faith knew he still struggled with nightmares and had little desire to engage with strangers. She had no need to add to his stress, which was why both she and Olivia agreed to wait one more year before seeking an apprenticeship for him.

Titus slipped out to return moments later with a representative of the watch. She recognized him as one of the town's coopers. He was shaped like the barrels he assembled day after day.

The middle-aged man checked the windows as he trudged along outside with Titus. "There are shoe prints in the ground, but there's no telling how long they've been there or who left them." He shook his head, which made his prominent jowls swing like an old dog. "I'm sorry you were disturbed, Mistress Clarke. It is likely some idiot full of too much rum. There are a few ships in on the river and those sailors get wild when they first get to town."

Faith's tone turned icy as she gestured at the damage. "That doesn't repair my window, nor does it relieve my fears. This is Williamsburg, Virginia's capital. Of all places, one should feel safe from ruffians."

The man shrugged. "No one can predict what men will do from one night to the next. There are not enough of us to cover the town from dusk to dawn. I will inform the other members of the watch to swing this way on patrol. That should keep the rascals from returning." He rocked back and forth on his heels as he took in her main room with its tidy wooden tables and chairs. The fire blazed fiercely in the grate, coloring the room in a warm glow. The flames rose and fell in a frantic dance as the chill breeze ebbed and flowed from the broken pane.

Faith suspected he would like to stay out of the chill and take in a brandy or two in the parlor, but she didn't offer him refreshment despite his pointed look toward her liquor cabinet. He smelled as if he had enjoyed a few tankards earlier in the evening. After he left, Faith and Titus worked together to restore order to the front room. Before long the room echoed with the tapping of his hammer, as he covered the broken window.

Olivia, along with Joshua and Faith's son Andrew, would be rising soon. It would take all of them to prepare for the day ahead. Their guests, asleep upstairs, would expect breakfast, as would the handful of men who came in regularly for food and news. Within a few hours, people would fill the room keeping them all busy. With any luck, some of them might have coins to pay their debts, although most paid with Virginia's paper dollars or with goods such as salt pork or potatoes.

"Let's finish getting ready," she told Titus as she examined the liquor supply. "Morning will be here soon enough."

He turned from checking the board he had placed over the hole in the window. "I'll get more wood after I check around the yard and make sure the gates are secure."

Outside the wind picked up in tempo to echo his words. Faith stood and watched clouds swirl across the sky, briefly obscuring the pale moon that did little to illuminate the night. As she looked east, light limed the edge of the horizon, promising the sun's return to the sky.

Movement caught her eye. Startled, she peered out the window. A large group of men crept through the sleeping town; some wore pale formal coats of British soldiers, while others wore the simple garb of sailors. The flickering candle of a streetlight revealed the red facings on their white uniforms, the colors of British marines. Her heart pounded as she watched them march down the road toward the Capitol and into town. This was not a group of sailors on leave; it was an organized company intent on creeping in unseen.

All thoughts of sleep evaporated as she watched them move stealthily toward the heart of town. Faith had heard rumors that the governor had been secretly visiting the Armory, checking guns and powder. Working in a tavern, she heard many things. She had hoped it was just talk.

As Faith edged back from the window, a soldier turned to watch as if he could see her. Faith froze until he turned back, his gaze elsewhere as he scanned the grounds while they continued down the road. She watched the wind drag at their coats, making some of the officers grab their tricorn hats. Before long, they disappeared from sight, fading into the shadows of the waning night.

Within what felt like moments, a series of shots peppered the night, obliterating the predawn calm. A muted boom told her that she had not been the only one to spot British soldiers creeping through town. An eerie glow appeared liming the edges of the capitol as it stood between them and the heart of town.

Titus joined her at the window. "Could there be a fire?" It was some distance away, but like all town dwellers, he feared uncontrolled flames.

Faith shook her head, jarred by what she had seen moments before. "I'm not sure." She hoped no one had set something ablaze. Given the wind, sparks would spread throughout town. Small explosions peppered the night, followed by a sudden repetitive throb.

"That's gunfire," Titus said grimly. "Hear those drums? That's a warning to the town; the British are up to something."

"At this hour?" Faith peered into the night to get a better look, but it was hard to see into town with the huge expanse of the Capitol blocking them from seeing further.

Will McKay rushed into the yard and up the steps to the porch, his chest heaving from effort. Titus opened the door to admit him. "The British are seizing our powder!" Dark auburn hair bounced across his shoulders in untidy curls, and a few loose pieces of straw drifted to the ground from his head. Faith suspected he had sprung from his bed in Georgia Clements's loft and run over. His shirt billowed out from the back where it had missed being tucked in. He leaned over, as he sought to catch his breath. "Troops are raiding the armory. They have a wagon from the Governor there. They're loading all our powder on it, while their sentries keep our folks out of the way. It looks like they plan to go east once they finish their thieving."

"East? Not toward the Governor's palace?" Titus looked dumbfounded, for a moment, before his face cleared with comprehension. "They're headed to the river. There's been a navy ship anchored out there. You need to inform the militia. We've got to stop them before they get the powder aboard the ship they must have waiting."

Will started to race off before Faith stopped him. "Grab a horse from the barn. You need every second to get the word out."

Titus followed them out to the porch and down the steps as if to follow. "I will saddle the black, he's the quickest. While I do that, you can button your breeches." He ran about, leaping over the picket fence with ease, before disappearing from view.

Will called out to him. "You need to get out your drum and let everyone know what's afoot." He glanced down, turning away from Faith to make some adjustments before a peppering of shots in the distance caused him to turn his head toward the Capitol. "Dunmore is a fool for doing this. Already the town is on edge, it will only take a spark to bring the rebellion to our doorstep. Men will not stand for it."

"And what of the women?" Faith responded sharply. "Do you see any wives and mothers sitting quietly while their loved ones risk their lives in this conflict?"

Will looked at her in surprise. "No offense intended. Although I thought you intended to stay neutral in this conflict."

"I wish there was no conflict and we could go back to our lives, but that is not going to happen. Whatever the future holds, it will change everything for all men and women within these colonies. There is no going back."

Will offered her a crooked smile, causing dimples to appear on either side. "You are right about that. I have to go rouse the militia. They may be able to stop this nonsense." The gentleness disappeared from his face as he looked into the darkness, the silence broken by muted shouts and the occasional shot.

An excited whinny interrupted them as Titus brought a horse around to the front, opening the gate gently while keeping a hand on the mare's reins. Her ears flicked as he whispered to her while stroking her back with his large gentle hands.

"That was fast," Will noted as he strode over to them. The mare eyed him but did not shy away. Will took the reins in one hand while running a hand comfortingly along her neck and shoulders. "That's a girl," he crooned. "We have a busy day ahead, but we'll get through it, my sweet, then there will be oats for you and a cool drink in the barn." He shot a glance over to the other man. "Do you always keep a horse at the ready?"

Titus shrugged. "It pays to be prepared."

"You're a good man. Freedom suits you."

"Freedom suits everyone, sir," Titus replied with a firm smile.

Will met his eyes before replying quietly. "So it does, Master York, so it does."

The sleek black mare's ears perked up, aware of strange sounds that permeated the night. Titus spoke softly to her and stroked her mane. "Ebony is quick, but a bit nervy. Give her a gentle touch and she'll respond."

Will nodded. "I'll take care of her, Titus. Thanks for the ride." He turned toward the gate, then turned back to look at Faith, who was nervously tucking a strand of hair into her cap. Their eyes met for a second before he leaned in to kiss her cheek before climbing into the saddle and racing off to warn the town.

Faith stood on the porch, hearing the hoof beats fade long after he had vanished from sight. The Scotsman had become a frequent and welcome presence at her tavern. She had come to look forward to seeing him come in to deliver broadsides for his mistress, Georgia Clements. If there were time, he would stay for a pint of ale. A few evenings a week, Will had brought a well-loved fiddle and played a few melodies to the delight of the patrons. He got along well with most everyone and helped Titus with some of the many repairs a busy tavern needed. She hoped he stayed out of range of the British. They would have no tolerance for his hotheaded rhetoric, and she did not want to lose anyone else close to her.

Titus faded into the velvet darkness of the night, around the back of the tavern. Within moments, the steady vibration of a drum broke the night; a sound picked up and echoed down the streets and into town.

Chapter Two

Voices filtered down the hallway from the main room of the tavern. A few days had passed since the governor had seized the powder and guns from the armory. Faith had watched as groups of local militia had entered the city, while British regulars had fallen back to the governor's mansion. Bits of gossip had drifted in with men wetting their throats with a tankard of ale. Drums sounded at odd hours adding to the unease she felt. Fiery debate continued unabated as it had since the first group of men crossed her threshold shortly after breakfast, led by her father-in-law, Ezra Moore. He had sweetened her temper at the disturbance with a small but solid bag of mixed coins and a half dozen bottles of wine. "My friend, Jefferson, assures me that these are prized by the French," he said as she gathered them in her arms. "I had some fine Spanish Madeira, but the governor claimed it. Otherwise, I would have acquired a few bottles for our cellars."

She nodded before handing half of them to Joshua, who went with her to the cellar to store them and lock them up safely from her patrons. Faith sent him back with a small keg of beer, before locking the cellar and following with a few bottles to take upstairs. She paused to catch her breath before delivering a fresh round of porter to where Titus stood watch over the bar.

"I'm not sure offering more drinks to this group is going to help keep the peace," He commented as he watched yet another man rise to revile Governor Dunmore's actions in detail and his ancestry in general.

Faith followed his gaze as it spanned the breadth of her main room. There were close to a dozen men seated in twos and threes at her tables. Some held tankards of short beer or ale, while a few, such as her father-in-law, sipped wine from her small collection of fine goblets. A farmer from outside town played cards with some young men Faith had seen in town, apprenticed to one of the shops, although she could not recollect which one. Near the fire, a man read a copy of the *Virginia Gazette.* Faith knew it was not the only one circulating the room although she hoped Georgia Clements's words were not too inflammatory. "Olivia will be ready to serve dinner soon. A good hearty stew with some of her bread should help soak up a lot of alcohol." She surrendered custody of the bottles to Titus, who locked them in the sturdy oak cabinet that served as a bar.

Ezra Moore sat where he could watch the rest of the room. Light reflected off his spectacles, concealing his eyes. With his wispy gray hair and genial half-smile, he resembled a plump, middle-aged cherub, rather than a shrewd trader of a variety of goods, as well as a well-to-do planter of tobacco. His plump cheeks were flushed pink, although it was unclear if this was from excitement or wine. Ezra had said little since his arrival that morning beyond dismissing his manservant to get a pint. Moore rose and circulated the room, murmuring pleasantries as he passed, offering sympathy to those who felt abused by the various burdens imposed by the king. Few realized how deeply Ezra had become involved in the cause of American Independence. She hadn't until he had paid off her debts with the understanding her tavern would also serve as a place to pass messages and keep horses ready for purposes he did not divulge. Now local merchants and farmers had filled her tables, mixed with members of the local militia. Angry murmuring peppered the conversations.

"They had no right," a blacksmith, his rolled-up sleeves revealing muscle from tending the forge, said as he pounded the table. "It's our powder, our guns. What will we do if the town is attacked by Indians or pirates?"

"I've heard the governor disabled our guns, too," another man chipped in.

"Well, maybe we need to go down to the governor's house and demand our powder back," one farmer said as he stood up unsteadily to face the gathering.

Faith leaned over to Titus to whisper. "He's had more than enough to drink."

Titus whispered back. "Maybe you need to mention to Master Moore that his followers may be getting too well-lubricated to act."

Ezra Moore rose and faced the crowd, which grew silent. "The powder is long gone, aboard a British naval ship. As for the governor, he remains hidden behind the gates of his residence, surrounded by armed men." He waited for his words to sink in. "In order to reach him, we must use our wits, our cunning, and our connections."

"Let's burn him out. That will show him he can't hide from us."

A few men cheered. Faith was disgusted. Having faced a fire herself not long ago, she found the suggestions horrifying. "And what of the small children living there? Would you punish innocent children for their father's sins? Perhaps it's time you went home until the liquor has cleared from your heads."

That quieted them, briefly, but long enough for her father-in-law to join her. "How long until you serve dinner?" he asked softly. "A full belly might soften their ire."

"I will go check with Olivia,"

He nodded, Faith left and went back to the kitchen; hoping revolution would not break out during her absence. As she approached, she could smell ham frying and coffee brewing. Stepping into the room, she called out to the other woman. "How long until we can serve? The men are getting restless."

"If you could lend a hand, it would be quicker," Olivia responded as she mixed ground corn to make a pot of mush.

Faith chopped onions and squash retrieved earlier from the root cellar to add to the stew that Olivia had begun and hung in a large iron pot over the fireplace for dinner. The large cauldron of meat, vegetables, and seasonings would cook for hours over the fire. They would stir it regularly to keep the bottom from burning. With luck, there would be enough to last through the afternoon. On the spider, a pot of bread cooked over the coals. Faith reached over and put more hot coals on the lid so it would cook evenly. The women worked in silence, each focused on the job at hand. Joshua, Olivia's son, spitted rabbits and placed them to roast over the fire.

Olivia handed her a platter of ham and biscuits. "We can start with this; the stew will be ready soon."

"Where did the ham come from?"

Olivia replied, "Master Crooks decided to settle his bill in pork. The cellar is full of smoked hams and shoulders."

Faith blinked. "How much did you get out of him?" Ever since Olivia had become an employee, her skills at getting payment for high tabs had become impressive. Faith let her handle some of the worst offenders.

Olivia smiled mysteriously. "Enough to cover a multitude of sins."

Faith grinned. "I had no idea he was ready to repent." She heard Olivia laugh as she shouldered the tray and took it up into the tavern to serve the men. She entered as Ezra was speaking to the group.

"Esteemed patriots of the American colonies," he intoned, his tenor surprisingly resonant in the crowded space. "The time for doing nothing has passed. We must act and let Governor Dunmore know that such acts of aggression will not be tolerated in these colonies."

The men bellowed their approval, holding their tankards in salute and shouting. "Here, here!"

Titus took the heavy tray from Faith's shoulder and turned to begin passing out plates of food. Faith began to quietly put away the heavier liquors. "Don't give them anything more than short beer," she whispered. Titus nodded his understanding, before hoisting the heavy tray to his shoulder to make his way through the room.

"Even as we speak, representatives of our fair town are meeting with Peyton Randolph. Master Randolph is a man respected throughout the colonies and is one of the few who the governor listens to."

Faith hoped her father-in-law knew what he was doing. Ezra Moore had saved her business last year, but at a cost. Clarke Tavern now served as a meeting place for those whose mind ran to revolution, a concept that still made Faith queasy. Many days she had looked out to see Titus waiting at her stable. He met men on horseback who never crossed her threshold. In the past few months, she had learned not to ask questions. As Ezra had told her during one of his impromptu visits, ignorance was her best defense against the British.

His face had looked earnest as he rose from inspecting the blossoms on one of the many pea vines climbing determinedly up one of the lines she and Oliva had strung to the fence. "Your best defense is your lack of knowledge. You are but a poor widow trying to make a living and raise her son. No gentleman wants to be seen as bullying a vulnerable young woman."

Faith rolled her eyes. Ezra had suggested she keep a pistol in her parlor desk, where it would be easy to retrieve. He didn't tell her directly, but Faith suspected he had a man somewhere near her business to keep an eye on things.

Faith tried not to think how close she had come to facing the harshness of British justice last year. The noose allowed no reprieve for the condemned. Even though she knew no one threatened her now, Faith still woke many nights trembling and covered in sweat, her ears sharply attentive to any unfamiliar noise.

As Ezra, then others spoke, she and Titus continued working the room, serving food and taking up tankards. Soon enough, bellies full of food and spirits turned the once fiery room of patriots into men more interested in wandering home for a nap.

She yawned as she watched Ezra deep in discussion with his cohorts; some of them undoubtedly part of the militia that had failed to stop the British from removing powder from the Magazine.

She drew close enough to hear the words of Ezra's companion.

"Our company is gathering, sir. They plan to march tonight to the governor's mansion and demand an explanation from Dunmore."

Moore's eyebrows rose. "Do you believe he will deign to answer?"

"He'd better," The man replied. "People are angry and frightened. There's no telling what they will do."

"Give our representatives a little time. This situation may be solved peacefully. Master Randolph still has some influence over the governor; maybe he can reason with him."

"Peyton Randolph is probably at home in bed," the man said in disgust. "He's not known for energetic action."

"He is head of the Burgesses and a very reasonable man," Ezra replied. "People respect him and will listen to him better than anyone. I have met with him once and will be doing so again tomorrow. He has requested to speak to Lord Dunmore. He's the most likely representative to be received. Hopefully, the governor will consent to meet with a small group of reasonable-minded men."

Faith kept her voice level. "The governor's temper has been notably ill of late. He won't like being questioned."

Ezra shook his head. "That's putting it mildly. He represents royal interests and diplomacy has never been his gift. It will take someone gifted with words to convince him returning the powder is in his own best interests. Perhaps we can persuade him that seizing our best means of defense against attacks by the natives only serves to inflame the populace."

Titus' voice was dry. "He may be more concerned about what that inflamed populace would do to him, given arms and a few barrels of powder."

"I would not go around sharing that idea," Ezra said quietly. "No matter how tempting the notion. Tempers are inflamed enough without suggesting a means of expression." Ezra's voice dropped to barely a whisper. "You may want to close early tonight and the next few. Tempers are high and ale has been flowing."

Faith looked at him. "I've dealt with drunks before. I operate a tavern."

He shook his head. "You've not dealt with anything like this. This town will be full of angry men, looking for someone to punish. There doesn't have to be a reason, and you've no husband to protect you."

Faith raised an eyebrow. "I can manage. I have for over a year now."

Ezra's voice was mild. "I meant no offense, Faith."

"I know. Titus and I will keep an eye on things, and I will warn Olivia."

Ezra patted her hand. "I'd best do what I can to calm the crowd." He turned back toward the men within the tavern. "I go to prepare for what tomorrow brings. Now is the time to look after your wives and children, make sure they are ready for when we must act. Who's with me?" A roar of assent echoed through the room. He headed toward the front door, taking a crowd with him. Within the hour, the tavern's main room cleared. Faith bolted the door once the last one exited. There was plenty of time to open it later for the supper crowd. She picked up abandoned tankards and dishes, left by men hurrying out to join their comrades. Normally Faith's son Andrew would sweep, but both he and Olivia's son Joshua were busy tending the livestock. Grabbing the broom from its resting place, she tackled the floor, while Titus straightened chairs and tables

"Do you want me to stay here, just in case of trouble?" He gestured at the deserted main room.

"No. We're a good distance from the magazine, much less the armed camp the governor has made of Tryon Palace. If anyone plans trouble, it will be there. I doubt anyone will come here to cause a ruckus." "If they want to start something, I have Jon's Brown Bess in my room."

Titus raised his eyebrows. "You sure you want to fire that in here?"

Faith hesitated before answering. "I prefer not to fire it at all, but if that's what it takes to protect us, I will."

"If you're sure, then I'll get to chopping more wood." The large man turned to walk down the hall to the rear door, to the yard, and to the outdoor kitchen where his wife, Olivia, would be preparing for the next day.

Faith went as far as the back porch casting her eyes about the yard. Already the angle of the afternoon sun cast part of the house into shadows. A slender maple sent out tender green leaves while seedpods whirly gigged across the ground whenever a breeze stirred them. Last night's weather had left several on the ground. The sound of voices came from the open kitchen door. Joshua and Andrew sat at a bench outside busily scrubbing Olivia's cookpots with ashes and vinegar.

Titus spoke to the boys as he strode toward the chopping block. Soon the sound of an axe striking wood rang through the air. For the most part, the day was over. Within a few hours, they would serve a cold supper of leftovers from dinner, as well as drinks to their guests and anyone who dropped by, and then hopefully, the night would pass peacefully.

Faith heard nothing the next day from Ezra about his meeting, although she heard plenty about Governor Dunmore, most of it rude commentary about his origins. By the second day, men were talking about the increased presence of British sailors at the governor's mansion, guarding him and his family. The lack of information was driving her mad, enough that she asked Titus directly what he knew.

Titus sat at the table in the kitchen, drinking a large tankard of short beer. Sweat made his shirt stick to his back as well as gave his face a shiny glow. Wood shavings sprinkled down his shirt and breeches. He took his time, taking a few more swallows before carefully placing the tankard on the table. "The last I heard, Ezra was part of a delegation going to talk to Governor Dunmore regarding the taking of the powder and guns from the armory, but that was day before yesterday. I've heard nothing since." He rose. "If you will excuse me, Mistress Faith, I have some harnesses to mend." He stepped out into the spring sunshine, walking steadily toward the barn out back.

Faith debated calling on her in-laws but decided against it. There was plenty to keep her busy here. She had a business to run and couldn't afford to dally in politics, no matter how curious she was. She filled her apron with peas from a basket in the kitchen before going outside where the air was more temperate. Faith paused to wipe the sweat from her brow. After all the cooking of the day, the kitchen was hot enough to be its own oven. She propped open the door, using a rock to keep it open. Sitting down on a bench nearby, Faith began shelling peas for the next day. After filling a bowl, she looked up to see Jeremy Butler striding toward her, his fair, corn silk hair tied neatly behind his head.

"Mistress Clarke," he bowed gracefully before her.

"Master Butler," she replied. Faith looked around him but saw no sign of his frequent partner, the unnerving Athena. "Where is...?"

"Elsewhere, my lady. She stays busy." He grinned at her look. Butler was well aware of the contentious beginning of their relationship. That he found it funny irritated Faith.

He glanced about, his silver-gray eyes restless as he took in her backyard, occupied only by the boys pretending to pull weeds from the garden while they eavesdropped. "We need to speak privately. Shall we visit your private room?" He stuck his head inside the kitchen door to greet Olivia and stepped out with a tray containing two goblets and a demijohn of her good French wine.

Faith frowned. Someone in the house had obviously known he was coming. She set her partially filled bowl down with the remaining pods beside it. The room was unoccupied, which she was sure he knew. She followed him down the path to the door and followed him inside. Although some months had passed since its resurrection, it still smelled of fresh timber and the dried lavender she suspected Olivia had placed inside. After last year's murder and fire, she still hesitated to enter it. Outside a mockingbird cried as if commenting on her dilemma. The room was dark compared with the light outside. Shadows cast dark pools on the floor recalling the violence of another time.

Butler strode inside and sat the tray at the small square table just inside.. She already knew Butler preferred French to local brews of Scuppernong or Muscatine grapes.

Faith took the other seat and let Butler pour them both a glass. Sunlight from the window hit the goblets, turning the contents molten gold. She lifted the glass and inhaled the rich, fruity aroma before sipping it. "I think this came from my cellar. Ezra typically sends a few bottles over when he gets a shipment in." Paying in wine or goods was simpler given the dearth of coins in the colonies. The British stranglehold on currency had caused much ire among those engaged in trade. Ezra didn't say specifically, but Faith assumed the steady supply of liquor was to cover expenses for his use of her tavern to entertain and meet people he didn't wish to receive at his home.

Butler looked faintly amused but didn't reply. He gave her a moment to savor her glass before speaking. "You are aware of the events playing out over the past few days."

She nodded before answering. "Governor Dunmore has seen fit to hand Williamsburg's powder and guns over to the British, regardless of how the inhabitants of this town feel."

Butler's eyes met hers. "He feared it would be used against him when the rebellion moves south. There is a war coming, Mistress Clarke, the likes of which you have never seen. England will never grant these colonies freedom without the shedding of blood. For all the posturing of learned men, we all know the time rapidly comes when each of us will have to take up arms. We all will have a part to play in the war for independence. There is no room for neutrality." He paused to pour wine for himself and Faith. Pale gold liquid poured from the bottle, the faint scent of summer grapes perfuming the air. He raised a glass, "To Virginia."

"To Virginia," she agreed before taking a sip. The wine slid down her throat like fine silk.

"My interest is information. To that end, I associate with men I despise and commit acts that the decent prefer not to acknowledge. Regardless of personal delicacies, I act to promote what I feel is the greater good, freedom for my country."

"You sound like my father-in-law," Faith said.

Butler paused to sip his wine. "I respect Ezra. He uses reason where many are driven by passion or fear. He is that rare commodity, an honorable man. That's why he is so invaluable in meeting with our impetuous royal governor."

"Do you think Governor Dunmore will return the guns and powder?"

Butler shook his head. "That would be too risky for him. My guess is he will issue a pithy proclamation saying it was in our best interests." He snorted in derision. "He's forgetting that these same men he believes so gullible are the same that fought alongside him during his altercation with the Shawnee last fall. He's a fool to antagonize them with his bluster."

Faith looked at him. "You don't think much of him."

"I don't think much of Royal Governors. It's a dirty system where the King grants favors to the gentry regardless of their lack of qualifications."

Faith sighed. Her head was starting to hurt. "We've always had a royal governor. All the colonies do what else would we have?"

Butler swirled his wine, watching the liquid move in the glass. "A governor of our choosing, Mistress Clarke. But to the matter at hand, you have a tavern within a stone's throw of the capital, where all kinds of men come for a meal and some respite. I've even seen a few lively games of dice at your tables. I was unaware that Quakers tolerated gambling."

Faith rolled her eyes. "I run a business. As long as no trouble is stirred up, I see no harm in it. Titus has been urging me to sell theater tickets as well."

Butler nodded. "It would increase your revenue. Mistress Vobe and Mistress Campbell do it in their establishments." He turned serious. "Already the British have come down harshly on Boston. You need to keep an ear out. I've seen British regulars here, pay attention to what they say and do. Ezra said you were to be trusted."

"Ezra has always been kind to me." Faith said. "But we are not here to discuss my father-in-law." She set down her empty glass and shook her head when he offered to refill it.

"You operate a tavern in close proximity to the capitol building. Not only that, but you have been careful not to voice an opinion in this conflict, which means men from both sides come here for a meal or a drink."

"You wish me to spy." Faith was dumbfounded. How had she gotten into such a mess?

"I wish you to listen," Butler said gently. "I have no intention of sending a widow with a child where there is great danger. However, you could do your country a great service by remembering what you hear within these walls."

Faith was silent for a few moments pondering the suggestion. Her eyes saw dust moats floating in a ray of sunlight emanating from a window. Within the room, the shadows dominated, growing as time passed. She'd known that Ezra's payment of her debt would come with a price, but she had hoped it would be minimal. Defying the crown came with a cost. The British were not shy when it came to executing those who defied the crown. Thinking about it kept her awake nights. For so long she had tried to walk the fine line of neutrality with little success. All those she loved and trusted believed in liberty, as did she. The time for neutrality had passed. "And if I do hear something of interest, how would I contact you?"

Butler's eyes met hers. "When you have a message for me, put a blue cloth in your front window and someone will find you." He fixed his pale eyes upon her. "Make no mistake, Mistress Clarke, once you cast your lot with me, there is no room for second thoughts. Your actions will help the cause of your country, but the British will regard you as a traitor should you be discovered."

Faith breathed quietly. "I have a son to think of. I will not go skulking in the night, like a burglar, doing things that will send me to the gallows."

Jeremy grinned, although his eyes glittered like a steel blade. "They don't hang women, they strangle and burn them. It's a very messy business." He raised a hand to silence her response. "I have people who are far better at skulking than you appear to be Mistress Clarke. Your task is simple. Serve your guests and keep your ears open. You have a well-stocked liquor cabinet and well-lubricated men talk. You merely need to tune your delicate ears to the tone of the conversations about you and relay what you deem useful to Will or Ezra. They will get it to me." He slanted an eyebrow and said dryly. "Not that I think you're a Tory, but I don't think you need to know where to find me."

Faith glared at him. He knew that Ezra had bailed out her tavern last year in exchange for a few favors. It was apparently time to call in a mark.

"Does Ezra know about this?'

Firelight silvered Butler's fair hair as it lightly gilded his skin, giving him a slightly unworldly appearance. "He suggested it. Ezra saw the potential in your little establishment ages ago. I dare say he may have been an influence on your late husband, to take up this trade." He looked about the small room, taking in the white-washed walls and stone fireplace. Sconces with unlit tapers hung from the wall, while on either side of the mantle a pair of stuffed chairs sat, waiting for someone to relax by the fire once it was lit. A tidy stack of logs lay near the hearth. It was not elegant, but it was clean and comfortable.

Faith was speechless. She had wondered for a long time why Jon had chosen tavern keeping, of all things, after deciding farming was not for him. He had never shared why and his death seven months after their arrival in Williamsburg had permanently silenced any chances for her to discover more. Butler's words made her wonder.

He watched her. His pale eyes reminded her of a cat eyeing a mouse. One hand cradled a glass of wine; the other was out of sight under the edge of the table.

"I'm not sure what would be useful to you." She said at last.

"You will know when you hear it. You have an uncommonly sharp mind, Faith Clarke. Don't be afraid to use it."

Faith pondered his words. She knew he was right, battle lines were being drawn within the town and throughout the colonies. The discord between colonials and the British was becoming impossible to ignore. But if she were caught . . . Faith drew in a shaky breath. "You know what will happen if I'm caught."

Butler caught her glance. His tone turned ruthless. "It's far too late to claim innocence now, Faith. You know your father-in-law uses this tavern to receive messages and send them on. If that's discovered, no one will relieve you of culpability. Ezra trusts you more than he does his wife. Your only choice is to help defeat the British so we can be free of King George's yoke."

The pound of feet outside caused them both to rise and face the door as it opened. Butler moved in front of Faith as he unsheathed a knife and held it at the ready.

Joshua, Titus and Olivia's teenage son, ran inside. "Mistress Clarke!"

He leaned over as his chest heaved to catch his breath. "You best come quickly, Master Ezra is dying."

Chapter Three

"How?" Butler lowered the knife but did not sheath it. Joshua towered a solid five inches over him, but the spy dominated the room.

Joshua shook his head. "Don't know, but he took sick night before last. Mistress Eugenia and Master Louis seem alright for now, but the doctor says to keep a check on everyone. He thinks it might be the cholera. Master Ezra called him a fool and sent him out. Nothing Mistress Genia does helps. She keeps dosing him with this and that, but he just gets worse. He called her a witch last night and told her to leave him be. This morning he asked for you. He hollered out the window at me to fetch you. Master Ezra says someone poisoned him. Deborah tells me that's what he says over and over."

Butler interrupted, "Who is Deborah?"

Joshua flushed. "Just a girl. She helps out in the house." He stared at his feet for a few seconds.

Butler studied him a moment. "Is she trustworthy?"

"Oh, yes sir. She knows everything that goes on, but she don't say nothing."

"Just to you," Butler said drily.

Joshua nodded. His ears turned ruddy as he studied his feet in apparent fascination.

Faith shot Butler a quelling glance. "I'm sure she's a lovely person, Joshua. Is there anything else we need to know?"

He looked up, horror on his face. "It's something awful ma'am. He can't keep anything down. There's blood all over the place." He shuddered. "No one should suffer like that."

Faith stood frozen in shock, trying to process the information. Why did Ezra think he was poisoned? It didn't make any sense. Everyone liked and respected him. "Why would anyone…?"

Olivia had entered the room quietly behind her son. Her features were unreadable as she listened. Her eyes met Faith's, "Just go. Ask questions later. I'll take care of things here."

Joshua called after her. "They sent a carriage for you, Miss Faith. It's just outside the gate."

Exiting the room, Faith stared blindly into the yard for a moment before spotting the carriage in the main street. She started as Jeremy Butler moved beside her. Neither spoke as they hurried across the yard and through the wooden gate in the fence that kept her side and back yard private.

Faith shivered as the wind penetrated the sleeves of her dress. She thought wistfully of the heavy wool short cloak on a hook inside her room in the tavern but did not pause for it. The Moore's footman handed her up into the carriage as Butler climbed in beside her. No sooner was the door closed than they took off for the grand house across town.

The jolting of the carriage threatened to throw her to the floorboards. Faith braced herself against the seat. Outside sounds permeated the interior of the cab; the clack of horseshoes as travelers passed, the cries of animals mingled with the calls of merchants at the market. All too soon, the carriage rolled to a stop. She heard the footman hop down to the ground. Within moments, the door swung open. Butler jumped out without waiting for the footman and raced ahead, swiftly disappearing around the house.

Faith accepted the footman's hand to step down outside the wrought iron gate. It stood ajar, as if the last person to pass through had been in too much a hurry to pull it closed.

Faith knocked once before opening the door herself. No one came out to see who she was or what her business might be. She paused outside the parlor, hearing the murmur of men's voices, her brother-in-law's among them. Voices drifted down the stairs in loud, angry waves shattering the hushed quiet of the house.

Her mother-in-law's voice was unmistakable. It was not until she had climbed up the main staircase and stepped onto the landing that she recognized the other voice as Jeremy Butler. As she approached the door of the Moores' bedroom, a short, stout man of middle years exited, almost running into Faith as he barreled past.

"Don't come back," Butler called after him. "You're no help whatsoever." Behind him, Eugenia sputtered like a leaky kettle.

"Dr. Ball is one of the best physicians in Williamsburg. You have no right to come here and disturb us like this. My husband is ill and needs help."

Faith stepped into the room, doing her best to ignore the smells of sweat, vomit, and blood. A basin of rusty fluid had been set on a table near the huge canopied bed. She could see droplets on the coverlet and floor, where a lancet lay discarded on the rug.

"Why are you here?" Eugenia snapped at her. "Do you want to carry this foul disease home? Go home before it's too late." She moved toward the door only to be blocked by Butler. "I need to recall the doctor before he leaves."

"That old bloodletter is more likely to kill him than heal him." Butler's voice was grim. Downstairs a door shut emphatically.

"There's little to be done for cholera," Eugenia informed him, "other than purge it from the body. That's what every doctor who has come has said. Dr. Ball is one of the most respected doctors in Williamsburg. Ezra refuses to believe any of them. He raves nonsense as if the fever has touched his brain."

"What makes you sure it's cholera?" Butler asked. "I've seen no signs of it in town. Believe me, if there were a cholera epidemic, the word would be all over town."

"All the doctors say..."

Butler interrupted. "How many have treated cholera? To my recollection, it's not been in the colonies in all the years I've been here, though I've seen it in Jamaica and on ships."

'What is it then?" Eugenia snapped. "Tell me, so I can help him."

"Poison." A voice whispered from the bed. A pale hand waved Faith closer. "Come here, I need to speak to you."

She approached the side of the bed, as both Butler and Eugenia fell back to give her space. "Someone is trying to stop the revolution here in Williamsburg. They have killed me and perhaps my compatriots. Find who did this to me. The cause is at risk." He coughed, wiping away blood from his mouth. "I don't know who else has been felled. You must do this to save the cause."

"Who did you meet with?" Faith asked.

Ezra's voice was little more than a whisper. "Members of the Common Hall drafted a letter to Dunmore, which a representative delivered to him. Later, he agreed to meet with a small number of us. He swore he had acted to protect the town and would return the powder within half an hour should the need arise. The Governor then called for a bottle of his prize Madeira to be brought in for us to drink to the well-being of Williamsburg and the entire Virginia Colony. Remembering my desire to purchase some of the shipment, he gifted me with a bottle in hopes of gathering together soon in more peaceful circumstances." Ezra's voice grew hoarser as he continued. Eugenia offered him a cup of tea. After a sip, he fell back on his pillows and continued.

"I fell ill later that night. I pray my comrades have not suffered the same fate. Dunmore has murdered me. Make sure he hasn't killed our cause. Do that for me, Faith. It's my last request."

Ezra wheezed at the end. Blood vessels stood out in blue bands on his forehead and in his neck when the skin sagged as if the vessel it contained had shrunk over the past few nights. He moaned as he writhed beneath the blankets. Eugenia grabbed the basin and held it where he could turn and retch into it, filling the room with the scent of misery and illness. Her eyes were red-rimmed with exhaustion. She looked up briefly to glare at them. "Leave."

Butler followed Faith downstairs and onto the back porch. They both took deep breaths of the outside air, clearing their lungs of the misery above. Off in the nearby trees, birds sang as if they were free of care. Their music softened the harsher sounds of wagons and horses making their way through town a short distance away.

"Go back to your tavern, Mistress Clarke. You have guests to tend to and this could get dangerous."

"I'm well aware, Master Butler." Faith said. "I face danger every day in my tavern, whether it's dealing with drunken idiots or listening for you. Don't denigrate what I do."

Butler blinked. "I wouldn't dream of it. But if it is a disease, I'm not risking you being further exposed. If it is poison, I need you to listen and see what you can find out. You are in the best position to discover who is plotting against our cause. There's a rumor going about that your tavern is sympathetic to loyalists, which means more may come in and talk. You need to be there to hear what they say."

"My tavern, loyalist? I serve all people. I'm not getting involved in this conflict. Who would say we were Tories?" Butler's face was expressionless, but Faith knew. Her already frayed nerves allowed her temper to flare up and explode. "You bastard, you spread that rumor, didn't you? Without thinking about how people would react in this town. The other day, someone threw a rock through my window in the middle of the night. What do you think will happen next?" Fear and fury spilled out. "You can slip off elsewhere when tensions get high, but I have to live here." Helpless tears welled up that she angrily scrubbed away.

Butler spoke softly. "I will replace the window. I admit I was not expecting such a physical reaction. If there is any trouble, I have people in place to protect you and your boy. Nevertheless, rumors such as this will make loyalists more likely to drop by. And in establishments such as yours, people talk."

Faith glared at him.

Butler gave an exasperated huff. "This isn't a game, Mistress Clarke. It's a life and death enterprise. We're up against one of the strongest nations in the world and they will stop at nothing to subdue a rebellion such as this." His voice softened. "There are risks in everything we do, but the prize is freedom for ourselves and our children. Remember that. Right now, we need to help Ezra. You are in the best position if anyone lets their guard down while downing a tankard with friends. See if there are any rumors regarding Dunmore. Taking down some of the most powerful patriots in

Williamsburg would be quite an accomplishment for the loyalist cause."

Faith nodded, trying to stifle the useless tears welling up at the fresh memory of her father-in-law's suffering. "What are you going to do ?"

"Check on the other members of the delegation, see if anyone else has sickened suddenly. I want to know if this is a strike against patriots or did someone hold a grudge against Ezra. I'm not sure if Dunmore did this or one of his allies." Butler's voice dropped. "Acquiring and administering poison takes planning. It is not an action done in the heat of passion. There is also the question of when it was administered."

"I saw Ezra earlier this week." Faith said. "He was fine. More than fine, he was planning to meet with Peyton Randolph to discuss how to negotiate the return of the powder and weapons from the governor."

"They did meet," Butler answered. "And had an amicable discussion, not that it got anywhere. Governor Dunmore refused to return the powder and arms to the armory. No one believes that pathetic excuse he offered of preparing for a slave revolt. Given all the acrimony, he's fearful that the populace will rise up and slaughter him in his bed."

Faith stared at him. "How's Master Randolph?"

"Fit and hale, the last I saw him, but I intend to confirm that he remains such," Butler responded.

"Do you think he could have…?

"No," Butler shook his head. Peyton Randolph may not be the most passionate revolutionary, but he is an honorable man. His brother holds Loyalist beliefs, but I would be surprised if he took such measures. Nonetheless, I will investigate both men. The poison had to come from somewhere. At this point, only God knows where." He looked off in the distance. "Our entire network could be at risk."

"Are you certain it's poison?"

Butler stared at her. "I've had cholera, though it's been many years ago. I was miserable for a good long time, but I didn't vomit blood. More than that, I trust Ezra's judgment. If he says he's been poisoned I believe him." He stood with her in the Moores' front yard, thinking before turning to her. "I need to check on the others."

"Could the governor have done this?"

Butler paused before answering. "Dunmore's in a tight place right now. He can see the resistance to Britain growing and it terrifies him. He likes to use troops when he can to quell resistance." His tone grew thoughtful. "He can be a right sneaky bastard, though. There's not much he might do that would surprise me, not if he believed it would benefit him." Butler's mouth tightened. "First, I must go check on the others that were in that meeting with Dunmore. Then I can better assess the threat."

As he stepped to take off, Faith said, "What should I do?"

Butler's voice turned bleak. "The only thing any of us can really do. Pray."

Chapter Four

Faith was not ready to return to the tavern. No matter what Butler said, she was going to do far more than pour ale and listen for information. Shaken by what she had seen, she could not pour drinks and smile at guests while her father-in-law's suffering remained fresh on her mind. She needed a distraction.

Outside, a warm gentle wind blew from the west, bringing scents of grass and early hay mingled with the earthy undertone of livestock. People bustled up and down the cobblestones, their feet making muted thumps on the ground. Walking among the men and women about their business, Faith felt isolated, as if an invisible wall kept her from joining in with those before and behind her. A woman passed with a basket of flowers headed home from the market. Despite their obvious beauty, Faith found no joy in them. Too many anxious thoughts crowded her mind.

Her feet carried her to Georgia Clements's house where printing the *Virginia Gazette* was in full swing on the main floor. The scent of ink perfumed the air as she walked into the shop. Mistress Clements bustled about the room checking to see if the ink was dry on the broadsides hanging about the room. An unfamiliar young, black man operated the press in the back while another young man worked on wetting and hanging paper until it dried to the proper level of dampness for printing.

"Hello, Faith," Georgia Clements greeted her just inside the door. "I'm happy to see you. I hope your family is doing well."

Faith nodded. "Yes, we are fine and how is yours?" Her eyes circled the busy shop.

Georgia smiled. "We have stayed busy. People have been clamoring for copies of Mr. Henry's speech. We also have a few ship manifests to print as well as our regular broadside." She smiled at a young man as he passed by with an armload of paper. "I don't believe you have met my son, Marcus. He's completed his studies at William and Mary for now and is helping out at the shop."

She looked about the room but hesitated to ask about the one person she most wanted to see.

Georgia's smile faded. "Will is not here today. He fell ill a few days ago. I put him in my spare room in the back so we can care for him. He's not strong enough to go to his place in the loft." She saw Faith's face. "It's all right Faith, he is doing much better than he was last night, but he's still pretty weak. Paul and I will manage until he recovers." Turning, she called over to the young man. "How's the press coming?"

"Just fine, ma'am," Paul responded. "We'll be good to go on the next sheet, once I finish securing the type in the galleys." Slender, dark fingers stained with ink, adjusted the metal pieces of type before securing them into position with strips of wood. He frowned thoughtfully as he eyed his work. "It's ready now."

Marcus brought over sheets of paper, which he carefully secured to the bed of the printer before stepping back. Soon the steady slap of the beaters inking the type filled the room, as did the acrid scent of ink. Paul methodically went up and down the lines of type, the syncopated slaps sounding much like the beats of a drum.

"He's a journeyman from Philadelphia," Georgia said. "He joined us last week and has gotten right to work, which is fortunate considering Will's illness. His brother Silas has been doing odd jobs around Williamsburg. Currently, he's repairing some steps at the chandler's shop, and then he plans to replace some rails on my back porch. However, that's enough about me. How can I help you?"

"I want to see Will," Faith said. "Where can I find him?"

"Faith," the older woman said gently. "He won't want you to see him like this. My new cook has experience treating illnesses. She has been taking care of him. He kept down some broth today and has been sleeping."

"New cook? What happened to Mathilde?" In the past months that Faith had become friends with Georgia, her cook had been a plump German woman of middle years, who had stayed on past her indenture to become a trusted servant.

"She met one of her countrymen at the market earlier this spring. The next thing I know she's getting married and heading out to the Ohio valley. May God keep her safe in the wilderness."

"So, who is your cook now?"

"I am,"

Faith looked over and blanched at the towering black woman standing just inside the doorframe that led to Georgia Clements' private living quarters. "Athena," she whispered. She had never forgotten the indomitable woman who had briefly imprisoned her at Jeremy Butler's behest.

Georgia Clements glanced back and forth between the two women. "I see you've met Mistress Wise."

"That's one way to put it," Faith said. She walked up to Athena, "I want to see Will."

"You don't need to see him," Athena replied implacably. "He's getting the first rest he's had in three days. There is nothing so necessary you need to wake him."

Faith became aware that they were becoming the object of attention within the shop. "Can we speak privately, please," she added when she saw the woman start to object.

"Very well, Mistress Clarke. We will talk, but you will keep your voice down." With that, Athena swept around and went back into the living area, her deep blue skirt swishing as she moved forward. Once Faith cleared the doorframe, the other woman shut the door firmly and led her to the back of the house. They walked past the parlor and back toward the rear door that opened to the back porch. Off the side, a door was slightly ajar. Athena reached to pull it closed before she turned to look at Faith "What is it you want to say, Mistress Clarke?"

"What's wrong with Will?" Faith softened her voice to keep the conversation private.

Athena folded her arms. "I don't see where that is any of your business."

"Could he have been poisoned?" Faith raised a hand to cut her off. "Let me finish. My father-in-law is ghastly ill. He believes he's dying of some sort of poison. He's been having severe stomach pain and vomiting blood. Nothing the doctors do helps."

"Poison," Athena said quietly. "That would explain some things. He took sick fast, vomiting, diarrhea but no fever. I was afraid he'd accidentally gotten something from the print shop in his system, but I couldn't see how. I've been dosing him with angelica and peppermint, which has eased him a little. If this is poison, I'd best prepare Cesar's cure for him."

"What is that?"

Athena stared at her with something akin to contempt. "Not all cures come from white doctors who attended fancy schools. From what I've seen, most so-called physicians kill as many as they cure. Cesar's cure dates back many years. Cesar was a slave so skilled at healing the sick that South Carolina freed him and provided a pension until the end of his days. Fortunately, he shared his recipe for everyone to make use of."

"How well does it work?" Curiosity made Faith ask. She had learned some herbal remedies from her mother and from Olivia, but Athena obviously knew some things she did not.

Athena replied. "Well enough. I used it on Jeremy when he stepped on a copperhead a few years back. He's still here."

Faith breathed in and out slowly, thinking of Will but also of Ezra. "Can I have some to take to Ezra? He's suffering terribly, and nothing Eugenia does seems to work. All the physicians want is to bleed him."

Athena snorted in disgust. "That sounds about right. They don't know what else to do so they drain a body of blood. Yes, I'll have my boy Paul bring you some when I've finished preparing it."

"Thank you," Faith said sincerely, and then what Athena said hit her. "Is Paul your son?"

Athena nodded. "Paul and Silas were born within an hour of each other. Once their father died, Jeremy was able to purchase their freedom."

"That's nice." Faith said, feeling a bit awkward.

"You have no idea," Athena said. "Although Olivia tells me you freed both her and Titus, which makes you a little better than some. Their father was my master for many years, and he took what he wanted. Jeremy probably never would have survived if a surveyor hadn't taken a shine to him and bought his indenture." Her eyes, dark as the night, shimmered with unshed tears. "You've never been separated from your children, sold like a bale of cotton, thinking you will never see anyone you love again."

"No, I haven't," Faith admitted. "I don't know what it feels like. I'm sorry."

Athena nodded then switched topics. "You say your father-in-law was poisoned and you think Will was too. So how did someone get to both of them?"

"Could Will have accompanied Ezra when he met the governor earlier this week?" Faith asked. "Ezra didn't tell me much, but Butler is checking on all the other men there."

Athena frowned. "I can find out. Only so many poisons cause a reaction like this. Arsenic is probably the easiest to get hold of."

"Arsenic!"

"Keep your voice down," Athena hissed. "That boy needs rest, especially if his insides have been torn up with that mess. He's lucky to be alive."

"I'm lucky to have you to care for me," a familiar voice called out from behind the closed door.

Athena swore under her breath. "Look what you did." Opening the door, she went into the room and checked the man lying on the bed.

Hesitating only for a second, Faith followed her in. Will McKay rested on a narrow cot inside the small room, which smelled of sweat and misery. The window was cracked open, letting in only a whisper of fresh air. A light-colored drapery shadowed the room as it blocked anyone from peering inside.

Athena gently brushed the hair from Will's face. "You need to rest and get back your strength." She adjusted a blanket over him.

Will's appearance shocked Faith. His eyes were sunken into his skull, while his skin had taken on a waxy hue. He shivered in the room although sweat had plastered his shirt and hair to his body. He wore a long white shirt, which was open enough to see dark curls plastered to his chest. His bare legs stuck out from the covers although a corner managed to cover his hips enough for modesty.

Will's voice was a horse whisper. "Have I been poisoned? Am I dying then?"

"Not if I have anything to say about it," Athena replied. "You're not dead yet and you've improved in the past two days. You will recover. Have you started pissing?"

"Can't you smell it?" Will frowned. He looked over in the corner where a stone jar stood. "I hope I didn't miss the pot."

"We'll take care of it," Athena said. "Can I get you anything to eat or drink?"

Will shuddered. "No. I feel like my innards have exploded. Please, don't give me anything else that makes me vomit. I've been purged enough that my stomach thinks it resides up against my nose." He moved restlessly under the covers. "My hands and feet feel like they are on fire."

Athena clicked her tongue as she checked his arms and legs. "Your insides have been emptied. You rest; I will bring you some broth later. You need nourishment to build your strength."

"Is there any Madeira left?" Will asked weakly.

"What Madeira?" Athena asked. "Mistress Clements doesn't keep any of that stuff. She likes a nice light ale."

"Ezra gave it to me. He brought it out to celebrate the progress we have made to the cause. The governor had given it to him after they met and discussed ways to end the situation. They had shared it at the palace, and then the governor made a gift of a bottle to Ezra as a way to thank him for his moderation in their talks. Truthfully, there wasn't much left by the time I arrived. He and his companions had already imbibed before heading home. Then we drank a few drams. Ezra seemed fond of it. It was a wee bit sweet for my taste, but I recognized it was of excellent quality. Dunmore wouldn't have anything less. Ezra sent me home with the rest of the bottle. I was going to save it for a special occasion, but if I'm dying anyway..." His voice faded away, replaced by a fit of coughing. As he wiped his mouth, Faith saw the blood. She did not argue when Athena pushed her out of the room and shut the door.

Faith swallowed hard, feeling a knot in her throat. Her eyes prickled. Will was so strong and vital; she had not thought anything could harm him.

"Here," Athena handed her a clean rag. "Wipe those tears." She led Faith out back on the porch that faced the garden. "Take a minute to get yourself together; I'm going to find that bottle."

Faith stood on the porch sniffling while tears streaked down her face. She wasn't ready to lose anyone, not Ezra and not Will. She didn't know whether to plead or yell at God for this situation. Opening her eyes, she took in the glorious abandon of blooms that filled Georgia Clements's garden. Amidst the deep green blades of young onions, early peas and lettuces were Dutch tulips, daffodils, and sweet Williams which blended together to perfume the air in a heady mix. "Not even Solomon in all his glory was clothed such as these," she murmured as she looked at the rich profusion of colors. Two sturdy apple trees filled the air with their scented blossoms drawing the attention of a crowd of bees. The low throb of them resonated in the air. Although Faith realized death and life continued beside each other throughout eternity, today it seemed bitterly ironic to see all the life emerging in the garden while those she loved struggled to live.

Outside the print shop on Duke of Gloucester Street, voices spoke and answered as people traveled in and out. A horse whinnied in the street as it passed by followed by the rhythmic jingle of a harness attached to a wagon. It was like any other day, filled with sunshine and possibilities.

Faith stilled as her mind took it all in. Anger boiled up inside, quelling the tears as the realization sank in. Someone planned this, poisoned the people she loved with malicious intent.

Athena joined her on the porch carrying an empty demijohn, missing its cork. Her face was grim. "The stable hand next door is dead. I think Will set the bottle down in the barn before he went up to the loft where he sleeps. Pete must have seen it and decided to take it and finish it. It finished him instead."

Faith stared at the dark glass. It looked no different from some of the bottles in her tavern's cellar, except for a sprinkle of white powder around the lip.

"What is that?" she reached a hand out to the bottle.

"Don't touch that, idiot. It's likely arsenic powder." Athena eyed it cautiously. "I'll take it to a friend who knows about these things." She wrapped the bottle in a piece of sacking and stuck it deep into one of the pockets hidden underneath her skirt. Wiping her hands on her apron, she met Faith's eyes. "Jeremy needs to know about this." She turned her eyes to Faith. "You need to keep your mouth shut and your eyes and ears open. We have a killer to catch and we don't want him to know he's being hunted."

Chapter Five

Sweat ran down Jeremy Butler's neck as he watched the activity in and about the governor's residence. Standing within the shade of a large beech, its branches concealed him from everything but insects that hummed around him with vicious intent. He waved off a flotilla of gnats from his face; they regrouped within seconds. Once he finished his current mission, he intended to find out if Athena had some potion that would discourage them. She never seemed to get bit. The warmth of the early May sun made the wig he wore even itchier than normal. He swatted a mosquito determined to dine on his flesh while he pondered his dilemma.

Getting into the Governor's mansion was going to be a challenge. Its construction placed walls of brick across nearly every opening. In addition, since the seizure of Williamsburg's powder, Dunmore had kept his residence well-guarded. Normally, that wouldn't be a huge problem. Most places had someone who would talk for the right price, except here. Butler had failed to lure any of numerous servants to turn. Either they were too scared or loyal to talk about Dunmore. Moreover, he would never blend in as another servant, not here in Virginia, where most servants' origins lay in Africa where they had been captured and enslaved.

He had watched the comings and goings from the enormous mansion most of the morning. Something was afoot, but he wasn't sure what. People had gone in and out all day, far more than usual. The unmistakable sound of children's voices drew his attention. Jeremy blinked as a well-dressed woman came out along with servants, some of which stayed busy keeping track of the younger members of the party. He had never met her, but he felt certain it was Lady Dunmore and her children. The governor had a large family.

"What are they doing?" He muttered, eyes narrowing on the scene. A large carriage pulled up outside the ornate gate that allowed entry to the palace. The light bounced off the metal as it swung wide open to let the family out. Two footmen jumped down and began swiftly loading members into the vehicle. A wagon came around the side loaded with boxes and trunks. He grinned as two of the smaller children started chasing each other across the green, followed by a determined nanny. Although he couldn't hear the words, he recognized the tone. The young man and lady were getting a scolding. Lady Dunmore, assisted by nannies and other staff, got all eight little Dunmore s in the carriage, which took off promptly, followed a group of soldiers on horseback.

Sliding out from cover, Jeremy headed toward the mansion hoping with all the uproar, he could slip in and find out if the royal governor had a hand in poisoning a few of the provincials he so despised.

Not surprisingly, the courtyard was quiet after the exit of so many. A few guards remained at the gate. Butler presented himself as a merchant looking to offer the governor some bottles of a fine wine shipment just arrived from France. In order to encourage his entrance, he offered a generous sample to the guards. It cost him a bottle of burgundy, filched from Ezra Moore's cellar, but allowed him inside where an elderly mahogany-skinned man dressed in elegant livery stopped him and inquired about his business before herding him into a waiting room.

Down the hall lay the governor's office. Jeremy could hear his voice clearly as the man who had answered the door told him of his presence.

The governor's Scot's accent was thick as he bellowed. "I've no time for merchants, Cicero. Henry and his militia are preparing to invade the town! I need troops to defend the palace. My family's lives are in peril."

Butler's ears pricked up. He knew of Patrick Henry although they had not met. Between his previous work for the Sons of Liberty and his current position to send useful intelligence to General Washington, he'd met some of the leaders determined to separate from Great Britain, but not all. He knew of the fiery Henry from his speeches and comments of others. His mind distracted by what he had overheard, Butler responded to his dismissal from the Governor's mansion with a polite nod before exiting out the door and sliding around to the large kitchen that lay separate from the main building. From the shadow of the main building, he watched as enslaved servants of the governor went back and forth from the kitchen to the nearby scullery. A slim young man emerged from the smokehouse carrying a side of meat, he jogged down the path to the kitchen, leaping nimbly over a pair of young girls busy cleaning the brick walkway with sand.

Logic dictated that the wine cellar was likely close to the kitchen if not directly below it. Butler found it by watching members of the kitchen staff go back and forth and backtracking the one he saw emerge with bottles.

Butler slipped into the arched doorway only to be blinded by the complete darkness of the room. Hastily cracking the door, he grabbed a taper from a nook outside and took it in with him, hoping no one would notice it missing. Using the flint and tinder from his pocket, he lit it before exploring further. The room was cool and smelled of damp and alcohol. Enormous barrels sat on their sides on sturdy boards laid across broad stands of brick. On another wall, wooden shelves lined an alcove. Glass from bottles reflected the flame of his small candle.

Someone could enter at any time and he would have no explanation of his presence. Given the number of bottles covering the shelves, he had little hope of checking the Madeira supply, until luck favored him. A brief flash of amber sent him looking on a lower shelf, where he realized the harder liquor was stored. The upper shelves contained wines and sherry. But this shelf held scotch, brandy, and Madeira. Squatting, Butler examined the bottles as well as he could, but all these were tightly sealed with no sign of tampering. A scratch at the door warned him his time was up. He pinched the candle flame and scrambled into the shadow of a huge barrel that smelled of beer. Crouching down, he prayed the servant would not look where he hid. A skinny boy with dusky skin and dark hair swept back with a ribbon slipped into the room and went straight to the shelves. Picking up a bottle, he trotted out, shutting the door behind him.

Breathing a sigh of relief, Butler crawled out from behind the barrel freezing when he heard a scrabbling noise that sent his heart racing. He hated rats, their scratchy claws and hideous squeaks. Three months in the belly of a ship from Ireland had left him with a permanent horror of them. Not caring if he made noise or not, Butler groped until he found the rough brick wall, biting down on a shriek as something brushed by him in the darkness. He plunged toward where he believed the door was and stumbled out into the afternoon sun. Taking a few deep breaths, he glanced about to see if anyone spotted him. Fortunately, no one was near. Brushing cobwebs from his jacket, he strode out toward the back gate, making an effort not to run to get away.

Butler had a few hidey-holes in town, but he longed for the warmth of familiar faces and the very small group of people he could trust. He had been in Williamsburg enough times to know most of the backroads and alleyways to get places. Having no desire to be seen in town in his current state of disrepair, he slipped around until he reached the backyard of Georgia Clements' print shop. The door to the separate kitchen stood wide open, sending the scents of baking bread and chicken out into the yard. His stomach rumbled, reminding him that breakfast had been far too long ago.

Athena glanced at him from just inside the kitchen door, kneading bread on the table. "Jeremy, don't come into my clean kitchen like that."

He stood at the door. "Then where do I go?"

Wiping her hands on her apron, she stepped out to look at him. "Where did you get all that mess on your fine clothes? I see soot and dirt and…" her voice trailed off as she stooped to look at the legs of his breeches. "You have rat poison on these."

"Rat poison?"

"Ratsbane, most likely. You need to take these off immediately. That white powder looks like arsenic and you don't want to have anything to do with it."

He signed exasperated. "More arsenic? I'm amazed there are any rats alive in Williamsburg. How is it I find the stuff everywhere but in a bottle of

Madeira?"

Athena shrugged. "It's easy to get. That's probably why someone chose it to get rid of Ezra Moore. Now get out of those clothes."

Butler looked about, but no one else was in the yard. He removed the coat and his stock as well as the wig. Shoes and stockings came next. He unbuttoned the bottom of his breeches and paused at the fly, before looking at Athena.

She snickered. "I raised two boys, took care of you for a while. There's nothing that surprises me except how white you are." Her dark eyes amused, she rose and turned her back. "Leave those in the yard and go around to my rooms upstairs. I'll send one of the boys around with a bucket of water and some clothes. And Jeremy?"

"Yes?" He said as he carefully slipped off his knee britches, leaving him with just his shirttails waving in the light breeze.

"Use the soap." He could hear her laugh through the door as he finished stripping and hustled around to a less exposed place.

Once he had cleaned up and dressed, albeit in a spare pair of Paul's clothes, he headed back to the kitchen. Pausing in the doorway, he watched Athena kneading bread dough with practiced ease. Her coffee-colored skin looked as smooth as satin. She looked no older than when she had taken him in twenty years ago. He had been a skinny Irish adolescent newly indentured to the man she called master. Back when she had a different name. She had treated him like one of her sons and he had never forgotten it or her.

Sensing his presence, Athena said, "Come in, I'll fix you a plate."

"Thank you," he said as he sat at the large plank table in the center of the room. A plate heaped with fried chicken, new potatoes, and asparagus appeared in front of him, followed by a tankard of ale. Butler gratefully took a swallow before digging in.

Athena finished getting her bread ready to rise while he finished. A piece of cake appeared in front of him. Butler felt the stress and tension ease from his bones. "No one cooks like you." He wasn't sure if she was flushed from the fire or with pleasure, but he liked to see her smile.

Sitting across from him, she looked him up and down. "Well, you clean up good. What have you been into?"

"Investigating the governor," He sighed tiredly. "I really don't know if he poisoned Ezra or not. Dunmore has a temper and he has trouble hiding it, but poison? And now I hear Patrick Henry is bringing in militia to demand reimbursement for the powder taken from the Magazine. If he brings a group of militia to lay siege to the Governor's palace, all hell will break loose."

"It won't come to that," Athena leaned in. "Messengers have been going back and forth to where Henry is camped at Laneville. The Receiver-General has been persuaded to offer him compensation for the powder. With any luck, Henry will take it and head off to Philadelphia with the rest of the delegates."

Butler sighed. "Let's hope for that." He was so tired. Ezra had run the information network in Williamsburg, leaving him free to check on other activities in Virginia and up the coast. If Ezra didn't recover, he would have to find someone else and he dreaded the task. Ezra had been more than a resource, Butler considered him a friend, one of a very few he trusted. If he died, Butler intended to ensure his poisoner faced justice, no matter what the sheriff might say. It wasn't just grief that kept him up nights, it was rage.

"Where are you, Jeremy?" Athena's voice broke through his thoughts. Ebony eyes looked intently into his. She knew how he hated to lose people. It was what had drawn them together: the slave who grieved the loss of a sold child and the young boy who lost his mother on the voyage across the Atlantic.

"I need to find out who did this to Ezra," he confessed. "If Governor Dunmore did it, I want to know why he singled out Ezra. None of the other delegates to that meeting are ill, unless they've taken ill on the way to Philadelphia."

"You're wondering if he knows Ezra used his contacts to send information to you." Athena looked thoughtful. "If he figured that out, he would already be searching for you and I've seen no signs of it. Silas has been doing some repair work in the governor's stables this week and he has heard nothing. Dunmore is scurrying around preparing for a rebel attack on his house."

"That doesn't mean he hasn't figured it out," Butler said. He pulled at the sleeve of his borrowed shirt. The twins were taller than he was which meant the cuff hung halfway down his hands, pushing them up was annoying. Finally, he gave up and rolled the sleeves up to his elbows where they would cease being a nuisance. There was little he could do about the breeches, which hung well below his knees.

"I wonder if we're looking at this the wrong way," Athena said abruptly. "While it's possible the governor decided to poison one of his opponents, I wonder if the answer lies closer to home."

Butler looked at her. "Why?"

"First of all, Moore seems to be the intended victim. None of the other men in that meeting with Dunmore fell ill. Will just had the misfortune of sharing a drink from the bottle that had been tampered with. I doubt anyone was targeting a man indentured to a printer." She continued, ticking reasons off on her strong, wiry fingers, the ends blunted with callouses. "The seal was broken on the bottle when Ezra brought it home. Anyone who visited him had an opportunity to drop in and then there is this." Athena rose from the table and went over to a large piece of broken crockery sitting on the floor next to the door. "Don't touch," she admonished when she set it on the table.

Butler looked at a small crumpled piece of folded paper, discolored to a yellowish-brown. A few granules of powder spilled out onto the crockery. "Where did you get this?" He eyed the whitish powder suspiciously. "What am I looking at?"

Athena smiled grimly. "Arsenic powder, more than enough to kill. Olivia brought it to me. It was on the ground outside of the Moore house, under the bushes. That woman doesn't miss much. She recognized it from Prentis' store."

"William Prentis?" Butler asked as his eyes narrowed in interest.

"That's where almost everybody goes to get rat poison," she said dryly. "But I'm guessing you've never settled anywhere long enough to have to worry about vermin."

Butler shrugged. "No." His life had not included a permanent home in a while, which was one reason working for Washington had been an easy decision. It gave his restlessness a purpose.

Athena continued. "Mistress Clements keeps an account there, so I stopped by to get some things for Will and spotted that Clarke boy in there getting some things for his Momma. He had quite the list."

"Did it include rat poison?"

Athena shook her head, "No. Nevertheless, for this to be at the house, someone had to have purchased it and I'm guessing they didn't want it known, either. Elsewise, why hide it under a bush?"

Fat popped loudly from the kettle over the fire. Athena rose to stir it. As she did, the rich scent of meat and vegetables filled the air. Her gaze went next to the rising loaves of bread near the fire to absorb the heat. Satisfied, she returned to the table. Her tone was flat. "What do you know about the wife?"

"Eugenia?" Butler thought a moment. "Not much. Ezra kept her out of his business. I gather she liked the benefits of ties to Great Britain."

Athena nodded. "She likes nice things. I've seen her at the milliner's quite often, buying lace, ordering gowns and caps."

"She likes Ezra to import lace and fine fabrics from abroad," Butler smiled like a cat given cream. "Those shipments were very useful in smuggling messages and other items as they traveled through the colonies to Williamsburg. I never realized how useful vanity could be."

Outside, the rising wind made the limbs in the young oak tree creak. With the wind came the scent of rain. Butler peered out to see the clouds gather like great grey puffs of sheep's wool, obliterating the view of the formerly blue sky.

"I'd best go before the rain rolls in." Butler rose to his feet. "Thank you for the meal and the clothes. Tell Silas I will bring them back in a day or two."

"Where are you going now?"

Butler's face lost its warmth. "I have a job to do. I'm off to the taverns to listen to the gossip and see what I can find out about our enemies." What he did not add was that he did not intend to rest until he put an end to whomever had harmed his friend.

Chapter Six

Faith swatted a fly irritably. Days had dragged by with little to no news. She spent her time plying her guests with food and ale all while hoping to hear something useful. So far, all that she had learned was that Dunmore had called British sailors to protect him at his residence from both unhappy residents and any of the local militias that were rumored to be headed to the capitol. The sailors who dropped by her tavern drank like fishes. Some nights she wondered how they could still stand after the innumerable tankards of ale and stronger drink. However, despite inebriated calls to tar and feather patriots and a few pathetic attempts to garner affection from her, no one spoke of poisoning.

When Titus came to relieve her from keeping watch over the liquor cabinet, Faith went down to the kitchen where Joshua tended the fire. "Where's Olivia?"

Joshua looked up from turning the spit. "She went down to check on Master Moore and Will. She said to tell you she will be back before dinner."

Faith nodded. Olivia was welcome at both residences. Her knowledge of herbs and preparations rivaled any apothecary. Faith had dropped off a preparation of Cesar's cure to the Moore's with instructions on what to do. A male servant stopped her entry telling her none but the doctor was welcome. He eyed the bundle of herbs doubtfully, but promised to let the mistress know she had brought it for Ezra. She had no idea what Eugenia had done with it.

Olivia stayed busy preparing herbal remedies for the patients, whether it was lavender ointment for aching limbs or various tisanes to ease queasy stomachs. She also kept Faith informed. Through her, she knew Will was keeping down broth and weak tea, although he still felt numbness in his hands and feet. Ezra had quit vomiting but had shown no other signs of recovering.

Faith leaned over and stirred the huge iron pot of bean soup that Olivia had started earlier. There was little for her to do besides stir the enormous pot and keep an eye on what Olivia had so meticulously put in place. Her eyes moved restlessly about the kitchen until a soft popping drew her attention. Faith couldn't figure out what it was until a strong scent alerted her to her mistake. The coffee! Hurrying to the fireplace dogs, she grabbed a heavy rag and lifted the roaster by its handle, shaking it madly. She had forgotten about the roasting coffee beans. The scent arising from the metal roaster was rich and powerful. "Please don't be burned," she begged as the beans continued to pop within the metal cylinder.

Behind her, the door squeaked as someone pushed it open. Olivia entered, putting down a couple of large baskets on the table. Her eyes took in the scene as her nose twitched. "I think those beans have seen enough of the fire." Her tone was dry.

Faith flushed. "I hope it's not ruined."

Olivia pulled out a basket rounded like a bowl. "Let's see."

Faith emptied the beans into the basket. They rattled as they tumbled out, different shades of brown, tan, and nearly black. The scent rose off them, filling the room with their rich earthy aroma faintly tinged with smokiness.

Olivia shook the basket gently, observing the contents. "I think they will do."

Faith let out a breath in relief.

"But perhaps, it would be better if Titus or I roasted the next batch."

Faith shot her a look, but Olivia's expression was bland as she changed the topic.

"I stopped at the market to pick up a few things for dinner. I picked up some cabbage and other young greens. If I remember correctly there are still some brandied cherries in the cellar, I may be able to do something with those."

48

"How are they?" Faith said as she set the roaster down. Her mind could not escape thoughts of Ezra and Will. Especially after Athena had discovered a man had died from drinking from the wretched tainted Madeira. Her mind could not contemplate losing either of them.

Olivia shook her head. "Not much change since yesterday. Will tried to come into the print shop and Athena sent him back to bed. He can walk to the privy and sit in a chair but anything beyond that exhausts him. His appetite is poor. Healing takes time."

Faith nodded. "I know. I keep hoping, praying for a miracle." She swallowed a knot in her throat. "What about Ezra?"

Olivia stayed quiet, as if gathering her thoughts. "I've been praying, Faith, as I know you have. But sometimes God doesn't answer the way we expect him to."

"Is it that bad?" Faith wished she could take back the words. Olivia's expression said what the petite black woman would not say.

Olivia hesitated for a moment before she put an arm around her former mistress. "With God, there is always hope. All we can do is pray for mercy. Who knows? He may stir tomorrow or next day and surprise us all."

Faith drew back, sniffling as she forced back tears. Sitting around would drive her mad. She needed activity, something to keep her from thinking too deeply. "Is there anything I can do?"

"Go see him. He needs his family."

Faith shook her head. "Eugenia won't let me in the house."

"I don't care what Mistress Genia says. She's under a lot of stress and she's never been one to keep her composure. Ignore those fits. You are family. Ezra needs you. Go see him, sit with him, and offer to stay awhile so she can rest."

Faith looked out toward the house. It was quiet now, but soon her guests would be expecting a meal. Men would come in for tankards of ale. "What about the tavern?"

"I will manage." Olivia pointed out the door. "Go."

Outside, a pale sun lit a rich cerulean sky. Faith stopped to breathe in the fresh, clean air and gather her thoughts. Her nose picked up the scent of sawdust from the wood Titus had recently chopped for Olivia's cooking fire, along with the fragrant scent of early lavender blooming in the herb garden. How could it be so peaceful, when so much was happening?

"God's ways are not our ways," she murmured quietly, and she was not in agreement with the Almighty. Faith went to gather a shawl and let Andrew know where she was going.

The tavern was experiencing a lull as it normally did between the midday meal and supper. People were about their business, which meant only a few lingered to read broadsheets from the Virginia Gazette or quench their thirst. Titus stood just inside the main room, keeping an eye on things. Faith nodded to him as she passed by and into the rooms that comprised her private quarters.

Joshua and Andrew gathered around the small table she used for accounts. A map lay spread out before them, a compass on top.

"What are you two working on?" she asked as she walked past them to grab a lightweight shawl off its hook on the wall.

"Navigation," Joshua answered. "We're trying to decide the best way to travel to Boston."

Faith smiled as she walked over. "Are you planning a trip?

The boys laughed. "No one can get in or out of Boston," Andrew said with a touch of scorn. "Everyone knows that. The Lobsterbacks have had every way in or out shut down for months."

Joshua looked apologetically at Faith. "He don't mean nothing. We thought we would try to figure out how you could get in without attracting attention."

"Good luck with that," Faith said. "The British have a very powerful army. I imagine it would be very difficult to sneak past them."

Joshua nodded. "Difficult, but not impossible. I'm sure there's a way."

Andrew chimed in. "One day, we will chase all the Redcoats into the Ocean!" He looked at the shawl on her arm. "Are you going somewhere?"

"I'm visiting your grandparents," Faith said softly. "Your grandpa Ezra has been very ill; I'm going to see how I can help."

The smile ebbed off Andrew's face. "Is he dying?"

She couldn't lie to him. "I hope not, but he is very sick. Your Grandma is doing everything she can to take care of him."

"Is she making him vomit? Doctors like to make you vomit or bleed."

Faith winced. "No, she's not doing that." At least, Faith hoped she wasn't. Ezra had looked like he had suffered enough on her last visit. "I will be back before supper," she said, tying a straw hat over her cap before she left.

The sun's brightness blinded her for a few minutes as she stepped out onto the small porch at the front of her tavern. The trees surrounding the street had leafed out into deep green umbrellas that shaded much of her walk. As she neared the walls that surrounded the Capitol, she looked onto the grounds. Except for a few soldiers, all remained quiet. A soldier tipped his hat to her as she passed; she dipped her head in polite acknowledgment. Despite the acrimony between Britain and the colonies, she saw no need to be rude. Most of the soldiers she served in the tavern were young men far away from home, ordered to the colonies to do a job. Parliament's poor choices were not their fault.

She sneezed as she entered Duke of Gloucester Street. Despite yesterday's rain, yellow pollen still permeated the air before creating streaks of yellow in the muddy street. The air smelled of mud and horse droppings, only faintly dispelled by the scent of grass and early hay. The air was warm and mild, enough that she let her shawl slide down her arms so she could feel the sun's warmth on her back. Wagons filled with spring crops crowded the roads along with travelers coming to the capital on business. Since the governor's dismissal of the Burgesses last year, they had met in other venues. Faith wondered if they would ever meet at the Capitol again.

The streets quieted as she walked further from the heart of town. Here, homes lay surrounded by maintained yards and fenced off from the main road. Within minutes, she stood at the gate to the Moore home. Faith paused as a man exited the front door. He turned to the servant behind him.

"Inform Master Moore that I will have a new will ready for him to sign in the morning." The man holding the door nodded and slid the door closed. He tipped his hat to Faith before swiftly striding away.

Faith knocked and was admitted by the same man, dressed in the finest livery Ezra's money could buy. "Hello George," she said. "I've come to see

Ezra." Before he could react, she walked swiftly behind him and up the stairs to the room where she had last seen her father-in-law.

The room was still as she entered. Heavy draperies covered windows cracked open and cast the room into shadow. She walked hesitantly toward the bed unsure of what she would see. No one else appeared to be inside. The bed draperies hung loosely around the mattress except for one side that had been looped back. Faith moved forward slowly hoping not to disturb Ezra. A soft wheeze indicated he still breathed. A lump rose in her throat as her eyes took in the shrunken form huddled under the blankets. He looked old and frail. Carefully, she stepped back and took a seat to be with him, even if he was unaware.

Her sister-in-law Martha Moore stepped in through the half-closed door. Her dark eyes glazed with tears as she looked at the figure in the bed. "I'm glad you're here," she whispered. Despite her recent arrival, her hair and dress were immaculate. A print of red and gold roses twined around the dusty blue silk of her full skirts in a style that likely came from France. Matching blue bows marched up her bodice to join ruffles that framed a wide square neck. While her face was pale and tired, a freshly starched snowy white cap adorned her dark curls. A matching blue satin bow had been pinned to the top, just over her forehead.

Faith nodded. "I am glad to see you as well." While she noticed the freshly pressed dress and cap, she didn't comment. Her maid undoubtedly stayed busy keeping her attire immaculate. For Martha, clothes were the armor that prepared her for battle whether it was social or familiar. The Moores were a powerful family where the language of clothing and social connections was an intricately woven web designed to build power and influence. While Faith lingered only on the periphery, she took time to put on a fresh cap and a clean apron before heading over to their town residence.

"Daniel and I arrived yesterday. We left the children with my family at their country home on the James River. We weren't sure what to expect from Eugenia's message. She had indicated some sort of stomach ailment, but this," she shuddered. "This is barbaric." In her hands was a vase filled with tulips and lily of the valley likely cut from Ezra's treasured flowerbeds out back. Their scent filled the room, almost overpowering the lingering odor of sickness and gastric upheaval. Martha set them on a dresser in a corner of the room before carefully sitting in an upright chair near Faith and arranging her skirts. "Maybe these will improve the air. No matter how many times the servants have scrubbed, it still smells of illness."

Glancing over at Ezra, Faith doubted much would change while poison continued to wrack his body. Even in sleep, his face was constricted in pain.

"Is there nothing that can be done to ease him?" she whispered, not wanting to disturb his rest.

Martha shook her head. "He's been dosed with everything known to man. He let them bleed him yesterday to lessen ill humors. The doctor still thinks it may be cholera, but Ezra insists he had been poisoned. Though I cannot imagine why anyone would do such a thing."

Faith shook her head in agreement. Tories and patriots alike respected her father-in-law. Amidst the tumult in the town, he remained a voice of reason.

Downstairs, voices broke through the stillness of the sick room. At first, it was a muted murmur, then the volume rose until it was clear a man and a woman were shouting at each other.

Martha winced. "Daniel and Eugenia cannot seem to come to any agreement. I hope they can come to terms before Zachary and their sisters arrive."

"What are they arguing about?" Faith asked as another voice joined them, followed by muffled bumps and thumps.

"Money," Martha said. "He went down this morning to go over the household accounts and make sure everything was taken care of. Daniel discovered many unrecorded expenses and Ezra's collection of coins emptied. His father taught him to keep track of things. He is very upset to find things so disorderly."

Before Faith could respond, a loud thump caused the walls to vibrate, followed by a shriek. She glanced at Martha who had leapt to her feet. Ezra remained asleep, still except for the rise and fall of his breath. Faith rose to join her. "What is happening?"

Martha shook her head, although her eyes looked worried. As she opened the door, the voices became clearer. Both women took the stairs down to the room where Ezra conducted his affairs where resounding thumps continued at an alarming rate.

The room where Ezra received visitors and conducted business lay behind a heavy oak door. When Martha hesitated in front of it, Faith moved forward and grasped the heavy brass knob, turning and pushing it open. Inside Ezra's normally orderly room, chaos reigned. Pieces of broken china lay scattered on the ornately patterned rug that Ezra had imported from France. Normally, the afternoon sun streamed through the set of tall windows behind Ezra's desk. Today, they remained covered with draperies, leaving the room cast in shadow. It was as if the room already mourned the loss of its owner.

"Let him go," Eugenia shouted. "You have no right to do this."

Martha flung open the door just as Louis put a sofa between himself and his stepbrother. Blood dripped from a cut lip that was already beginning to swell. A torn ruffle dangled from one sleeve of a silk embroidered coat, fit a bit snugly.

Daniel went to follow him, but Eugenia grabbed his arm. He struggled to shake her off, but she clung to his arm like a dog with a bone.

"This is my house. I will run it as I see fit," She hissed, raising her free hand to strike his cheek. "How dare you come and disturb us when your father lies so ill."

Daniel Moore stared down at her, his grey eyes, so like Ezra's, were like a field of ice. His normally scholarly features were flushed with anger. "How dare you and that spoiled boy of yours take advantage of a gravely ill man who has spent years keeping you in silks and imported laces? That son of yours," he nodded at where Louis cowered, "needs to keep his hands out of my father's possessions."

"I have taken nothing besides that which I have a claim to," Louis sputtered. "Ezra gave me a few baubles to settle accounts. As we all know, money remains in short supply in the colonies."

Daniel snorted in disbelief. "My father did not run up debts. He always told me that running up debts was a step on the way to ruin. He minded his accounts and kept them paid. He looked at Eugenia in disgust, gesturing at her exquisite floral printed gown. "I've seen the accounts. Your spending on garments and embellishments goes beyond ridiculous, enough that he put you and your son on an allowance. Since he has fallen ill, you've been busy lining your own pocket and indulging this useless piece of flesh." He gestured at Louis, who took refuge behind his mother. "That ruby on his pinky belonged to my mother; hand it over before I break a bone removing it."

Louis sniffed as he adjusted his wig, which had slipped to one side in the melee. "No true gentleman manhandles another." His eyes darted about frantically as he looked for a way to escape.

Eugenia glared at her stepson. "Ezra gave that to him."

"Liar," Daniel's voice was cold. "His will states that it goes to his oldest daughter, my sister Rachel, who will arrive in a matter of days. You helped yourself to it as you have to a good many of my mother's valuables. I assure you there will be an accounting."

Eugenia replied. "When Ezra recovers he will set you right. He has always provided for us. He would not wish me or Louis to do without now while he is unable to tend to his affairs."

"He sent for his solicitor to change his will before he dies." His tone turned sarcastic. "I wonder my lady, what compelled him to do that?"

Eugenia fell silent as shock filled her features.

"Now, hand me the ring." Daniel moved to go around Eugenia

Louis stood frozen behind his mother. He licked his lips as he put his hand into the side pocket of his pale rose jacket, the cuffs stiff with embroidered posies.

Daniel edged closer to the younger man. "My father wrote to me of his concerns over you, how little interest you took in learning a business or furthering your education. He quit paying your tuition because he discovered you were spending your time at the card tables rather than attending classes."

Eugenia hissed. "How contemptible of you to judge us. You know nothing of us. Until this malady struck Ezra, we were so happy."

"I'm sure you were, every time you went to your mantua maker." Daniel stood so that he blocked any escape. His gaze met Eugenia's in challenge until she looked away.

Louis' gaze took in the design on the rug as he flushed. "I had intended to return to William and Mary after a short reprieve, but Ezra had already cut me off by then. We had discussed me joining his business once I had recouped my losses." His face turned sad. "All we can do now is pray for his recovery from this dreadful ailment."

"Until then, I will be managing my father's affairs and there will be no more pilfering of items that do not belong to either of you. If I discover any, you will not remain under this roof." Daniel's voice was grim.

Eugenia turned pale. "You would not dare."

"Try me." Daniel held out his hand. "Now hand over my mother's ruby."

Daniel's eyes looked like Ezra's, although Faith had never seen such a cold gleam in her father-in-law's gaze. It unnerved her even though he remained focused on Louis, whose expression resembled a rabbit caught in a snare. Wrestling the ring off his finger, he gave it to Eugenia before shouldering past Martha and Faith on his way out.

Eugenia slapped it into Daniel's open hand.

Faith winced at the sharp sound. Although she stood slightly behind Martha, her height provided a clear view of the altercation. She wished she were anyplace else. Although she did not know Ezra's older children well, they had always been courteous to her. It rattled her to see the normally quiet Daniel in a rage.

"You have no right to do this," Eugenia said. "We are not strangers, we are family. Would you cast us adrift?"

Daniel smiled grimly before replying. "My father put me on a ship when I was fifteen so I could learn shipping from the ground up. At sea, it doesn't matter whose son you are, but how well you do your job. Everyone's survival depends on each man doing his best. There is no dead weight and fools are not welcome. By the time I came home at twenty-one, I had learned what it takes to survive and succeed. I have no use for frivolous peacocks, and I will not allow anyone to take advantage of my father. You will follow my rules if you wish to remain."

"I have expenses," Eugenia sputtered. "In Ezra's absence, I have had nowhere to turn to take care of things."

Daniel threw her an exasperated look. "My father took care of everyone in this house. He has indulged your whims for years because you made him happy. For that reason, I tolerate your presence. But mark my words, Madam, there will be limits on your and your son's expenditures. Every expense must be approved by me."

He held her gaze. In the altercation, his stock had become loose, its snowy ends dangling down the sides of his dark jacket. Daniel paused to tuck loose strands of hair back into his que. Never one to wear a wig, his dark brown hair was tied back with a simple black ribbon. As he spoke, his breathing slowed as he paused to regain some control before continuing. "From now on, he will see proper physicians who will tend him and not dose him with unfamiliar tinctures and potions."

"I have done everything in my power to care for him," Eugenia said. Grief radiated from her as her temper faded as well. "No one can say otherwise." With that, she left the room, continuing up the stairs where her husband slumbered. Muffled sobs could be heard amidst the sound of her footsteps dragging upstairs away from the confrontation.

Daniel handed the ring over to Martha. "Take charge of this until my sister arrives. God knows what else they have pilfered while my father lies helpless." He swore as he strode over to where Ezra stored his liquor and grabbed a bottle of whisky. His hands shook as he poured two fingers worth and tossed it back.

Faith remained silent through all the drama. In truth, her mind was still spinning from all she had overheard. Stillness settled over the room although a sense of disquiet remained. She hesitated, not knowing whether to go or stay given the acrimony she had just witnessed.

"Why are you here?" Daniel Moore had finally noticed her presence.

"I came to see Ezra," Faith said softly. "I wanted to see if there was anything I could do."

"Such as?" His tone was cool although the hand he used to sweep stray strands of hair from his face shook.

Faith twisted her hands in her skirt awkwardly. "I don't know. Perhaps I could sit with him for a while so others can rest."

Daniel shook his head tiredly. "There are enough members of the Clarke family here without me having to keep track of one more. My father is well cared for. My brother and sisters should be here within a day or two to help tend him. You are not needed here."

Martha looked at her husband briefly before turning to Faith. "I know how fond Ezra was of you. It was kind of you to come. If there is any change in his condition, I will send word."

Faith nodded before turning to go. Her throat felt tight from emotions she dared not express, but Martha was right. There was nothing she could do.

Chapter Seven

The sun's heat was a relief after the boiling tensions within the Moore household. Escaping the house, Faith strolled home, thoughtfully considering all she had seen and heard. A battle was escalating amidst Ezra's heirs, his children versus his current wife and her surviving son and she didn't know who to believe.

As Faith approached the gate of her home, a thread of music touched her ears. Someone inside played a fiddle, low and sweet. Its plaintive sound whispered its way into her soul releasing the weight of repressed pain.

Faith caught her breath. She knew only one fiddle player who visited Clarke Tavern. The melancholy notes of *Over the Hills and Far Away* trickled through the windows opened to catch a passing breeze. She burst through the door as the next verse began.

Will McKay stood near the fireplace, his instrument tucked under his chin, eyes closed as he played. Delicate notes, as if plucked from the heart, filled the space, expressing feelings too intimate to be uttered. The taproom stayed silent as a church, save for the haunting melody resonating from the strings.

The occupants sat as if held in thrall, speaking in hushed tones as Will continued to play. Titus pulled a chair out for Faith. She sat down, too stunned to think. When he stopped playing, his audience thanked him with generous applause and offers of drinks, which he refused with a smile.

"I'm not quite up to much liquor," he said, joining Faith at the table. Joshua set a mug down in front of him. "Thank your mother for me," he called after the boy.

Faith stared at it, unable to identify what he was drinking. "What is it?"

"Cesar's cure," He said as he sipped. "I feel like I've drunk a barrel load over the past week. That and light beer are all Athena will let me drink." He frowned thoughtfully. "She locked up the whisky, said it wasn't good for me right now." He shook his head. "Every Scot knows good whisky solves a lot of ills. Nevertheless, I am not keen to cross her. She looks like she could wrestle an ox." He sighed and raised a hand to brush a stray lock from his forehead. He'd gotten thinner over the course of days of illness. Violet shadows underlined his eyes, but his voice was clear. "I don't think I would have survived without her." He eyed the taproom, which contained a half dozen or so men. "Let's go back to the kitchen so I can pay my respects to Olivia. She's been kind enough to bring things to tempt my appetite." He rose awkwardly, using the table to steady himself as he gained his footing. Joshua left off from gathering dirty dishes and handed him a well-worn black music case. Will thanked him and laid it on the table, before carefully tucking his fiddle inside. He moved slowly toward the doorway out of the taproom and into the hall.

Faith rose to follow him then looked back at Titus. He was busy filling a tankard. As amber liquid flowed from the cask and into the earthenware tankard, Titus's eyes rose to meet hers, he nodded and angled his head toward the door for her to follow Will. Faith mouthed a thank you before leaving the bar to him and Joshua.

Will moved awkwardly, unsure of his steps and hesitant of his footing. Faith stopped walking before she ran into him. She thought about offering an arm to support him, but kept her mouth closed. He would not appreciate her observation of his weakness.

"I move like an old man these days," Will said quietly. "But I'm grateful to be moving at all. Athena says it will take time to regain my strength."

"I imagine so," Faith replied, not knowing what else to say.

"I returned to the print shop today and set some type while Paul hung some broad sheets to dry. Georgia has been busy selling advertisements for the *Gazette*. More people want to keep themselves apprised of events in the colonies."

Will grew quiet as he started down the steps to the yard. His free hand gripped the rail tightly as he carefully placed each foot on a step. Sweat beaded his brow, causing a stray auburn curl to stick to his face. Lines of strain formed on either side of his mouth as he continued down. At the bottom, Will stopped and drew in a few deep breaths before continuing down the red earthen path that led to the kitchen. He surprised Faith when he passed the kitchen and continued into the yard towards a small copse of trees at the back of the yard.

"Where are we going?" Faith asked.

Will took her hand in his. "Wait." A quiet smile framed his face as they continued through the rich green grass to the trees.

Outside, the afternoon sun cast a coppery eye on the horizon, painting the clouds in colors of gold and bronze. Off in the distance, doves cooed as they sought mates for the coming year. A light breeze teased the leaves emerging on the trees, making them rustle against the larger branches.

A plank bench rested under the shade of an oak that was framed on either side by thick branches of other trees. The emerging leaves created a private spot that was virtually invisible from the back porch.

Will sat down heavily, pulling her beside him. The music case rested on the ground beside him. He leaned back against the tree, looking out over the yard.

Faith watched Will's face as she waited. Illness had aged him and he looked frail. She suspected it would take time for the poison to leave his system. She was simply grateful he was alive.

Will broke in on her thoughts. "I've had a great deal of time to think over the past few days. About what I wanted to do with my life, what mattered most." His glance was almost shy. "You see, I've spent most of my adult years running from one thing to another. I came here because I had no other options and I came as a servant, bound to another for a span of years. I didn't know what or who I would find once I arrived."

His long slender fingers, rough with callouses and stained with ink, stroked her hand. "I knew when I met you, something in my life had changed. I really didn't want to admit it." The light caught his eyes, causing gold flecks to appear amidst the dark green iris. "I've lost a lot of people I loved, Faith

Clarke. More than I've time to share. But if this poisoning has taught me anything, it's that life can end at any time and I've wasted too much time not saying what's in my heart."

Faith shivered at the intensity in his voice. His free hand reached out and freed a strand of hair that was peeking out from her cap. Will curled it around his fingers, stroking it with his thumb.

"Your hair is like fine silk. To watch it catch the light is a little like watching the setting sun hit the clouds, coloring them gold and russet. I've no right to say these things. I'm a man bound for four more years before I can promise any sort of life, but I can't wait any longer." He turned and stiffly knelt on the ground. "Will you wait for me? I promise to love you like no other and to spend the remainder of my life showing you how deeply you are loved, Faith Clarke."

Faith drew in a deep breath, having forgotten to breathe moments before. "I love you too, Will. I can wait."

"Thank God." He paused for a moment before a faintly embarrassed look came over his face. "And now that you've agreed to be mine in four years, can you help me up? I fear I've misjudged my ability to get up and down unassisted."

Faith laughed as she offered her arm. "Yes, I will."

"Remember those words. You will be called upon to repeat them in a few years."

She leaned over to kiss his cheek after resettling him on the bench. "I will remember, and I pray you will too."

"There's no danger in that," He answered softly. "Thinking of you helped me survive."

Chapter Eight

Jeremy Butler sat near a window, nursing a tankard of ale while watching the activity on Duke of Gloucester Street. He had enjoyed a meat pie along with the huge slice of yeasty bread that came with it. Within the comfortable public room, a half dozen men also enjoyed the hospitality of the tavern keeper. Not far from where Butler sat, a pair of men were engaged in a game of checkers, each intent on analyzing the other's moves. Near the silent fireplace, a man used light cast from the window to read one of the Virginia Gazette's latest broadsides. Duke of Gloucester Street ran east to west, allowing the light to linger unfettered by buildings for hours before the sun sank in the sky. Most men occupied themselves with either eating or drinking or dice. Butler did not turn away a thick slice of cake covered in strawberries and cream offered to him by the pretty tavern maid. He smiled his thanks and turned back to the window, ignoring her hopeful smile. She was almost young enough to have been his daughter, had he any children.

Butler had time to kill. He could do nothing until evening's shadows fell. He nursed his ale and took time to appreciate the sweet delicacy of the berries. Reflections in the glass allowed him to keep an eye on the action within the tavern as well. Already the tavern miss had found an admirer. Her laugh joined with one slightly deeper, most likely the young man apprenticed to the weavers. Butler shook his head. Had he ever been that young? Outside, a rider and horse rode slowly down the street either headed home or seeking a room for the night. He continued eastward toward the capitol, where both the Raleigh and Christiana's Campbell's taverns lay, as well as the small establishment of a certain stubborn woman he knew.

By Butler's estimation, down the street apprentices were scurrying about Prentis' store, preparing to close for the night. Among them, members of the Prentis family tended to the family business. His surmise was confirmed when he spotted the older man, John Prentis, walking slowly down the street towards his home. According to his sources, a younger cousin, Robert, sometimes worked late. Butler hoped he was not inclined to do so tonight. He wanted to get in, uncover the information he wanted and be out before the night watch was any wiser.

Luck was with him, Prentis younger entered the tavern heading to a table already occupied by another gentleman who greeted him and invited him to join in a game of cards. That suited Butler just fine, it meant William Prentis' shop was unoccupied and he could search the ledger to see who at the Moore house had bought Ratsbane.

After paying for his meal, Butler also strode down the street, well past his intended target before crossing the road and heading down a side street before crossing into an alley. A light wind blew across the walkway, scattering dead leaves left from the winter. A pair of doves cooed from their perch on the roof of a small stable, content with their state of the world. A few hours of sun remained before night would fall on the town. Butler walked slowly as if he were simply heading home after a long day's work. The soft sound of singing caught his ears, the soft cadence of a lullaby likely conceived in Africa and carried across the sea to this place, far from home.

Shadows cast dark fingers out from the doorways and porches of buildings he passed, weaving bands of darkness as they joined the wraith-like darkness that fell from the trees that lined the path. Darkness swiftly overtook the narrow alleyways between businesses, welcoming only to the scurrying feet of rats seeking what humans had left for them to scavenge.

Butler's nose wrinkled at the unmistakable scent of urine nearby where someone had decided to make use of a tree not long ago, mixed with it were the usual town scents of beer and ink and animal waste. Fortunately, the wind was blowing away from him and soon relieved him of its acrid scent. Soon he arrived at the tidy brick building where the Prentises operated their business.

64

Although the streets had quieted as the sun set, small numbers of people lingered in the streets. The torch lighter had started his rounds to light the torches that lined the street. The roar of the flames in the distance warned Butler he would arrive shortly.

Down the street, men sang drunkenly as they exited Chowning's Tavern. Amidst the cursing and singing a child cried out, probably woken by the ruckus. It soon shushed hopefully comforted back to sleep, or so he hoped. He'd spent a night or two sleeping in barns and sheds, alone and hungry. Butler wished that fate on no one. Uneasy, he fingered the small locket he kept hidden about his neck. It was his one treasure, a small miniature of his mother, long since dead. Given as a gift from the man he presumed fathered him and his sister.

A large chimney occupied most of the back of the building, allowing only enough room for a small door that opened on a well-kept yard on the side where a large fenced garden took up most of the space. Butler recognized a few herbs, fennel, and hyssop, lavender, and foxglove. Beans ran up a trellis in profusion. Shadows cloaked the majority of the space although the bright blooms of nasturtiums and marigolds were visible as they bloomed in sweet profusion along the edges near the house. His nose picked up the delicate evergreen scent of rosemary before he spotted the modest shrub coated in shadows from the house. The narrow stoop stood bare, its surface swept clean of leaves and dirt. Everything about the building indicated it was well cared for. He moved forward then halted as he realized the door stood ajar, creaking as it moved slightly in the breeze.

Butler remained in the shadow of the house, listening for sounds of life. One of the apprentices could have stayed late, putting out stock for the next day. He waited, watching the shadows lengthen and darken as day ended. No sound came from within. Perhaps someone had been careless? There was no way he could be certain, and he needed some light for his search.

He looked about, both in the yard and across the fence into the street. No houses stood close by which left a disquieting amount of empty space. In the street, the clop of horse's hooves paired with the rattling of wagon wheels, a few murmurs of voices of men heading down toward the Raleigh Tavern from the sound of it. After the men passed, Butler went to the back door, wincing as a board squeaked beneath his boots. He slid inside, pushing the open door just enough to get inside.

Compared with the late afternoon sunlight outdoors, the interior of the shop was pitch black. Temporarily blinded, Butler stopped once inside waiting for his eyes to adjust. A faint whisper of sound was his only warning before someone crashed into him, sending him slamming into a shelf before hitting the ground. An array of objects crashed over him, hitting him again and again. The door slammed behind him leaving him alone in the dark.

He rolled into a ball, trying to protect his head from the onslaught of containers and crockery that broke and sent clouds of herbs and preparations into the air. Butler couldn't stop coughing as the powdery fog engulfed him. He stumbled to his knees, cursing as sharp edges dug into his skin. Stunned, he crawled underneath a table seeking refuge from falling tools, tinctures and heaven knew what else.

Once the avalanche stopped, Butler slowly crawled out from under the table. His nose burned and he coughed, caught in the dust of whatever had been in the broken jars that had almost buried him. His head throbbed dully as he slowly rose to his feet, taking stock of his injuries. Nothing felt broken, but his body felt every place something had hit him. Broken crocks littered the floor. They had once contained whatever items the merchants had stored there. Reaching up to check the stinging along his hairline, Butler winced as he pulled a fragment of porcelain out of his hair, smudged with blood. The ambush had taken him by surprise. No one knew of his errand. He must have surprised a burglar although there was not much of great value in the shop to steal. Regardless, he had pressing business of his own.

Using the light from the windows, he made his way to the small room at the back he had remembered from before. Light from a crescent moon provided some light through the front windows, partially shrouded by draperies. Mindful of the night watches' patrol, he kept to the inner walls of the building. Watching his steps among the rubble, he stepped inside. The room had been tossed. A table lay on its side, various items thrown onto the floor. Butler cursed. This made his job ten times harder. As he turned to go around the fallen table, his foot encountered something soft. He glanced down at an outstretched arm, its hand curled against the hardwood floor.

Butler's blood chilled as he knelt down to get a better look. Although the room remained cast in shadows, he could see a white shirt covered with a leather vest. The head lay at an odd angle partly covered by a large broken jug. The bitter metallic tang of blood assaulted his nose. The head lay in a puddle of it. Someone had smashed the man's head hard enough to snap his neck. Butler leaned back, his breath coming in sharp gasps. Only fate had kept him from joining the poor wretch into eternity. Looking about, he realized the shelf where he had once spied the ledger was now bare.

Butler hurriedly scanned the floor, mindful that every moment increased the danger of being caught and blamed for the murder. A tiny beam of moonlight gleamed through a crack in the draperies and caught something in the man's clenched fist. Butler eased it from fingers still faintly warm and pliable. He beheld a scrap of paper, a corner from a book perhaps. Butler could not read it in the dim light, so he tucked it into his vest pocket. The victim could not have been dead long, given the lack of stiffness. Butler was sure the man was dead but checked his throat for a pulse anyway. There was nothing, the man's eyes were sightless, his soul long gone. He'd probably come in to work thinking he would go home as he always had. Cursing himself as a superstitious fool, Butler closed his eyes and murmured *media vita in morte sumus.*

The pound of footsteps out the front warned him it was time to leave. He ducked below a counter as faces peered in through the cracks in the curtains. Shouts broke out as someone took in the damage. Butler heard the cries for the watch as he abandoned caution and leapt for the door, running as he hit the yard. Cries of men and dogs roared behind him as Butler raced to the fence, scrambling over it and into the woods that opened out behind. He ran blindly, stumbling over roots and fallen logs before sense took over. Pausing behind a huge tree, Butler stopped to catch his breath and consider his options. His hunters hadn't hit the woods yet, the baying was still somewhat distant. He would need to emerge and find a place where his scent would blend in and his presence be unnoticed. Through a break in the brush, he spotted the solid silhouette of a wall. Butler made for it as quickly as he could without tripping over another tree root.

Emerging behind a barn, he took a moment to catch his breath. Out in the yard, the soft, rich singing of slaves filled the air as they returned from the fields and to their homes. In a nearby corral, a couple of horses nickered as he passed. Their tails swished to shoo away the last of the evening's gnats.

He had little time before his pursuers broke through the woods as well. Moving slowly along the wall of the barn, he looked about. The servants appeared occupied with caring for their master's cows and horses. Butler paused a moment, slipping into the dark recesses of the barn before the men finished with the livestock and came inside. Hay and chaff lay mounded in one section, making his nose drain. He didn't dare sneeze. Hunkering down in a stall, Butler took a few deep breaths, trying to calm the pounding of his heart. The barn smelled like livestock, hay, and manure. He hoped that it was strong enough to hide any traces of his presence from the dogs he heard out in the yard. As the barn door opened, he clearly heard one of the hands say, "We haven't seen anyone come through. We've been here feeding the cows and slopping the hogs for a while now."

Tension thrummed through Butler's shoulders as the sound of voices and dogs faded away. There was always a chance that someone would hang about, waiting. He would have, had the roles been reversed. As he knelt inside the stall, sweat ran down his back even as his breathing returned to normal. Next to him, a horse nickered companionably. Butler glanced up at her warm brown eyes watching him from her side of the barrier.

"Shhhh," he crooned, hoping she would remain calm and not betray his presence.

The mare turned back, her head ducking down below where he could see. Through the planks separating them, he could hear her hooves shift about as she moved in the stall. She didn't seem worried. Butler let out a slow breath. If he was lucky, no one would want to use the stall he lay in. He could wait until the men had finished with the livestock and slip out, no one the wiser.

Outside, the bucolic lowing of the cattle painted a pastoral scene in his mind, one he did not trust. Butler wanted to take off, out of the confining barn and out where he could move freely, but he didn't dare go anywhere while he could still be seen and identified. Blood stuck to his face and hands, some of it his own. There was no way he could blend into a crowd until he cleaned up.

The barn door squeaked as its hinges flexed to swing the door open. A steady clop of hooves informed him that someone was leading a horse in for the night.

A voice spoke into the darkness. "Them folks be long gone. I doubt they will be back tonight." A long pause then. "Titus and Olivia speak well of you. I decided to trust their judgment. There's only me and my boy Sam here with the stock. After I drop these pails of water in the trough, we're headed down to the creek to get some more. It should take a while before we're back." The door shut, leaving Butler in the darkness. He rose and crept toward the door. Looking out through a crack in the wall, he spotted a black man wearing a large straw hat carrying a shoulder harness with pails on each end. Walking beside him was a boy in breeches and a shirt like his, carrying a smaller yoke with buckets, heading down a path away from the barn.

Butler eased the door open and slipped out into the twilight. He nearly tripped over a bucket of water left by the barn wall. Taking off his shirt, he splashed water on his hands and poured some over his bent head, shivering at the chill but grateful to be rid of the sticky blood. After rubbing off it with his shirt, he donned it and slipped back into the woods to meander home.

Chapter Nine

The bell let out its mournful toll early as most men and women were heading to work or engaged in other activities. Faith paused in the midst of doing her accounts, which was her habit after breakfast and before her overnight guests flew the coop. It took a few moments for the sound to penetrate her concentration and register what it was. Rising from her chair, she walked into the main hallway, where the last of her guests were headed to the main door of her establishment as well, all of them puzzled by the clamor.

Out on the porch, the clanging became more resonant before it stopped, its tone gradually fading away. Her remaining guests headed down the steps and out into town, some talking with each other as they strode toward the Capitol building that lay between them and the main thoroughfare of Williamsburg.

Faith brushed her apron down with her hands before looking over at Titus who had followed patrons out of the taproom. "I'd best see what news required that response." She told him. "They wouldn't be doing that without a reason. I hope no more militias are coming to harry the governor."

Titus's face was still. "That's not the only reason that bell sounds, Mistress Clarke."

Faith's heart jumped in her chest before becoming leaden. He was correct. The bell not only rang to summon folk to church and share news, it also proclaimed the death of important members of the community. "No," she said softly, not wanting to consider the possibility.

"Look," Titus said, pointing to a figure just emerging on the path that led into town.

Faith squinted against the bright morning sun at the man in a white wig and servant's livery walking swiftly toward the tavern. George, the proper, middle-aged man who Ezra relied upon for everything from carrying messages to brushing his suits, was coming toward them. Faith stumbled down the steps to meet him in the front yard of the tavern.

He pushed open the gate and stepped inside, raising eyes red-rimmed with grief. "Mistress Clarke, "he began slowly, his breathing labored.

Faith interrupted, "He's gone, isn't he?"

George nodded tightly. "He began failing in the early hours of the morning. We gathered the family. This morning, word was sent to the vicar at Bruton Parish."

"I'm family," Faith said tightly. "Why did no one come before now? Did it not occur that I or Andrew might want to say goodbye?"

The valet looked uncomfortable. "I'm sure no slight was intended, Mistress."

"Then you don't know Eugenia very well," Faith snapped.

Titus interrupted. "Have they planned the funeral yet?

Faith didn't stay to hear the answer. She felt like she could not breathe. Ezra was gone, Pain pummeled her heart in a cold wave, making her shiver. She wanted to scream and shout but there would be no point. Vaguely she heard Titus and George speaking, but nothing was intelligible. Roaring filled her head to the point of explosion. Ignoring the men, she went around to the back of the tavern,

The porch lay covered in veils of shadow from its pitched roof, allowing her some privacy. Faith sat down on the steps as her legs gave out. Her fingers gripped a side post, barely registering the sting of rough edges on her palms. Her breath came in great labored gasps that radiated from the depths of her soul. Despite the severity of his malady, she had always assumed Ezra would recover.

Wrapping her arms tightly about her body, she rocked back and forth, as soft keening sounds emerged from her lips as the pain refused to remain contained. Tears stung and dribbled down her cheeks to drip down her chin as she looked about her, blinking away tears that threatened to blind her.

Dew dappled the grass, sparkling like crystal where the sun had penetrated through the limbs of one of the trees. Olivia's hens strode about the garden, hunting for bugs, tiny chicks in tow, cheeping as they followed their mother up and down the rows.

Olivia's rich contralto floated out from the kitchen door as she worked on preparing the next meal for the day. The scents of rising bread and cooking meat were also in the air. No matter where Faith looked, life continued as it always had. It didn't seem fair. She looked up into the bucolic sky where a few cottony clouds floated in a chamber of deep blue. "Why?" She asked the Almighty. "Why did he have to die? Surely you could have spared such a good and decent man."

There was no answer. The sun still shone, the birds still sang. Faith sighed. Why were there no easy answers? A faint breeze whispered across the yard, brushing over her damp cheeks like a gentle caress, as it caused the nearby flowers and grasses to wave gently back and forth. A few flower blossoms brushed her face before falling into her lap. Faith started to brush the petals to the ground before picking them up to stare at them. The pale blue of forget-me-nots filled her palm. She quietly tucked them into a pocket.

Standing up she walked out into the yard, seeking solace from the bucolic setting. As she walked along the dirt path worn in the grass, she realized her steps were taking her to the private room Ezra had so painstakingly rebuilt, providing her with needed income and him with a place to meet quietly with his allies in the patriot cause.

The paint still looked new. Ezra had insisted on not only painting the room, but also the entire tavern so that it matched, even the walls of the narrow alley that connected the two. He had even put up a new sign advertising the tavern. Clarke Tavern had become not only his investment, but also his legacy. As she gained control of her grief, she realized Ezra's actions had ensured that Andrew and she would survive the muddled wake of her husband's unexpected death, which had thrown her into the world of business unprepared.

Wiping her face on her apron, she drew in a few deep breaths, ignoring the pinch of her corset. No matter her loss, life continued and there would still be guests to attend. Wallowing in grief would not help anyone. Slipping back inside, she walked to her room, intent on putting herself back together before heading to the taproom. Already, low murmurs and the clink of tankards told her there were guests. The deep timbre of Titus' voice resonated through the walls as he tended the bar.

Faith poured water from the pitcher into the basin and taking a clean cloth, wiped her face. The cool water felt soothing to her flushed skin and burning eyes. Again, she breathed, knowing she had no choice but to present her guests with a calm façade.

Reminders of Ezra's generosity were everywhere. He had insisted on painting the interior walls a soft creamy white last fall, which brightened the interior. In one corner, the tile stove stood, polished and ready for any cold snaps. Deep red curtains hung from the window, tied back to let in the light. On the wall was a silhouette of Andrew that his father had gotten done the year before his death. Beside it was one of her, he had paid for as well. After John's death, nearly two years ago, Eugenia had clung to the silhouette of him she possessed with evangelistic fervor, vowing it would never leave her home.

Faith's life revolved around this tavern, a place she would not have if not for the generosity of her father-in-law. Ezra had paid off the debts John had run up opening the business and asked little in return, except her help in his more secret activities. Now he was dead. "I will find out who did this," she whispered in the empty room.

A tap on the door outside her room caught her attention. "Who is it?"

"Olivia. May I come in?"

"Yes." She watched as Olivia entered and took a long look at Faith. She carried a crystal glass filled with amber fluid. Brandy fumes tickled Faith's nose.

"I suspect you need this,"

"It's early for spirits."

Olivia's ebony eyes glittered from grief she held within. "Not on a day like this. You need a shot to steady your nerves before you head over to the house."

She meant the Moores' house. Faith didn't want to go but knew she should. "There's going to be a lot of upheaval."

Olivia chuckled grimly. "There's no doubt of that. Master Moore's sons have never cared much for Ms. Genia. She doesn't care much for them either. Now that Ezra is gone, it's going to get ugly."

Faith downed the liquor quickly before second thoughts stayed her hand. The brandy burned down her throat, leaving a sensation of warmth and faint queasiness.

"Daniel seemed to think she had something to do with his poisoning," Faith said quietly.

Olivia raised an eyebrow. "If Eugenia wanted him dead, she would have picked a more subtle poison. She knows her herbs. Whoever set out to kill Ezra chose something that could be gotten quick and took no skill to administer."

Faith looked at Olivia thoughtfully. "You know her pretty well, don't you?"

Olivia's cat-like eyes crinkled slightly. "You cannot live and work with someone for years and not get some sense of who they are. Miss Genia took me when no one else would. She taught me what she knew of herbs and healing, then she gave all of us to you. Not many folk would have chosen to let us all go together, but she doesn't believe in breaking up families. I won't forget that."

Faith nodded. Olivia had been a slave most of her life before Faith had manumitted her and Titus. She didn't talk much about her past, although Faith was aware that she had come over from Jamaica as a child. She knew suffering and separations that Faith could not even begin to imagine. She would feel no need to protect a person who had once owned her. Olivia noticed things about people that others did not. Faith had learned to rely on her judgment.

Olivia went over to Faith's clothes chest and removed the sheet of muslin laying over it.

"What are you doing?"

"You can't go over there dressed like you've been waiting tables, Miss Faith. You need to look respectable, like a member of the family because that is who you are. Ezra liked you and he would want you there."

"You're right." Faith removed her cap and began the task of removing her apron and jacket, carefully removing the long pins that held the sides together. Once she had stripped down to her petticoats and stays, she looked at what Olivia had revealed. It made sense, even if the sight of the patterned gray fabric made her throat tighten. She had worn that dress often in the days and months following Jon's death just over a year ago. It was the closest to mourning that she could do at the time, that and the black aprons and ribbons Eugenia had supplied.

Olivia noticed her expression. "We don't have time to make up anything new."

Faith nodded. "Nor do we have that kind of money. It will do, Olivia. I shouldn't be so foolish about clothes." She looked it over. "You've worked on it."

Olivia shook her head. "Not me. One of the ladies at the millinery shop. Ezra's son's wife agreed to pay for the alteration so you would look respectable for the funeral. I think Ms. Fanny did a fine job adding the lace."

Faith nodded. The seamstress had done more than add lace. The sleeves and neckline reflected changes in style over the past year. Black ribbon made it even more sober. White lace filled in enough of the neckline that it wasn't indecent. With it was a pair of black kid gloves and one of her hats, dyed black and trimmed in black ribbon. "You've been busy. Thank you." Faith had focused so intently on the death that she had not thought about having proper clothes. Olivia had saved her from major embarrassment.

Olivia smiled before gesturing for her to sit. "Let me brush your hair."

"Preparing well is your best armor," she replied as she began removing the pins that held Faith's hair in place. The pins rattled as Olivia set them down on the top of her writing desk.

As Olivia brushed slowly and methodically through Faith's scalp, the tension began to ease from her body. Faith realized that this had been Olivia's purpose, to calm her before the arduous journey.

As her breathing eased, her mind began to work. "Olivia, do you believe someone murdered Ezra?"

The other woman paused. Olivia was no longer a slave, but she remained cautious about what she said. She rarely volunteered information. After a moment, Olivia answered. "Yes, I do, Miss Faith. It's the only explanation. Something about his passing just doesn't make sense to me."

"Someone suggested it might be cholera."

Another pause. "I've seen cholera, when I was a child in Jamaica. It's not something you forget." Olivia's voice was grim. "If there was a cholera outbreak in Williamsburg, more people would be sick or dying. It would spread through town like a wildfire. This struck Ezra. I don't believe that was an accident. I spoke with Athena. She's pretty sure it's arsenic."

Faith's voice was quiet. "She showed me a bottle that had arsenic powder around the rim. She said Ezra had given it to Will after they shared a drink after the meeting with Governor Dunmore."

The brush hit a snarl, causing Faith to stifle a yelp as it pulled on her scalp. She reached down to grip the seat of the chair for support. The rough bottom scraped her fingernails providing a faint distraction from the ongoing torture.

Olivia muttered an apology as she separated the brush from the unruly knot. With a few quick motions, she twisted Faith's hair into a neat knot and pinned it into place with pins.

Olivia helped her dress, shaking the wrinkles out of a simple dove-gray petticoat that went over her everyday petticoats. Pulling out a jacket with a coordinating pattern, Olivia helped her get her arms in the sleeves before leaving her to pin it in place. Faith took the fresh white cap Olivia handed her and tied it about her head, grateful that the other woman had already attached black ribbon to it.

"Thank you. You have always been a great help to me."

Olivia's eyes gleamed like jet in the shadows of the room. "You freed us and allowed us to make our own decisions. I will never forget that, or how you tried to help Stella."

Faith nodded. She had not realized that Olivia had a sister until she had been accused of murder last year. Her regret was that Stella had died alone in the gaol and there had been no way to save her.

"Time for you to go," Olivia said, gesturing to the door. Titus and I can manage here. The boys are busy with dishes. They will be back soon."

"Andrew," Faith hesitated. Here was another death for him to accept. His father's death over a year ago had been difficult. Neither of them had expected it. Now he was ten years old and the man he considered his grandfather was gone.

"Talk to him when you get home," Olivia said. "We won't speak of it here."

"Thank you," Faith said before removing her apron. Her footsteps echoed in the hallway as she walked back to her room. Peering in the small mirror that hung from the wall, she wondered what she should say. The face that stared back looked pale and tired. Ezra had been the one she went to when she needed to discuss her problems. She didn't know what to say to Eugenia. She put on a clean apron. She didn't bother pinching her cheeks for color. It seemed ridiculous considering her errand. Ezra was dead. Her eyes burned as a knot appeared in her throat. Faith swallowed hard. There was not time for tears and Ezra would expect her to support Eugenia and Louis, though she doubted he needed anything from her. Rumor had it that Eugenia was intent on finding him a wealthy bride. Faith shuddered at the thought of Louis playing the role of husband to any poor girl. It was none of her business, she reminded herself. And there would be no large social gatherings to attend during their period of mourning. Tying her kerchief in place about her shoulders, Faith took a deep breath. There was no putting this off. "God have mercy on us all," she murmured as she strode out the door and down the street to the place her father-in-law had lived his last days.

Chapter Ten

Jeremy Butler paced like a caged animal within the confines of the room above where Athena reigned as cook for the widowed Georgia Clements. After the ruckus at Prentis' shop, he had remained out of sight, lest someone recognize him. He longed to be out and about town gathering intelligence. Despite the debacle a few nights ago, he knew little more than he had before, other than someone was desperate to cover his tracks.

He could not sit still knowing an enemy roamed freely, able to strike at any time. For all he knew, the entirety of his carefully built network of patriots was at stake. Ezra's poisoning had been both deliberate and brutal. But why? There were patriots that were far more outspoken in Williamsburg and Ezra was discreet in his leanings. He doubted the governor had had a hand in it. Dunmore was volatile and sneaky, but he was no coward. Slipping a man poison smacked of cowardice. Besides, if Dunmore wanted to kill a patriot, there were more vocal critics of his regime. Butler mentally considered other prominent Tories in town; there were plenty, but few had been in close contact with Ezra, except Peyton Randolph. He frowned. Randolph had gone up to Philadelphia for the Second Continental Congress not long after the meeting he, along with Ezra and others, had held with the governor. From what he had heard, Peyton Randolph was not the most enthusiastic of revolutionaries. Randolph was gone, but his staff might know something. Olivia or Titus very likely knew the slaves over there. Despite the restrictions that went with being enslaved, the black community was close-knit. They looked after each other in a way Butler envied.

His restless mind continued seeking suspects. Ezra had excelled at sending and receiving information, all under the guise of his business interests. As far as Butler could tell, his work remained undiscovered by the British and their allies. Butler rubbed his head restlessly. Maybe he was looking in the wrong direction. Athena had suggested that the attack might be personal, rather than politically motivated.

Without hesitation, he considered Ezra's wife, Eugenia. Butler despised her. Eugenia's Tory loyalty had nothing to do with politics and everything to do with her desire for all the luxuries trade could provide. Despite Ezra's mild reprimands, she curled her nose at anything deemed provincial. To Butler, she seemed like a spoiled, willful child rather than a middle-aged woman with adult children. He had no doubts she could poison someone. She was quite knowledgeable about herbs but would she risk losing all the benefits that being the wife of a wealthy merchant brought her? The Moores entertained lavishly and dined with the governor at his residence. Ezra indulged her love of gowns and jewels. Widowhood might not offer those kinds of opportunities.

Heat from the constant fire below kept the room so warm Butler felt like he was on one of Athena's spits. Outside, a mockingbird chirped as it lit on the sill of the open window. It tilted its head as it watched him taking its measure. Butler took one stride toward it before it winged away across the yard and into a nearby copse of oaks. "Cheeky devil," he muttered. Were it not for the heat, he would have pulled down the sash to keep birds out of the room, having had to chase out a few sparrows the day before. Lying low a few days had not felt to be such a burden until he had heard the tolling of the bells. Butler had realized what it meant before Silas had come up to bring him breakfast and share the news.

Frustrated, he paced back and forth in the tiny apartment. Against all odds, he had hoped Ezra would recover. Butler claimed few friends and Ezra Moore had become one. Butler could find no one to speak against him. Even his opponents in the House of Burgesses spoke of him with respect. Killing him made no sense. Grief channeled into rage as he silently swore to avenge his old friend. To die in battle was one thing, but to die slowly from the agony of poison was quite another. He intended to find the guilty bastard and administer some justice of his own after he found out why.

A quiet knock on the door drew his attention. "Who is it?" he said softly, picking up a walking stick he used on occasion. In addition to its sturdy length, a sword nested inside made it doubly useful. Butler eased forward on cat feet carefully avoiding the squeaky board that ran close to the center of the room. Anyone who broke in would discover him more than willing to beat the stuffing out of him or her. Today he made little attempt to leash his temper. He longed for something to transmit his rage to. He slowly lowered his weapon when he heard the woman on the other side of the door.

"It's Athena," she said before opening the door and slipping inside. "I wanted to see you." Although Butler had known her for over twenty years, she never seemed to age. Her beautiful coppery brown skin was like the finest satin, and only the faintest of creases appeared at the corner of her eyes, which appeared only a shade or two darker than her skin. She was nearly six feet tall and rounded in a way to please any man. He suspected that was how she had ended up in her former master's bed. He had never asked, and Athena refused to talk about the life she had left behind.

She thoughtfully eyed the stick in his left hand. "Expecting trouble?"

Butler set it to one side. "You can't be too careful. You taught me that."

"I also taught you to think before you act-or did you forget that part?"

Butler shook his head. "No ma'am. I've just been shut up here too long. I need to get out and find out what is happening."

Athena looked thoughtful. "That might be possible. So far no one has come up with a plausible description of the man who broke in and killed that young man."

"He was dead when I got there," Butler said. "If I had been there a few moments earlier, I could have stopped it from happening." Frustrated, he punched the side of the wall. Athena raised a brow at him.

"Did that help?"

"No," he growled softly as he rubbed his aching knuckles against his breeches. "My whole organization could be in danger while I sit up here. If I had stopped him then, this would be over."

Athena raised a hand to silence him. "I know that, Jeremy. You told me when you dragged in here a few nights ago. However, folks in town don't know there were two men there. Talk in town is that someone broke in to rob the place, was discovered by the apprentice, killed him, and ran off. The Prentises are heralding the man as a hero to his family for defending the place against a vicious burglar. They're even paying for his funeral."

Butler drew an exasperated breath while raking his hands through his hair, which he hadn't bothered to tie back this morning. "So the boy is a hero for being in the wrong place at the wrong time. Did anyone but me notice the account book was missing?"

Athena nodded. "It's been mentioned, but right now they're trying to put the shop back together so they can continue in business. From what I hear, much of their stock was destroyed. The good news for you is that all anyone can recall is a man running off in the dark. No one got a clear look at you."

"So, I'm free to head out and find out who killed Ezra."

She nodded. "That's one of the reasons I came up here, that, and to let you know that the funeral will be in a few days, once the doctor is finished with him."

"Doctor?" Butler was confused. "He's dead already. What need does he have of any physician?"

"Ezra's sons have demanded an autopsy. His wife is having a fit about them cutting him open. I'm surprised you didn't hear her all the way over here."

"Doesn't she want his killer found? An autopsy would provide proof of the poison. How can she not see that?"

"Maybe she does," Athena said. "If they say it was cholera, she's a wealthy widow with a nice house in the heart of Williamsburg. If they say poison, then the question is who killed him?"

Butler stilled. "Do you believe she could have done it?"

Athena smiled grimly. "I don't know her. Nevertheless, money can be a powerful motive. You've spent time in that house, what do you think?"

Butler paused. His visits to Ezra Moore's home in Williamsburg had been rare, simply to avoid a recognizable pattern. His observation of Eugenia had been seldom, but he had taken note of her expensive taste and the tension between Ezra and her over her spending. Eugenia loved clothing and furnishings imported from Europe. Ezra seemed to handle it with a mixture of amusement and resignation.

"My wife likes to keep the European economy afloat," he had once commented.

Most of their meetings had taken place either in the private room of Clarke Tavern or in places where there was no one who would note the meeting. Butler wondered bleakly how he could ever replace him. He looked up to catch Athena watching him.

"I don't know if she did it or not," he admitted. "Olivia told me that she was skilled in the use of herbs, so she would know how. I just don't know why she would." A floorboard creaked underneath his foot. "We need eyes in that house, someone whose presence would not be questioned."

"You're going to send your little innkeeper to spy on her mother-in-law." Athena had tangled with Faith last year. It had left both women with a wary respect for the other.

"No one would question a family member going to help in a time of bereavement. Athena nodded. "That's true, but can you trust her judgment so close to home?"

"Do I have a choice?" he replied, staring up as if the pitched ceiling offered answers from above.

Chapter Eleven

D ust motes danced in the air, invisible except for the shafts of pale sunlight drifting in from the windows on either side of the sanctuary of Bruton Parish Church. Amidst the crush of petticoats, Faith felt packed like a fish in a barrel. She, Eugenia, and Ezra's son's wives were packed into a pew in the women's section on the south side. Ezra's sons, Zachary and Daniel occupied Ezra's seat in the government section of the sanctuary. Louis Clarke, Eugenia's remaining son, sat by them. Faith could barely see them amidst the rabbit warren of columns, private pews, and other seats filling the space. Not even the overpowering scent of Eugenia's perfume could mask the unmistakable scent of unwashed bodies crowded into a warm room.

A dull headache formed within Faith's skull as she looked upward at the raised platform where the priest would speak, and men would come to speak their eulogies over her dead father-in-law. The muted throb did nothing to distract from the noisy murmur of voices as people entered to fill the pews both on the main floor and upstairs where she knew Olivia was.

Her eyes burned with tears she refused to shed. She had wept in the early hours of the dawn, smothering her sobs with a pillow so as not to disturb anyone. Today she would honor a good man and look for clues to the identity of his killer.

A breeze drifted in the windows, offering a hint of air in the crowded space. Through the wooden floorboards, she felt the vibration as the organ began to play, muffling the shuffling of feet as people continued to enter. Her mind turned to the endless mechanisms of mourning that had permeated the day.

Early, she had choked down a cup of coffee and joined the family at the Moore house on Francis Street. Everyone from Lord Dunmore to the footman wore a black ribbon of mourning. After prayer and reading of scripture, six servants including Titus, lifted the closed coffin and set out for Bruton Parish, followed by Ezra Moore's friends and family.

The dusty procession down Duke of Gloucester Street had been miserable. Despite the rancor between Eugenia and Ezra's other children, they had agreed he deserved a funeral worthy of his standing. The wailing of the mourners had penetrated her skull early in the day, aided and abetted by the merciless white-hot gleam of the early morning sun overhead.

She swatted irritably at a fly that buzzed about her face. Perhaps she should have worn a veil like her mother-in-law. Next to her, Eugenia sat dressed in full mourning; black dress, petticoats, gloves, hat, and veil. Louis had lent her his arm during the procession from their home to the church. Like Faith, he had eschewed full mourning and had tied a black armband over his dark blue jacket. Faith wore a black knot around the waist of her gray overskirt. Olivia had dyed her straw hat black as well. Ezra's family had provided black ribbon and gloves to family and friends. They sat in the place allotted to Ezra due to his place in the House of Burgesses. Faith found it ironic that despite the dismissal of the Burgesses last year, to a man they held onto every privilege granted the office. Nonetheless, she was grateful for a seat in the crowded building even if the hardwood quickly numbed her bottom despite layers of petticoats and skirt.

The doors at the back creaked closed as the last people entered the room. Upstairs, Faith knew Titus had joined Olivia and Joshua. He had been one of six servants assigned to carry the casket down the road and into the church. Faith had heard him instructing the men how to lift together and balance the load. He had done this before. She remembered him carrying Jon to the churchyard for his simple funeral, where Ezra had stood beside her lending silent support over Eugenia's hysterical sobs.

Her throat knotted painfully at the memory. Nothing about the church had changed in the year since that last funeral. Faith swallowed against the pain rising from the depths of her soul. Her hands clenched as she fought for composure. The black kidskin of her gloves stretched tightly across her knuckles, reminding her that she was on display along with the rest of Ezra Moore's family, business associates, and friends. It was too warm for the layers of clothes she wore. Her corset was already beginning to stick to her from sweat. Her nose took in the scent of too many bodies in an enclosed space. Her vision grayed briefly before she took in a breath.

Despite the warmth, Faith could not permit herself to faint. She bit the inside of her mouth welcoming the sting that jolted her back into sensibility. She had been surprised to see British officers among the crowd before she remembered how carefully Ezra kept his patriotic leanings under wraps. It made his death all the odder.

Faith's eyes slid over to the dark veiled figure beside her. Her mother-in-law had said barely a word since she had come downstairs for the walk to the church. One of Ezra's friends had offered a prayer for the well-being of his soul before they set off.

Although she heard the sermon and moved in tandem with the prayers, it was as if time stood still. She bowed her head in prayer and focused on breathing in and out. It would be over, soon it would be over. Ezra would be buried, the guests would return to the Moore home and feast from the spread the servants had prepared, drink fine wine from his cellars and leave to go about their business as if nothing had happened.

She knew her thoughts were unfair. Some of the mourners seemed genuinely grief-stricken, but many had come for the show. Faith hated it; the black handkerchiefs, the well-rehearsed wailing of mourners, and the endless march through the street as if a macabre celebration were being staged. Nowhere was there time to privately mourn a good and decent man taken too soon.

Zachary Moore rose from within the pew. His brother Daniel followed him. Both wore plain black coats with a black band at the arm. She was not surprised that they would choose to speak. Ezra had a warm relationship with all his children. They walked slowly to the podium, the elder, Daniel, in the lead. Next to her, Eugenia stiffened as she watched them walk up the steps and turn to face the audience.

Daniel faced the congregants; his face looked pale against the severe black of his jacket, blending in with the white of his cravat. Zachary stood just behind his shoulder. Both looked grim. "I come here to celebrate my father, Ezra Abraham Moore, and to mourn his passing. To name his accomplishments would take far longer than time will allow. Suffice it to say he was in all honorable, whether it was in his dealings with the government, commerce, or to the people he passed in the street each day. Whether man, child, or stray dog, he was honest, fair, and kind.

To me, he was the best of fathers. He led by example, but he was always available to lend a hand or an ear. He taught my brother and sisters and me how to ride a horse, add sums and appreciate a fine glass of wine. He made sure we heard the word of God and respected it. Even when he disagreed with a man's views, he accepted a man's right to follow his own conscience.

It is why it is inconceivable to me that such a man could be foully murdered in his own home among those he loved and trusted best. You may have heard he died of a fever that came on suddenly. The esteemed doctors within this holy house have indicated they thought such a thing, but I believe the words of my father, spoken before he died. He said he had been poisoned and begged those he trusted to find his killer." Daniel's eyes bore into Faith's. She stared back, horrified by what she was witnessing.

"My father was not the victim of strangers, set up at a chance meeting. No, he was set upon in his own home, slyly by one who hoped to live in luxurious fashion on the rewards of his work. Someone close to him, knowledgeable in the uses of herbs and draughts, knew when and where to place the fatal dose and then waited for him to die an agonizing death while she cried crocodile tears and waited to inherit."

I implore you, good citizens of Williamsburg; don't let my father die in vain at the hands of a heartless poisoner. Grant him justice so that he may rest, and we may know that although we lost him far too soon, he received the justice he deserves."

The large sanctuary echoed with gasps that quickly evolved into a hum of whispers too indistinct to hear, but hard to ignore. It swept through the room like a swarm of insects filling the once empty space. Faith held her head high, eyes forward, nudging Andrew to do likewise when his head swiveled around to look at the people around them.

"Why are people staring at us?" he whispered. "I want to go home."

She did too, but knew they had to stay until the service concluded. "Shh," Faith replied. "We will be home soon. We have to say farewell to Grandpa Ezra."

Andrew subsided but he didn't look happy. Faith didn't blame him. This was too much for a nearly ten-year-old to take in. If she could find Olivia or Titus after the service, she intended to send him home with them and save him the spectacle of filling the grave.

Ezra's second son walked up the steps to the podium as Daniel walked down the aisle and out the door, the sound of it closing echoing through the sanctuary. Unrolling a small scroll of foolscap, Zachary began to read. "My father was a good and honorable man who provided for his family and cared for his community. I will miss him all the days of my life." he fumbled with something in his hands, it was Ezra's pocket watch. Faith swallowed the knot rising in her throat. Many times, she had seen Ezra take it out and examine it. It was a solid reminder of the man that had passed. Taking as deep a breath as she could with stays, Faith looked back up at the podium. Now wasn't the time to grieve. Here she had to keep her guard up, she would mourn later with good friends in private. Zachary lacked the fire of his brother, but Faith preferred the awkward honesty of his words. Strands of dark hair worked their way out of his club to curl around a face mildly scarred by pox. Ezra's wife and a daughter had died from the disease, but Zachary had survived. The other children had escaped the disease.

Beside her, Faith heard the soft sobs of Ezra's daughter and daughters-in-law. Eugenia remained frozen in her seat, barely breathing. Across the room, Louis sat frozen in the pew.,his gaze glued on the podium.

The minister rose to his sermon, speaking words of comfort and reconciliation that fell on a shell-shocked audience. Except for the rustling of a few rapidly beating fans, no one appeared to move until the organ recessional jolted them into action. Along with the sound of shoes and boots across the wooden floor, whispers drifted across. Too low for words to be distinguished, but nonetheless, the tones stung like flies. Faith stood awkwardly and tried to negotiate the door amidst so many wide skirts.

Louis saved her the trouble by opening the door and helping her out before turning to Eugenia. Louis took his mother's arm and led her out of the church, supporting her as they walked slowly to the place where Ezra would be interred. As Faith approached with Andrew, it struck her how the family had divided on either side of the hole. On one side were Ezra's grown children, their faces stony and cold, although Martha and one of Ezra's daughters held black-bordered handkerchiefs to their eyes.

On the other side, Eugenia and Louis stood, looking very much alone. Eugenia, too, held a black-bordered cloth in her hand. It rose from time to time up under the dark veil. Faith crossed quietly to stand near them, cognizant that in so doing she was implying Eugenia's innocence. A dark voice in her mind noted that Eugenia could have easily doctored the bottle. She had the knowledge and easy access. The lingering question was why? Faith had no idea.

The minister's cough drew her back to the open grave. She bowed her head as he prayed. Behind her, she heard murmured voices, some grieving, others raised in prayer. Titus's deep bass softly called to God. Faith felt comforted by his presence.

After the final prayer and ceremonial tossing of soil on the coffin, Faith walked back to the Moore house where the next few hours were a blur of food and drink as people dropped by for the traditional offering of food and to acknowledge the passing of a man respected by his community. Faith suspected most came for the food and an opportunity to sample the liquor cabinet. Eugenia retired upstairs almost immediately, leaving Ezra's children to deal with the crowd.

The brothers gathered in Ezra's old office while Martha bustled about making sure food and drink were offered and that anyone in danger of becoming too well lubricated was escorted out by one of the staff.

Faith eyed the ormolu clock on the mantle and wondered how long she had to politely accept condolences before she could escape to the relative sanity of her inn. All around her people ate and drank and gossiped as if they were attending a macabre party. She wandered about the downstairs rooms filled with few people she knew. She accepted condolences with a brief nod. She avoided the enormous table of food in the room normally reserved for balls. People swarmed like flies, piling their plates with food. Faith recognized none of them. She suspected many had come in for the opportunity of a free meal. As she crossed the entryway, she glanced up the stairway wrapped in black fabric. Eugenia stared down at her from over the rail before gesturing for her to come up.

The steps creaked softly under the leather of her shoes, almost completely muffled by the noise of the supposed mourners below. Faith followed her mother-in-law to a small room Eugenia used to write letters and attend to household business. She had never been inside before. She paused before the entryway to see what Eugenia was doing.

"Come in before someone sees you." Eugenia's voice had lost its cultured enamel and sounded rough and exhausted. She collapsed into a padded chair, its legs covered in gilt.

Faith stepped in and sat in a simple wooden chair across from her. Her eyes took in the elaborate floral wallpaper that surrounded the small room. The large pink flowers with their encircling vines made her feel like she was being slowly smothered. A large window went from floor to ceiling letting in the afternoon light. Pastel draperies ran the length of the wall framing the window.

Eugenia sighed and gestured at the doorway. "Ruth, please bring us some of that light Rhenish wine. I have need of something to settle my nerves."

Faith caught sight of a young dark-skinned woman, her hair covered by a light-colored cap. She glided soundlessly into the room, her skirts brushing the polished floor as she brought in a decanter and two glasses, setting them down on a small table between them, carefully missing the china figurine taking over the center of the space.

Eugenia took a healthy gulp, gasping slightly as the alcohol hit. Faith took a more measured sip feeling the burn down her throat. It wasn't wine, but brandy, probably from Ezra's private collection. She looked over at the other woman, noting that she had slightly more color in her face. "How are you doing?"

"Terrible, I don't think it could get much worse." Eugenia shuddered as she took another drink. "I'm treated like an enemy in my own home. They want me gone, but I'm not leaving. Ezra promised to always take care of me. This house is mine and all its contents. I will not leave." She smiled grimly. "They think I don't know what they plan late at night, but I have ears they don't see." Eugenia looked away for a moment to the light that trickled through the window. Her voice became low and choked. "I did everything in my power to save him."

Light flickered through the draperies, muted slightly by the leafy limbs of a tree. Dappled sun spilled on Eugenia's face revealing a network of fine lines and shadows. Age had caught up with her as Ezra lay dying. Faith felt a rush of pity as she looked at her once indomitable mother-in-law. Eugenia rocked back and forth soundlessly. "I didn't kill him." She paused, fighting for control. Her face contorted with grief she didn't want to reveal. Her eyes glittered as she glared over at Faith, as if daring her to contradict.

"I know." And in that moment, she did. Faith could see no reason for Eugenia to poison Ezra. He provided for her generously. For all their differences, they seemed to care for one another.

"His sons seek to lay blame on me." Eugenia reached out and grabbed Faith's hand, holding it in a death grip. 'You have to prove I did not do this. You must."

Faith struggled to free herself. Eugenia held it in a crushing grip. She stared at her mother-in-law, seeing what she had missed earlier. Beyond the grief of loss, Eugenia was deathly afraid. She carefully peeled the death grip from her hand and returned it to the other woman's lap. "Ezra's own physician remains convinced he died of cholera."

"Ezra insisted that someone had killed him. Everyone who drank the governor's Madeira with him that night fell deathly ill within a few hours. Ezra's own valet we buried yesterday." Eugenia put her head in her hands. "Ezra's sons have never liked me. I never thought they would go to these lengths to claim their inheritance."

Faith was dumbfounded. "You think they killed their father?"

"They will inherit most of his worldly goods, short of my widow's portion. If I am convicted, they receive that as well. Who else had cause to harm him?"

"What of those who disagreed with his support of the Patriot cause? That's who Ezra believed guilty."

Eugenia sniffed. "He suspected Governor Dunmore. The royal governor is an honorable man and loyal to his king. No one loyal to the king would stoop to poison, it's uncivilized."

She leaned forward, her eyes narrowed. "If anyone did this, it was the patriot rabble he foolishly associated with. There is no loyalty among rebels. Ezra didn't think I knew about his secret meetings in your shabby little tavern and around town, but I heard the whispers. He was a fool to dabble in this revolt and look where it landed him. Dead! Betrayed by dirty sleeved printers, and farmers that he had no business consorting with. She drew breath to continue as the door was flung open.

Daniel Moore strode in, followed by the sheriff. "There she is, the killer of my father, arrest her!"

Faith jumped at his bellow. Ezra's eldest son's eyes gleamed with fanatic rage as he glared at the two women. He glanced at the glasses and bottle at the side table. "You celebrate your victory too soon, Madam. I know you poisoned him, but I will make sure you do not profit even if it takes me to the end of my days." He removed a slender vial from his pocket and waved it in Eugenia's face.

"Look at this."

A small cork held pale yellow powder that had settled in the bottom. Faith had seen these before at many of the shops in town. Yellow arsenic. It was used to eliminate rats and apparently, people too.

Eugenia looked surprised then tried to shrug it off. "That has nothing to do with me."

"It was found in your still room; where you have been so busy making preparations and tonics for my father."

"I made peppermint tea to ease his digestion. I don't know how that got there. I don't keep rat poison with my herbs."

"So you say." Scorn laced his tone as he passed it to the sheriff. "You know what this woman has done. My father deserves justice. Will you not give it to him?"

The sheriff turned to Eugenia who looked even paler than before. "Mistress, one of my men found that bottle. Do you mean to tell me it's not yours?"

"I've never seen it."

Both women had risen to their feet. Faith stared at the sheriff and Ezra's son. There was something they were not telling them. Sheriff Johnson's face was grim.

"There is also the matter of your husband's finances. Did you not cash a check at the bank, just two days ago?"

Eugenia flushed. "I did. My husband has always taken care of me. He signed a check for me just before he died."

Daniel's face flushed in rage. "My father was in and out of consciousness for days. He couldn't have knowingly done that."

"I know my husband," Eugenia shot back. "I knew his wishes. Even in illness, his thoughts were on providing for his family."

Daniel sneered. "Your greed knows no shame. Even as he drew his last breath, you were fleecing him."

The sheriff intervened, raising a hand to silence the embattled pair. "We will settle this matter civilly. Mistress Moore, please come with me so we may discuss this matter in private." He swiveled to point a finger at Daniel Moore. "You will hold your peace young man. I will make no prejudgments about anyone, nor will I allow rumors to run rampant in my town." He looked at Faith.

"Mistress Clarke."

Faith nodded. "Sheriff Johnson."

"Your father-in-law always spoke well of you. He believed you did an admirable job in revealing the truth surrounding Master Bullard's death last year."

Faith didn't like to think of how close she had come to being blamed for murder last year. She nodded. "My father-in-law thought well of many people."

Eugenia shot a pleading look at Faith as she exited the door. "Find the truth. My son would have wanted you to take care of me."

She was right. Jon would have, had he been alive. Faith's husband had been gone nearly two years and still his ghost arose at odd moments.

Outside the door, voices reached a crescendo as awareness that something unusual was occurring swept through the house. The crowd that had gathered around the buffet table and bar moved into the hall to watch Eugenia being led down the stairs of her home by the sheriff and his men.

Eugenia held her head erect as she met the eyes of prominent members of the town and their wives. Through the years she had been to many teas and balls at their homes. Her expression dared them to speak as she walked past at a steady pace, her feet making barely a sound on the ornate rug that ran the length of the entryway. Faith remained a few paces behind, watching as Ezra's eldest descended to be met by his wife and younger brother.

Martha was clad in a gown of deepest wine trimmed in black. She parted through the crowd swiftly to greet him. "Daniel," her rich contralto was barely audible as she reached to touch his sleeve.

Daniel's face contorted as he fought for control. His voice cracked as he reached to grasp his wife's hand. "I had to," he breathed, "For Papa's sake."

Martha nodded as she grasped his hand, rubbing it gently between her two. "I will take care of our guests, do what you must." Her eyes followed him out the door as he strode to open it for the sheriff.

He nodded and looked over at his brother. Zachary Moore's eyes were puffy, but he appeared calm in the midst of the maelstrom. "Take care of our father's business," Daniel said before he strode out the front door following the Sheriff and his men as they led Eugenia to the gaol, while the guests gathered like vultures waiting for the right moment to swoop in.

As Faith went to follow them, Martha touched her arm. Faith looked at the other woman's concerned face. "This is not what my father-in-law would have wanted."

The other woman nodded. "Go, see she is settled. I will send her maid over later to make sure she is comfortable until this matter is settled."

"Was this necessary?" Faith hissed.

Martha looked at her. "This is not the time to discuss this. The house is full of guests."

Faith wanted to scream at them to leave. The sheer hypocrisy of the moment enraged her. Vultures filled the entryway and adjoining rooms, gorging on food and drinking Ezra's wine while spreading gossip that had nothing to do with the man himself Those who truly grieved had nothing but the dregs of relationships and the fading memories of what was gone forever.

People spilled out of the main door and onto the tidily kept yard to watch Eugenia being loaded into a waiting carriage. Faith wondered who had arranged for it. Regardless, her mother-in-law allowed herself to be handed up into it followed by the sheriff. Daniel Moore would have followed except for the staying hand of the sheriff.

Faith was too far away to hear the exchange of words before Daniel nodded and stepped away. He glanced at the throng of onlookers before striding around back of the residence far from the painful presence of prying eyes.

Chapter Twelve

"What are you going to do?" Olivia asked as she put the finishing touches on a pie before turning to slip it into the brick oven built into the wall. Sweat made tendrils of her hair curl at the edges of her scalp like a halo.

"I don't know," Faith replied. She had come home from the Moore house shocked and exhausted. She had ridden with her mother-in-law to the jail in the jolting wagon. For once, Eugenia had nothing to say. Neither did Faith. Within moments they had stopped at their destination. As one of the sheriff's men handed Eugenia out, she looked back at Faith before stopping to stare at the Gaol.

Thinking about it made Faith shiver. Despite the house attached to it for the Gaoler, one's eyes automatically went to the stern brick walls that enclosed the cells where those awaiting trial were imprisoned. Exiting the carriage, she had watched as Eugenia walked across the snow-white gravel towards the gate of the fence that enclosed the property. Her back was rigid and straight, and she did not look back, but Faith had seen the plea in her eyes before she left.

"I have to do something," Faith said. "I cannot leave her to rot in there."

"She won't rot. She's got money to make her stay more comfortable."

Olivia brought a bowl of peas to shell before joining Faith at the table in the middle of the kitchen. Her hands busily processed them into another bowl, the round peas clattered as they rolled down the sides and into the base of the bowl.

Faith reached over and swept a pile of pods in front of her before joining in the shelling. The steady rhythm of work helped her sort her thoughts.

"Court will be in session in a few weeks."

Olivia nodded. "If the judge gets here when he's supposed to." She slid a pile of empty pods to the side to be taken out later.

Faith thought about the poison. "Did Eugenia keep arsenic in her still room?"

Olivia blinked. "Is that what they said?" She shook her head. "I worked for her a good many years and I never saw her use arsenic. She was particular about what she handled." She paused to gather her thoughts. "I never asked who had taught her so much about healing, but I learned to trust her judgment. I've worked beside her as she helped deliver babies in the slave quarters, set bones, and tended illnesses. She never wanted anyone to know but she tended to all the enslaved folk whether in town or at the farm. She saved my life after the fire."

Faith digested this information slowly. Olivia didn't talk about the fire that had scarred her so badly. She didn't know how Eugenia passed her days when not immersing herself in society functions. Apparently, she didn't know much about her mother-in-law at all.

A fly buzzed as it came in through the open door, propelled by a slight breeze. Despite the air from the door and windows, warmth permeated the kitchen, fed by the constant fire required for cooking.

A log popped, propelling a short spray of sparks within the fireplace, quickly extinguished against the heavy black iron pot suspended over the flames. Olivia rose to give it a quick stir before adding the peas they had just shelled. The rich scent of beef rose to fill the air.

Olivia began dusting the table with flour before rolling out the pie crust. "Another pie?"

"That was rabbit; this one's a fruit pie." Her arms rolled the crust in a steady rhythm until it suited her.

Faith rose to help but Oliva waved her off. "I got this. Can you check the bread? I put it in the oven before you arrived."

Faith nodded and peeked into the oven. Four loaves of bread had turned light golden brown. Grabbing a thick cloth, Faith moved them from the oven to cool on the side, leaving the pie to continue baking.

She watched the other woman add sweetened blueberries to the crust she had shaped into a pan, and then topped it with another crust, sealing it and cutting slits for the steam to escape. "That should take care of everything." Olivia wiped her hands on her apron before looking back at Faith.

"Mistress Genia has never gotten along well with Master Ezra's children. They played nice for him, but now that he's gone, there's no reason to hide."

"I saw that." Faith had been shocked by the animosity. Although she had never been close to Ezra's children, they had always been cordial. She had not expected the explosion of acrimony following Ezra's death. Now her mother-in-law awaited trial for his murder.

"Does Eugenia lock her still room?"

Olivia shook her head. "No. There's never been any need for that. No one wanted to deal with her if they messed with her things."

Faith brushed off her clothes. "Can you manage without me?

Olivia looked dubious. "There's a full crowd in the main room, Miss Faith."

The back door of the tavern slammed, startling them both. Boots thudded over the porch and down the steps, running towards the kitchen. Faith turned toward the door just as a young man bounded in.

"Faith!"

She was bundled into a hug before she could speak. Once the hold was broken, she caught her breath and looked at the intruder. There was something familiar about the eyes and mouth. The straw hat looked like one her father favored, and he was dressed in the plain fashion as Quakers did. It had been three years since she had seen any of her family. Taking a guess, she said, "Seth?

He grinned, showing the good teeth they all had thanks to their mother's insistence on daily cleaning with willow twigs. Seth Payne had gotten tall and filled out. His hair was a shade or two lighter than hers and tied back with a thin leather strap.

"I've come to help you with the tavern." A well-worn satchel lay at his feet, undoubtedly containing all his worldly possessions. Whatever this was, it was not a short stay.

Faith nodded, wondering what the real reason was that her parents had sent her seventeen-year-old brother so far from home. She suspected a letter would arrive in due time alluding to the reasons her younger brother was now her responsibility. Nonetheless, she was not turning away a spare pair of hands. There was plenty he could do, and his timing was opportune.

She turned so he could see the woman standing by the fire. "Seth, this is Olivia. Do what she tells you. I have an errand to run."

Before either could object, she darted out the door, leaving the two of them staring at each other.

Chapter Thirteen

The Moore house appeared subdued in the swelter of the afternoon heat. The front yard appeared deserted, with not so much as a bird to be seen in the trees. Overhead clouds gathered, obscuring the sky and filling the air with moisture. Skirting the yard, Faith cut through using a narrow path that snaked through a grove of trees nearby. A faint rumble of thunder echoed overhead.

Olivia's admission had jarred her mental picture of Eugenia, making her feel faintly ashamed. After Eugenia's obvious disappointment in her son's choice of wife, Faith had avoided her whenever possible. Jon's passing had only eroded the relationship. Now if she couldn't prove otherwise, her mother-in-law would be executed and there would be no opportunity for any sort of reconciliation. Her thoughts touched on Andrew. He had lost both his father and the man he considered his grandfather. He didn't need another loss.

From past visits, she knew that Eugenia's still room lay just outside of the main house near the kitchen garden, within easy reach of the many herbs grown there. A servant worked in the garden weeding what looked like cucumbers, while another watered spires of lavender. She was just wondering how to sneak around them when the dinner bell rang calling them inside. Relieved, she waited a moment for any stray workers before slipping inside the fence and into Eugenia's domain.

The room smelled of dill and onion, blended with other scents she could not readily identify. She stood still waiting for her eyes to adjust to the dimness of the room. Dust motes danced through bands of sunlight coming through a window too high and narrow for anyone to climb through. As her vision sharpened, she took in her surroundings. Bundles of herbs hung from the rafters drying. It was too dim to identify them all and not necessary to her purpose. A mortar and pestle lay on a narrow table against one wall. On the other side was a series of shelves containing jars and baskets. She picked up a lidded basket and peered inside. At first, she didn't recognize the darkened leaves, and then she inhaled and took in the rich scent of tea. Apparently, Eugenia was hoarding tea. Amused, Faith returned the basket to its place and picked up a jar. Its dark contents slid about loosely. The seal was broken, so she gently pulled the cork and took a sniff. Her nose burned from the powerful scent of liquor infused with cherries. "What have you been doing in here?" She murmured. It had never occurred to her that her mother-in-law bottled liquor. Replacing the cork, she put it back before turning her attention to the table.

A few bundles of dried plants lay on the table as if someone had been disturbed in the midst of their task. As she gently teased the dark green leaves apart, the scent of basil wafted up. The window allowed just enough light for Faith to look about without burning a taper or leaving the door open to announce her presence.

Her ears caught a faint rustling in a corner. Remaining still, her eyes scanned the shadows looking for a cause. A faint flash of movement made her heart jump until she identified a squirrel as it leapt back up to the rafters, pausing to chitter at her in irritation before slipping out from whence it came.

Her breath came out in a rush of relief that she hadn't been discovered. Faith continued her search. Bundles of herbs hung from the rafters, drying until needed for the kitchen or sickroom; heads of garlic braided together by their tops, round globes of onion bound in a similar manner. Faint glimmers of whiteness shimmered like pearls in between strips of darkened, dried stalks. Ducking her head, she made her way to a set of shelves in the back, intending to check out a series of ceramic jars. Just as her hand touched one, it spun and hit the floor with a resounding crash. As she lifted her head, she bumped into a swath of dill, causing its dry, fernlike fronds to cascade down on her, its distinctive scent filled her nose. She sneezed explosively, inhaled, and sneezed again before subsiding into coughs.

"Well, that should bring someone running," a voice said from a darkened corner.

Faith jumped, smothering a shriek of fright.

"Screaming is only going to make it worse," Jeremy Butler, stepped out of the shadows. He looked at her in amusement. "You don't have much experience in this do you?"

Faith glared at him just as footsteps pounded on the gravel path from the garden.

"We need to go," Butler gestured to a narrow door set into the wall. "Now," he emphasized reaching for her hand.

Faith hesitated, and then let him lead her to the door and down a narrow ladder which led into darkness. "Where are we going?" she whispered.

"Root cellar," he whispered back. "We can slip out through the outer door." He stepped down and helped her off before whispering, "Watch yourself. It's tight quarters in here." He drew her aside from the faint light that limned the cracks in the door. Upstairs the floorboards creaked under the weight of footsteps moving swiftly, searching for them.

Darkness surrounded them along with the musty scent of earth. Cool damp air seeped from the walls making her shiver. As her eyes adjusted to the dimness of the room, she saw that it was crowded with barrels and crates lined with straw. From the rafters hung vegetables, some braided together by their tops, other in canvas sacks.

The door above them cracked open and Butler pulled her further into the shadows of a huge cabinet. Faith held her breath as the opening widened, spreading the revealing light across the space.

"I don't see anyone here, "a woman's voice said. "It may be mice."

Another woman replied. "You better hope there's no mice getting into Ms. Eugenia's things, she expects one of us to stay the night down here to catch them."

"Why can't she just get a cat?"

The unseen woman's laugh was deep and rich like molasses. "Because she's scared to death of cats, that's why. But don't tell anyone I said that. We'll both be in trouble."

"That doesn't make sense, Cora, why be afraid of a cat? It's not like it's a bear or something."

"If I were you, I wouldn't dwell on it. There's no point in trying to figure out why she thinks what she does. It doesn't change a thing."

The door about them shut just as a droplet of cold water dripped on Faith's neck and ran down her back, causing her to startle, making the cabinet next to them shift. Butler reached out and caught a small jar before it hit the ground.

Faith's eyes met his. "I'm sorry," she whispered.

He shrugged. "Let's see what this is."

The ceramic jar's lid lifted off easily, its cork liner offering only a tiny squeak of resistance. Their heads bumped as each tried to peer inside.

"Ouch," Faith whispered, rubbing her head.

"Wait your turn, "Butler responded as he tilted the jar to get a better look. "I can't see a damn thing,"

"You don't have to," Faith responded. "Use your nose."

Butler shot her an undecipherable look before complying. "Mint?" He asked before handing it over to her.

Faith took another whiff before nodding. "Peppermint, I'm pretty sure."

"Well that wouldn't kill him," Butler muttered.

Faith looked at him irritably. "Eugenia is many things, but stupid isn't one of them. If she wanted him dead, she wouldn't have used rat poison."

"Let's get out of here," Butler murmured in her ear. "Before someone decides to come down here to deal with the mice."

Faith followed him, walking carefully to avoid bumping into anything else. When he flung the cellar door open, she expected to be confronted, but as she stepped into the yard, it appeared deserted. Butler gently shut the door before pausing to look about. They were in a side yard by the huge brick house. The neatly clipped lawn stretched out before them, the tide of green unbroken except for the sprawling branches of an oak. The stylized iron fence traveled for some distance around the property. She followed

Butler into the shadows of the tree and out into a small grove of young trees. "Where are you going?" she hissed, worried someone was about to overhear.

Butler walked over to a gate that opened to a graveled pathway and opened it wide enough for both of them to exit. The gravel path took them back to Queen Street. Faith followed him past a few houses before pausing to ask, "Where are we going?"

"Mistress Clements's home is nearby; it would be the most convenient place to talk, unless you have a better idea."

Faith didn't, although she didn't care for the odd look Will gave when they both entered by the rear gate.

Butler looked at him. "It's good to see you back on your feet McKay."

Will nodded looking from one of them to the other. "What brings you here?"

Faith suspected the real question was, what were the two of you doing together, but that remained unspoken.

"We all want to know what happened to Ezra. Far better to discuss it here than out in the street."

"And you both happened to be walking up the street at the same time."

"Not exactly," Faith said. "We..." her voice trailed off as she tried to figure out how to explain ending up in Eugenia's root cellar.

"Similar errands brought us to town," Butler finished. "Now where is Georgia?"

Once inside, they settled in the small room that served as a small office and parlor, behind the print shop. Athena appeared with a young dark-skinned girl carrying a tray of cakes and small sandwiches. Athena set down the pot along with cups and a cone of sugar before stepping back. "Mistress Georgia will be here soon. I'm sure Mistress Clarke will be glad to pour in her absence. I have other responsibilities," she said before drifting outside back to her kitchen.

Faith took up the pot carefully and began pouring into the cups; the rich scent of mint filled the air. She passed each man a cup, letting each one break off however much sugar they wanted. Will broke off a generous lump, Butler none at all. Georgia Clements sat down and took a cup, breaking off a thumb-size lump with practiced ease.

She smiled over at Faith before taking charge. "So gentlemen and Mistress Clarke, I assume we've gathered to discuss murder." Her tone was dry as she filled plates and handed them about. "We're still looking for who wanted to kill Ezra, although poor Neddy didn't deserve to die either, even if he did nick your bottle, Will."

Will winced. "I had no idea that Madeira was spiked. I'd intended to finish it myself. If he hadn't taken it, I'd be the one dead."

Butler leaned forward in the ladder chair he'd appropriated. "I think you and Ned were collateral damage, as was Ezra's valet, Theodore. The question remains, who wanted Ezra dead?"

Faith's voice was soft. "I'm not sure I believe Eugenia did it."

"Why not?" Butler asked.

Faith frowned, and then set down her tea. "She has too much to lose. Ezra already gives her everything she could want. She lives a life of privilege. I don't see her throwing that away on a whim."

"She will be a very rich widow and she's a Tory. She could have done it as a service to King George. Maybe she discovered his work for the patriots, maybe she wanted more than Ezra was willing to provide. Perhaps she has become a secret ally of the British." Butler ticked off the reasons on his fingers on strong, square hands. He raised a brow waiting for her rebuttal.

Faith laughed. "The only person Eugenia is interested in serving is herself. She favors England because of the quality of goods. She scorns anything made in the colonies."

Georgia noted. "Depending on the particulars, her widow's portion could be generous."

"Not if Ezra's sons have a say in it," Faith responded. The acrimony she had witnessed had been sickening. "They despise her, and the feeling is returned. I had never realized how much they resented each other. She'll be fortunate to receive her widow's portion from them, much less anything else."

"What about the sons?" Will asked. "Could they have wanted their father gone?"

The others looked at Faith.

"I'm not sure." She paused to gather her thoughts. "Both Daniel and Zachary married well. They are men of means without Ezra's wealth. His daughters I've barely met, but they seem affluent. They all seemed greatly grieved by his passing." Faith paused to blink the sudden sting in her eyes. Ezra's death remained a raw wound.

Georgia poured a dollop of whisky into Faith's cup. "I think you could use this,"

Faith took a swallow, feeling the burn in her throat. "What about the governor?" she asked"That is where the Madeira came from."

Butler shook his head. "I found no tainted bottles at the palace."

Athena interrupted. "That just means no one was trying to poison him."

Butler sighed. "I'm sure Dunmore has many people who would like to see him dead, but since he had no ill effects from drinking with Ezra and the delegation, I'm pretty sure no one tried to poison him."

Will looked at them, "That leaves us with finding Ezra's enemies."

Butler ruffled his fingers through his hair tiredly. "Most leaders of the patriot cause are in Philadelphia right now and have been for a while. Not that I've observed any rivalries to that degree. Besides, they are more likely to express their ire in anonymous letters in the paper."

"We graciously accept paid submissions," Georgia said before taking a sip of tea.

"So, who does that leave us? Someone nearly killed me and I want to know who." Will stood up and walked about restlessly. He didn't use a cane in the small space, but his legs weren't working well. He took his seat after a few minutes, pouring from the bottle into his tea.

Athena frowned at him before confiscating the bottle and placing it out of reach. "You need to give yourself time to recover."

"And how long will that take?" Will snapped. "It's been two weeks and I still tire quickly and my eyes blur after a few hours of setting type. I'm no use to anyone as an invalid." His hands fisted briefly before he forced them open and took a breath. "I don't like feeling weak," he said softly, staring down at the floor.

"I wouldn't call you that," Georgia replied. "Your strength is what allowed you to survive. That and Athena's concoctions. You are stronger than you were a week ago. You will recover in time."

"I hope so," he muttered. Athena put a couple of scones on his plate and pushed it towards him. He took one and bit into it, chewing in silence.

Butler looked at the people gathered around the tea table. "What we need is more information about what was happening before Ezra was poisoned. Whoever it was had to have access to the bottle. Dunmore opened and drank from it before giving it to Ezra. Unless he's a master at sleight of hand, he couldn't have done it. There's no reason for him to kill Ezra. He was among the more agreeable of the delegation. Dunmore would have wanted to keep him. Besides that, he's busy fortifying the Governor's castle. Now if Patrick Henry had shown up that would have been a different matter."

"So," Faith said, taking up the thread. "Not Dunmore. Most of the powerful patriots are in Philadelphia, so not them."

Athena interrupted. "You're forgetting all these people have servants to do their bidding. They didn't need to be present for that. And servants buy ratsbane all the time for their households to take care of rodents. There is nothing unusual about it."

"Someone didn't want a record revealed of what they purchased at Prentis." Butler noted. "Their account book was stolen a few nights back."

"I heard about that," Faith shivered. "Some poor apprentice was murdered. The night watch almost caught him, but he escaped. That would have brought this sorry mess to a close."

Butler coughed as Athena caught his eye. Setting down his cup on the table, he continued his thoughts. "Mistress Clarke, you need to check on your mother-in-law, see what she can tell us." He raised a hand to ward off her objection. "Even if she didn't poison him, she may know something that can help us find who did. And it's in her best interest to talk if she wants to avoid a grisly end."

"Athena can connect with servants at the Moore household. They see everything." He looked over at her. "Let me know what you hear."

Georgia asked. "How am I and Will to help in this endeavor?"

"Keep doing what you already are."

"Nothing," Will grumbled.

"A great deal, actually. "You two take the temper of the town. People come in with their letters and advertisements and that tells you a great deal. Listen to them and make note of any useful tidbits."

"And what are you going to do?" Faith asked. It irritated her to be ordered about by Butler of all people. Although she realized his plan made sense, it was his self-confident arrogance that irritated her. She had a feeling he knew it too from the faint smile he gave her before answering.

"I will be seeing who might benefit from Ezra's demise. He received a handful of visitors that evening, maybe one of them had a reason to kill him."

Georgia rose. "I need to be out front. Silas is a fine worker, but the intricacies of running a print shop take time to learn."

"Indeed, we all have tasks to attend to. " Butler rose as well, nodding as he slipped out the back.

Faith had risen as well, dusting crumbs from her apron. "I have left Olivia long enough. I need to go help her and then find a time to visit Eugenia."

As she turned, Will touched her hand. "Let me walk you out." He flushed as he struggled to his feet before joining her. They walked out of the room. Within a few minutes, the back door closed softly behind them.

Faith knew Will wanted to talk to her. She paused on the porch, allowing him to catch up to her before turning to face him. Asking after his health would only make him angry so she waited in silence for him to speak.

He leaned against the outside wall, allowing it to bear some of his weight. "You've been busy with this business with your father-in-law," he noted.

Faith nodded. "It's been hard." She swallowed. "I still can't believe he's gone and all this business with poison."

A pained expression crossed his face.

"I'm sorry," she whispered. "I know this happened to you too."

"Aye," he answered. "I feel its effect every day."

"You're getting stronger."

He sighed. "That's my hope, Faith." He clenched his hands together. "This wretched tingling drives me mad sometimes."

"Does Athena know?"

Will nodded. "She doses me regularly. That woman knows a lot about healing. I trust her more than the doctors that Mistress Clements has called. They want my blood."

"But that's not what I want to talk about." His eyes caught hers. "Be careful, Faith. There's a ruthless killer out there. I'm not able to protect you as you need. I couldn't bear it if anything happened to you."

Faith reached out to touch his hands, feeling the calluses built up from hard work. "I'll be careful," she promised before leaning over to kiss his cheek. "I have plenty of reasons to want to be around."

He turned to capture her lips with his, gently like the brush of butterfly wings. "I dream about the day you can be mine."

"I dream too," she whispered before stepping off the porch and heading back to the tavern and the responsibilities that waited for her there.

Chapter Fourteen

Athena knew most of the alleys and backways in Williamsburg. Between her and her sons, they had the town covered. Although most people recognized her as Georgia Clements's cook, there were times she wished to go unnoticed.

The enslaved staff at the Moore house regarded her as a healer. She had quietly tended to many small injuries of the enslaved servants within the community as was her custom wherever she was. Athena had learned how to treat illness and injury from women at the plantation where she had raised her children and spent over twenty years of her life. Knowledge passed down from woman to woman, never shared with those who held them in bondage.

She tried not to think too much about those days. Her life was her own now. What time she didn't spend working with Jeremy, she spent chasing leads to find her daughter, sold and sent away despite her pleas. It was a wound that never really healed; listening to your child scream for you as you were held helpless, unable to keep her from being taken.

Athena shoved the memory aside before it engulfed her. There would be time later to check with people newly arrived from other places to see if anyone had seen her Rosie, named for the rose-shaped birthmark on the side of her neck.

The Moore house looked as stately from the back as it did the front. Its well-tended gardens filling the back yard with blooms and scent. Athena watched from the shadows of a stand of birch trees for a few moments, biding her time and seeking the person most likely to be able to answer her questions.

A faint wisp of smoke rose from the chimney of the separate kitchen, indicating that the cook was at work, preparing food for dinner later that day. Athena had covered a pot of stew to simmer over the fire at Mistress Clements'. She would have time to fix bread and some cabbage before mealtime. She had left her assistant, Peggy, to watch the fire while she roasted coffee beans. She had come from the New York Colony after her manumission and had proved a very useful set of hands.

Athena ducked her head to keep from hitting the low doorway into the kitchen. Inside, Edith was checking a spit and reminding a boy to keep turning it less the birds on it burn on one side and be underdone on the other. She was startled when Athena's shadow fell over her then relaxed slightly when she saw who it was.

"Hello Edith," Athena said, setting down her basket of herbs on a bench away from where the other woman was working. "I brought some sage and parsley. We have plenty in our garden."

Edith nodded, her expression cautious as she nodded to the statuesque woman who had just walked in. She returned her focus to the dish she was engaged in making. A spider skillet stood by the hearth, its insides shiny with fat. Edith's sturdy hands were rolling balls of chopped meat into flour before dropping into the pan. Once the pan was full, she moved it closer over coals still red with heat. As the pan sizzled, a rich satisfying scent filled the air. Edith wiped her hands clean and looked up at her visitor.

"No one's turned sick, why are you here?" With that Edith began chopping mushrooms. "I have gravy to make to go with that forcemeat, so if you've come to talk, it will be while I finish making dinner. Not everyone is free to go as they please."

Athena nodded "If you would like, I can chop those onions for you. Athena picked up a large steel knife and began by cutting off the blossom end.

"Small dice, Master Louis complains if there are big chunks." Edith watched her work for a few minutes before continuing her own work. Barely five feet in height, Edith ran her kitchen in a deft and efficient manner. Her square frame carried enough compact muscle that lifting heavy pans and pots took little effort from her.

Athena remained quiet as they worked together to prepare gravy for the meatballs simmering over the fire. Soon the sauce was mixed together and bubbling from a pot that hung inside the large stone fireplace.

"Peggy will take food over to Mistress Genia at the gaol," Edith said. "Mistress Martha has already sent over a bed tick and blankets. She's been rearranging furniture and giving orders like it's her house now."

"Really," Athena said. "I didn't realize she was so familiar with this place."

Edith sniffed. "Oh, they come three or four times a year, mostly so Daniel can rub shoulders with the gentry. Mistress Martha, she likes to entertain about as much as Mistress Genia. She can be real sweet when she wants. It took her no time to get the staff to show her the good silver and china. They've been using the very best even though Master Ezra's not been gone a week."

"They got here pretty quickly before he took ill, didn't they?" Athena murmured as she gathered the finely diced onions together in a bowl and added them to the pot Edith indicated.

Edith snorted. "They had been here and then left to visit her sister's in Yorktown. Master Ezra took ill that very night and they came rushing back."

Athena hummed noncommittedly. Edith was ready to talk to someone, and she saw no reason to interrupt.

Edith used her wrist to wipe sweat from her brow, before checking on the contents of her pot. Below, on the glowing grate a Dutch oven sat with coals on its lid to ensure even cooking of whatever rested inside. She cut a glance up at Athena as she straightened and backed away from the fire. "Every family grieves differently. These folks want to punish each other. It's sad to see. Ezra Moore treated us decently. I don't know what these folks will do."

Athena remembered how frightening it was not to be free, to have to constantly worry what would happen when the master died. "Have they said anything?"

Edith shook her head, a tear dripped down her face. "Mistress Martha likes my cooking. She says she wishes I could be at her home." She shook her head. "This is my home. I don't want to go anywhere."

"Mistress Eugenia will likely get this house," Athena said. "She won't let you go."

"We will see." Edith composed herself. "We pray for the family at our church."

"Your church?"

"Brother Gowan leads us in worship every week. He does the Lord's work when he's not working for Mistress Vobe. He checks in on all of us. You're welcome to join us for prayer next evening."

Athena nodded. Perhaps meeting Brother Gowan might prove useful. But for now, she had other business. "How do you think arsenic got into that bottle?"

Edith straightened and tucked a few stray hairs under the green cap she wore. "Let's step out for some air. I'd enjoy not breathing smoke for a minute or two."

Going out into the enormous backyard with its pleasure and kitchen gardens was a relief from the relentless heat and smoke in the kitchen. Even with windows and doors propped open, it was sweltering hot. Edith removed her cap and fanned the air, showing a tidy braid pinned around her head.

Not until they stood outside did Athena see the unusual color of Edith's eyes. Rather than a shade of brown or black, they were a dark golden green. Although middle-aged, Edith remained a remarkably handsome woman.

"None of us had anything to do with it," Edith's tone was blunt. "Don't stir something up that will cause trouble. You know if there's a chance to blame us, they will do it. Leave it be. Master Ezra's family can sort themselves out."

Athena nodded. "That could happen, but if she didn't do it, then the killer is still around and might not be through."

Edith nodded. "Uh huh. We buried Theo underneath that row of pines. He used to like to slip out there, sit on a stump, and whittle. He was a good man. He didn't deserve to die. I'm probably the only one who remembers he came from the French West Indies. He spoke the language too, which was why Ezra bought him. Theo wasn't even his first name. The man the Moores bought him from gave him that name."

Edith looked up at her. "A body should get to keep their own name or at least pick out a different one if they wish."

Athena nodded. "If we find the killer, he can be punished."

Edith nodded before turning to go back to the kitchen. "I don't know who did it. Only Theo and Master Ezra had keys to the liquor cabinet. Not even Miss Genia can get into it without one of them helping."

"Do you know where the ratsbane came from?"

Edith snorted. "You can buy that at any of the stores, everyone in town has mice trying to get into their cellars. Nellie just got some to keep them out of the attic. The family heard them rustling around at night. Miss Martha had a fit about it."

Edith paused before the open door of the kitchen where fingers of white smoke wafted out. "But Miss Genia never kept it with her herbs. It's odd that the sheriff found a vial of it just lying on the floor." She stepped over the threshold. "Porter and Julius do the most errands. They might know something, but I didn't tell you that." With that she went to her fire, first checking her pan and then stirring the gravy, her back to the other woman.

Athena didn't pursue her. She'd gotten all the little cook was willing to share. Although she would wager Edith knew more about the goings-on in the house than she revealed.

Eyeing the progression of the sun in the sky, Athena knew she would have to continue her investigation later. It was time for her to return to Mistress Clements' home and prepare their dinner. She was fortunate that she had found a position that paid well and allowed her a great deal of freedom to poke about. She would hate when it came time to leave.

Before returning to her kitchen, Athena stopped by the marketplace in hopes of finding something to tempt Will's appetite. He needed to build his strength to recover from the poisoning, yet his appetite was picky. She was hoping to find fruit to put with dumplings for him. This time of day the choicest items had already been acquired by the early crowd, but maybe there was still something worth claiming.

In a corner where the roof was also sheltered by a slender maple tree, a plump country woman sat with a basket of wild strawberries. Tiny, sweet, and richly red, they drew Athena like a magnet.

"Guten Morgen," the woman said before switching to English. "You like my berries, Ja? I pick them in the forest last night and keep them here in the shade where they stay sweet all day. You try one?"

Athena paused before picking a tiny red jewel from the basket. She closed her eyes in delight, before putting on her business face.

The German woman had a shrewd brain as well, but after a little negotiating, Athena left with an apron full of rich sweet berries to make a treat for her ailing patient. Hopefully, with a little care, he would return to the hale young man who had been so kind to her and her boys.

As she ducked through the gate of the picket fence, she smelled the heady scent of roasted coffee beans, mixed with the savory smells of dinner. Peggy could mix together a pan of biscuits while she dealt with the berries. In the yard, one of her boys chopped wood for the fire. Jeremy and her other son would be home for supper. A wave of contentment washed over her as she strode back through the garden to her domain.

Chapter Fifteen

Faith knew she was in trouble before she crossed the threshold of the kitchen. Oliva was stirring a pot with vicious intent. When she spotted Faith, she straightened and caught her eye.

"We need to talk."

She looked at Olivia uneasily wondering what was wrong. "Yes, Olivia?" Despite the tidiness of the kitchen, there was a lingering scent of burned meat in the air. The fireplace had blackened smudges on the normally immaculate grate.

Olivia's tone was as even as always but her eyes blazed fire. "If you expect to run a business, you cannot just take off when the notion strikes. We have guests to feed, animals to care for, and chores that cannot wait. There aren't enough of us when you are here and leaving me with that boy..." Olivia paused to take a breath.

"He may know how to slop hogs and clean stalls, but he knows nothing of how to operate a tavern. I have spent my day trying to manage him and this tavern. It's too much. You said Titus and I would have a voice in this business, so hear my words. We need help and you need to train Seth. I have enough work in this kitchen without chasing after your brother." She stopped to take a long drink. After swallowing, she wiped back tears. "I can't do all this Faith. You abandoned me during one of the busiest times of day for us." Her hands shook. "Seth spilled gravy all over a member of the Randolph family. Titus smoothed things over by clearing his bill. He let that fur trader from the Ohio Valley leave without settling his bill. We'll never see that money and he gave away those theatre tickets we've been selling. Something has to change now if you expect me and Titus to continue working here."

Faith winced. "I'm sorry, Olivia. I wasn't thinking. Ezra's death has caused so much chaos."

"Then quit creating chaos here."

"I won't leave before dinner again, "she promised. "Do you really think we need more help?"

Olivia rolled her eyes. "We have for a long time. You can afford to hire some more hands. I know a few folks who would be happy for work."

Faith nodded. She knew they had been stretched thin but had avoided looking for additional help. Interviewing people seemed such a tiresome task. Now she was here with her right hand threatening to quit. Guilt didn't even begin to describe her feelings. "Send them to me. I will put them to work." She looked about the kitchen. "Did something happen here?"

Olivia sniffed. "I was so busy dealing with Seth, I burned some pork shoulders. It left a fine mess in the hearth."

Faith sighed. "I shouldn't have put you in that position. Where is my brother?"

"Titus took him out to the barn. That boy does know how to care for animals." With a sniff, she returned to the fire.

"I will go talk to him and then see what needs doing in the tavern," Faith said as she retreated out the door. Olivia rarely lost her temper and was very rarely out of sorts. Faith walked past the kitchen garden that helped keep them stocked in food to the small barn behind. Already the summer squash was blooming, although a few rogue morning glory vines had begun twisting themselves amongst the stalks. They would have to be pulled before they strangled the plants. Inside the barn, she heard the rise and fall of Titus's voice.

She paused at the open door. "Hello, everyone, how goes it?" The interior of the barn was dim compared with the sunlit yard. It took a moment for her eyes to adjust to see the two men inside.

Titus was currying a gray dappled mare while Seth forked hay into recently raked stalls. "Hello, Miss Faith. It's good to see you home." His smile gleamed in the dim interior before he returned to Seth. "Be careful of that mule.

Brandy can be a bit cantankerous."

"Brandy?" Faith said. "That's one of Master Graves' mules. Her name is Brandy?"

Titus nodded. "The other one is named Gin."

Seth commented, "I guess that is short for ginger."

"If you say so." Titus continued running the comb over the horse who nickered and rubbed her muzzle affectionately against his shoulder.

Faith walked up to her brother, nearly missing being covered in a load of hay. "Perhaps we could take a moment to talk."

Seth continued forking hay. "I need to finish tending the stock first."

Titus exited the stall. "We're about done here, Seth. Go talk to your sister. I'm sure you have catching up to do."

Seth set down the hayfork before casting a wary glance at his older sister. "We don't have to do this now. You have a business to run."

"I do," Faith said. "And I need to figure how you fit in, since you said you came to help out." She gestured to the door. "There's a bench out here. Let's sit and talk for a moment or two."

Shade dappled the wooden seat. Clouds gathered overhead, causing patches of gray in the otherwise blue sky. Faith wondered if it would rain later. Right now the air hung heavy with moisture making clothes feel sticky.

Seth didn't sit, but leaned against the tree trunk looking like he would rather be anywhere else. His gaze drifted across the yard toward the narrow dirt path that ran into the woods behind the tavern.

"Why did our parents send you here?" Faith asked bluntly. "They've never seemed overly concerned with how I was faring after Jon's death. Why now?"

"Pa thought it was the best solution," Seth said as he walked slowly over to the bench. He kept his eyes on the ground, avoiding meeting hers.

"To what?"

Seth plopped down beside her, placing his elbows on his knees and facing down. "He thought it best I leave before the wedding." He fumbled with his hands before letting them drop between his knees. "Patsy Stoddard loves me, I know she does, but her parents betrothed her to Judge Downey." His eyes looked pleadingly at Faith. "He's an old man, over 30, and has two children from his late wife. I don't care how much land he has, he doesn't deserve her."

"What does Patsy say?" Faith asked.

He looked at her, his eyes sad. "She has refused to speak with me since the betrothal was announced. I went over to her home and was met by her older brother and father." He rubbed his face, his rolled up sleeves revealed the yellowed marks of faded bruises. "I didn't intend to get into a fight, but they wouldn't listen."

Pa said they agreed not to call the sheriff if I went away." He sighed and pulled out a much-worn letter. "I wasn't going to go until she sent me this."

Faith asked him gently, "What did she say?"

Her brother remained quiet for a space of moments as if gathering his thoughts. "She told me to go away, that my behavior was an embarrassment to her. That marrying him gave her a good position in society and if I cared about her happiness, I should accept that." He folded the letter and put it back. "I didn't believe it at first, and then I went and waited outside the milliner's window. Patsy was there with her sister. She saw me outside the window. When she opened it, I went up to her and she slapped me and told me to leave her alone."

His eyes were the dark gray of storm clouds. As she looked at him, she saw they glittered with unshed tears. "I left for Virginia the next day."

"I'm sorry," Faith reached her hand to cover his.

Seth shrugged her hand away. "What's done is done. I'm here now and I'm sure there's plenty of work to be done. Let me work in peace. I don't want to talk about it anymore."

She gestured to the woodpile. "There's always a need for wood to stock the fires."

She left him hefting the axe, splitting wood in steady rhythm.

Faith spent the next few days supervising her brother in the work needed to run a tavern. She heard murmurs about Eugenia's incarceration, and Ezra's sons making connections with their father's associates, but otherwise, people in town seemed to be waiting on the trial coming in June.

Faith hired a young free woman named Ellen and accepted an indentured servant her sister-in-law Martha sent over, asking her to find the boy some work. Henry said he was sixteen, but she suspected he might be younger. She gave him a room over the barn to share with Seth and let Titus supervise them both. Faith hoped a few weeks of Olivia's meals would put some meat on his bones.

While her days filled with the rattle of dice and the filling of tankards, her mind struggled to piece together what had happened to Ezra. Despite her personal feelings, she couldn't see Eugenia killing him. It didn't make sense. Faith was also well aware that no one would try too hard to prove her innocence.

Nevertheless, it caught her off guard when Titus came out into the garden late one morning when she was pulling out mint that had invaded her bed of thyme and sage. The plant kept sending runners where it didn't belong no matter how severely she pruned it. Dew had long since dried in the rising heat of the day. Faith had noted the ungainly growth of green before breakfast and decided to come work on it after her guests had been attended to.

"Miss Faith, you're needed inside." The large man strode up to her, careful not to step on any of her plants.

She straightened up, wiping the sweat out of her eyes. "It's too hot to be out here long anyway." Already her shift was stuck to her back, glued in place by her corset. "What needs my attention?"

"Someone wishes to speak to you. You will understand when you get to our main room." With that, Titus jogged back across the yard, up the steps, and back into the tavern.

Faith frowned before following him inside. She stopped by the well to draw up a bucket, drinking thirstily before taking time to wipe off her face and hands.

At this time of day, past dinner and before supper, there were few inside except for men engaged in cards or dice. Most men were tending their business before the sun went down. As she walked down the hallway, the low murmur of voices drifted out, but nothing sounded worrisome.

As she turned to face the entry into the large front room, nothing caught her eye at first, until she spotted a familiar face seated at one of her tables near the front window, opened to help cool the room.

Louis Clarke sat fanning himself with an elaborate feathered fan composed of ostrich feathers. His hair for once held no powder and was tied back in a simple club with a stark black ribbon. His suit, although cut from fine cloth, was less ornate than his usual attire. It was gray with green stitching, decorating the cuffs and edges of his coat. Every few inches, a spray of embroidered violets emerged from the abstract lines of stitching. Hand-painted buttons not only adorned one side of his jacket, but around each sleeve as well. As she came closer, she could see he still wore one of his ridiculously embroidered waistcoats, this one a subdued plum with more of the green patterned stitchery. He rose as she entered. "Dear Faith, I am glad to see you." He gestured about the room, which was populated only by a few men playing cards by the hearth. "You appear to be doing well."

Faith nodded and stood by him, choosing not to sit when her brother-in-law-did. Her eyes took in the partially emptied bottle of French wine, as well as the remains of a meal. "What brings you here, Louis?" She had no doubt he was running up a tab that he would likely never pay.

Louis smiled sadly. "It appears you are the only family I have left. Ezra's children have taken over the only home I've ever known, while my mother languishes in the confines of the gaol. You're the only one I have left to turn to."

Faith resisted the temptation to roll her eyes. Louis didn't look to be suffering much although the dark circles under his eyes and the restless drumming of his fingers indicated some disquiet. "Why are you here, Louis?"

"My mother needs your help," he paused before continuing. "She didn't kill Ezra. They were a contented couple. Surely you know Eugenia is a godly woman respected throughout Williamsburg. And you know she is not capable of harming anyone."

Faith looked at him.

Louis had the grace to look away. "I realize she could be sharp-tongued at times, but her intentions have always been above reproach." He fiddled with his napkin before signaling to Titus. "Another bottle, my good man."

Titus looked over at Faith, confirming that this was all being put on a tab.

" I'm sure my brother-in-law's thirst can be satisfied by one of our local brews," she replied.

Louis frowned at her, wrinkling his nose as he cautiously sipped one of her better Muscatine wines. "The French and Italians have perfected winemaking for thousands of years, Faith. Must you serve me this?"

"Importing wine across the Atlantic costs a pretty penny, Louis. So, unless you're offering to pay for it, accept what is offered."

Looking affronted, he forced himself to swallow. "You know I'm short of cash, given the current crisis. I'm lucky they still allow me access to my rooms." He leaned forward. "No matter. I've not come about myself, but my mother. Court will commence in two weeks' time and she has no one to help her. She needs your assistance."

"Surely this is a matter for her attorney."

Louis took a moment to adjust the lace spilling out from his cuffs. Its pristine whiteness had to come from an excellent laundress. His expression turned serious. "Ezra's children would like nothing more than to be rid of her. Already they have taken over his business ventures. Visitors have come to talk with both sons even though we are a house in mourning." He leaned forward. "I have heard Martha planning with Zachary's wife Beatrice, for entertainments once it is suitable to do so. It is as if my mother no longer existed. Mark my words; they have been planning this for some time." Louis paused. "I know I have not always been the best of relations to you, but I've always respected you. When Jon passed, you held steady and now run a respectable business." He offered a self-deprecating smile. "My abilities don't lie in finding hidden truths. I'm better at entertaining and games of chance. If my mother is to prove her innocence, she needs someone with the mind to do it. She's asked Master Wythe for help, I'm hoping he will consider taking her case." He looked up from where he had been adjusting his ruffles. "Please help her, for Ezra's sake."

Faith sighed. "I can make no promises. I'm not even sure I will be allowed in the gate."

"They will. Martha likes you." Louis beamed cheerfully. "She has always admired your ability to successfully run a business here in the capital. I suspect she wishes she could do something similar, not that Daniel would ever dream of his wife dabbling in commerce."

"I don't know about that," Faith said carefully. "I will check on Eugenia after I have fulfilled my responsibilities here at the tavern. I'm not a woman with a great deal of idle time on my hands."

Louis leapt up and grasped her hand. Faith managed to free herself from his plump, moist hands. She wiped hers on her apron.

Louis's eyes darted over to the corner where men continued to roll dice. "I look forward to hearing what you have discovered dear sister. Now I have other business to attend to."

"I don't run tabs for gambling debts," she said in his ear before he wandered out of range. He pretended not to hear her as he went over to the other men.

Faith collected steins and plates before heading out to the kitchen. Joshua and Andrew would have plenty of dishes to wash when they returned from school. Already she could see that Olivia had laid out pots of ash and vinegar as well as some rags to aid in scouring pans.

As she stepped inside, she was surprised by a new face. Alongside Olivia was a young woman, taller and darker than Olivia. Underneath a white cap, a thick dark braid peeked out. Oliva looked up and smiled.

"Dorcas, I would like you to meet Mistress Faith Clarke, she owns our tavern."

Faith nodded at the younger girl, "Nice to meet you, Dorcas. I hope you enjoy working with us."

"Why don't you go out to the garden and find some fresh onions. They would work well in the dish I'm planning for tomorrow." The girl went out, basket in hand.

Faith raised an eyebrow. "Where did she come from? And what happened to Ellen?"

"Her family lives north of town, I met them at the market. I knew they were hoping she could find work here in town. I sent Joshua down to get her once we had spoken. Ellen is busy inside, emptying chamber pots and making beds. We have enough work to keep them both busy. I've given them a room in the attic to share. We're already seeing more people come in for the markets and when court convenes, there will be more people coming to get their cases settled."

Faith said nothing, but scanned the well-ordered kitchen. Out in the garden, Dorcas worked steadily at her task, a basket at her feet for the vegetables she harvested.

The garden, instead of looking half-wild with weeds, had neat rows of vegetables and herbs, the dirt paths were clear of weeds and easy to see.

Olivia commented. "I can focus on cooking for our guests while she tends the garden and handles other chores. Ellen prefers to clean than work in the kitchen, so I've set her to tending the rooms upstairs and down. With summer coming, we will be much busier. Titus is training your brother to carry trays back and forth and how to treat guests. He's already pretty good at laying fires and tending stock. Henry is young but he's handy with the animals and fixing things. He said his father taught him a few things before he passed." She paused to brush a stray curl back from her eyes, faintly crinkled in concentration. "If Ezra leaves you any people in his will, you may want to plan how best to make use of them."

"Slaves?" Her voice sounded as horrified as she felt.

Oliva looked at her. "It's a possibility, you know that."

She had avoided thinking about Ezra's will. It was hard enough to admit he was dead, much less consider how his household would be divided among his heirs. "I don't know if he has named me in his will."

Olivia didn't reply but her expression said plenty.

Eager to change the subject, Faith said, "I will go to the gaol after supper. It's time I spoke to Eugenia."

"What do I do if your brother-in-law returns?"

"Local wine and beer only. Serve him the same food as any other customer." She walked out toward the tavern's back entrance. "And we're not staking him in any games of chance."

Olivia muttered under her breath.

"What?" Faith said, pausing at the door. It never ceased to surprise her that Olivia sometimes used words not usually uttered in polite company.

123

Olivia paused and set down the iron spoon she had been using to stir the black pot bubbling over the fire.

"Don't let him be a leech."

Faith laughed. "I have no intentions of that. I'm well aware that Louis has spent most of his life being overindulged. But he is family, and while Eugenia is in jail, he is at loose ends."

"Henry has seen him at Ms. Vobe's dicing and going on the edge of town where they have the races." She paused. "He got kicked out of Raleigh Tavern last week because he ran up such a bill. Don't let him do that here."

Faith nodded. "I'll warn Titus not to let him get too high."

"I already did," Oliva said as she turned to her next task, dicing the onions that Dorcas had gathered. The girl had come in quietly before going back out to weed the hills of potatoes.

Faith raised an eyebrow.

"I'll just say it. You can be too nice to people, especially Jon's family. You need to be careful."

"I'm not turning them away. I need to check on Eugenia. The gaol is not known for its comforts."

Olivia sighed. "No, it's not. And I doubt the Moores are going to go out of their way to help her. Master Ezra knew how to manage money and if she's convicted of his murder, there will be more to share."

"Has it come to this?" Faith said. "That justice is measured in money and wealth?"

"When has it not?" Olivia's tone was cynical. "The wealthy can always find someone to free them from their responsibilities. It's the poor that suffer, guilty or not."

Faith held her tongue. She knew what Olivia was referring to. Her sister had died the previous year; her only crime was that of being a slave. She had been able to do nothing for her. It still stung. "I intend to do what I can."

"Then go. I have enough help to manage tonight."

Chapter Sixteen

The gaol had not changed in the months since Faith had last visited someone in its cells. It still smelled of bodily functions and despair. As the sun continued its descent to the horizon, long shadows from nearby trees lined the dirt path leading from the road to the facility. She paused before walking up the narrow wooden steps to the door next to the section housing prisoners. Thick red brick insulated the home from most of the noise but presented a grim reminder of its purpose. A chimney stood between her and the barracks, but out from it stood the wall that formed the outer perimeter. Built high of sturdy red bricks, it stood as a grim reminder of the builder's purpose. Inside the accused waited for judgment, whether high or low born, everyone stayed in the cells in back of the home of the gaoler.

Faith knocked on the solid wood door, the sound echoing in the partially enclosed space. A dark-skinned woman peered out a crack in the door. Faith smiled politely. "I need to see one of the prisoners."

"Master Pelham is busy right now," She started to close the door before Faith put her sturdy shoe in the crack while holding the door firmly.

"I'm sure one of his sons can let me in to see Mistress Moore. I can inquire myself if you're busy." Faith's smile probably showed too many teeth, but she was done being ladylike.

The servant looked like she wanted to argue, but a voice behind her said. "It's all right Amelia, I'll take care of it." As Amelia backed away with a disgruntled swish of cotton skirt, a middle-aged woman with a tired face opened the door and looked at Faith.

"Mistress Pelham," Faith began.

"I heard you speaking to Amelia. My husband is busy with music lessons at this time and must not be interrupted. I will send John out to let you in to see Mistress Moore with the understanding you will keep your visit short."

Faith stepped back and nodded. "I only wish to speak with her briefly."

"So be it." The door closed firmly, steps sounding on the wooden floor of the entry.

Within a few moments, a boy around Andrew's age stepped out with a large iron key in his hand. "This way, Miss." He trotted to the door set in the brick wall which extended well over Faith's head. The enormous lock slid open easily with a turn of the key, the heavy door swung out with a faint groan. He looked over at Faith. "Mistress Moore is on the far right. I'd walk fast past the others if I were you." Obeying his own words, the lad jogged over to the cell nearest the interior wall. Faith wrinkled her nose at the scent of unwashed bodies and walked swiftly behind him, ignoring the jeers and pleas from faces in the door grills of other cells.

No face peered out of Eugenia's door, nor did anyone speak. A shiver of unease went down her spine, Hoping nothing untoward had happened to her mother-in-law during her incarceration.

After a moment of wrestling with the key, the door swung open. Faith stepped inside, pausing to adjust to the dimness. Her nose took in the scents of lye soap and lavender as well as faint body scents that could not be avoided in such an enclosed space.

"Have you come to escort me home?" Eugenia asked. She sat upright in an upright wooden chair. A Bible lay in her lap.

Faith doubted she had been reading, given the poor lighting. As her eyes adjusted, she took in the room. Her previous experience visiting the gaol had informed her of its box-like and Spartan design. Eugenia was fortunate to have some furnishings provided for her. Despite Daniel's accusations, he had allowed his wife to send over a bed and a chair for the older woman's comfort. Eugenia still wore her black mourning, but her hands and face were clean, as was the delicate lace cap on her head. Faith walked closer to her mother-in-law, her steps echoing on the wooden boards that formed the floor. Eugenia watched her approach with no expression. She remained in her chair, waiting.

"I can't do that," Faith replied. "You have been accused of murder and must wait here until your day in court."

"And when will that be?" Eugenia snapped. "I have been caged in this hot room for days. No one comes to check on me, save for my maid, who tends to me and brings scraps from the table for my meals. Meanwhile Ezra's sons," she hissed, "use my house as if it were their own."

Faith looked about. "You have far more than most tenants of the gaol Eugenia. The trial will be in two weeks' time. If you are to return home to the life you treasure, you need to tell me all you know about Ezra's movements before he took ill."

Eugenia stared at Faith outrage visible on her face. "I have done nothing wrong. Yet here you are here to badger me about Ezra, recently cold in the grave."

Faith stared back at her, unimpressed. "I'm the one person who is willing to try to prove your innocence. Talk to me or not, I have plenty of other tasks to fill my day" She turned to knock on the door to exit.

Eugenia let out a breath. "The previous evening, he spent meeting with other members of the delegation to the governor. He told me little except that he hoped they could find a peaceful resolution before one of the hotheads, like Patrick Henry, reacted with force." She rose, placing the Bible on the seat.

"Ezra didn't sleep well that night. I found him downstairs reading this Bible before his meeting. He asked me to keep it safe for him and pray for a productive outcome, which I did after my morning toilette." She patted her hair. "It's very important to keep up appearances even in trying circumstances."

Faith resisted rolling her eyes. Eugenia walked about the enclosed space as she spoke, smoothing her gown as if expecting to entertain company soon.

Eugenia sighed. Exhaustion had left its mark in lines more prominent on skin turned waxy and sallow. Dark circles extended under her eyes and the small bags that had appeared to join them. "Ezra went to the Raleigh

Tavern to meet the other men chosen to talk to Governor Dunmore about the arms and powder taken from the arsenal. He left early and didn't return until hours later with a few companions. They stayed drinking and talking for hours."

Faith's attention sharpened. "Who was with him?"

Eugenia snorted. "How would I know? He entertained them in his study; it was not a place for a lady to intrude. I could hear the sound of their boots and their voices from my bedchamber upstairs."

Faith stifled her impatience. "Who would know?"

Eugenia shrugged. "His manservant was the first to die. Poor man keeled over in the night. No one realized it until the next morning. Ezra was terribly ill throughout the night with a churning of the stomach and unsteady bowels." Her nose wrinkled in distaste. "It was terrible. He woke me well before dawn, moaning and shouting that someone murdered him. I sent for the doctor and brewed a concoction of peppermint and chamomile to ease his stomach, but nothing seemed to help. Two of the kitchen staff took ill but recovered. Louis was unwell, but recovered in short order after taking one of my tinctures." She paused thoughtfully. "I have not had time to seek new staff. I hope Martha is not acquiring slaves in my absence. They have to be carefully selected."

"Maybe you should hire staff and pay them an honest wage," Faith suggested with just a hint of sarcasm."

Eugenia stared at her. "Why would I do that? An enslaved person is a lifelong investment. You really have no head for business."

"Indeed, I prefer to treat my staff like human beings."

Eugenia huffed and glared, but did not reply.

Faith bit her tongue to keep from saying more. Now was not the time, but one day soon she planned to have a discussion about the evils of owning people. "When did Martha and Daniel arrive?" she asked, changing the subject.

Eugenia frowned. "They had stopped by for a few days the previous week before continuing to her sister's in Yorktown. They returned after the incident at the Armory." She picked up a fan to push air onto her flushed face. "Such an overblown affair. The governor is within his rights to do as he sees fit for the colony. It has always been this way."

Faith pressed on. "So you, Ezra, Louis, and possibly Martha and Daniel were all at the house? Was there anyone else?"

"Louis may have been there briefly. I don't see him much. He spends most of his time at the store he has been managing for Ezra. He sometimes sleeps in the rooms over it."

"What about servants? Who besides his valet tends to his office space?"

Eugenia shrugged. "Eleanor dusts the downstairs, while Arthur minds the fires and cleans the fireplaces."

"Have there been any disagreements recently?"

Eugenia fanned herself. "No, there have not, not anything unusual." She glared at Faith. "Why are you asking these things? It's unseemly." She fanned harder. "No one had a reason to harm Ezra. He was a good man, loyal and law-abiding. It had to have been an accident!"

"An accident?" Faith said incredulously. "How does arsenic accidentally get into a bottle of Madeira?"

Eugenia turned to look at her. "Is that how it was done? Ezra doesn't normally keep Madeira, he prefers port. But that bottle came from the governor. It was the highest quality."

"Did you drink any?"

Eugenia shook her head. "I don't expect you to understand the distinction, but no, I did not. Madeira is a drink for gentlemen, not ladies."

Even with her life in the balance, Eugenia held onto her snobbery.

Faith's tone sharpened with irritation. "So, anyone there could have slipped arsenic into the bottle while it stood on the sideboard."

"No," Eugenia said hoarsely. "Not in my home. None of the servants would dare," Eugenia's voice rose in agitation. "Either his patriot associates grew jealous and tried to end him or everyone is mistaken, and he died from cholera, as his physicians insist."

Faith walked over and grasped the older woman's shoulders. "You know better, Eugenia. It wasn't cholera or any other illness. Someone put rat poison in a bottle of Madeira after he left the governor's palace to return home. The question is why?"

Eugenia knocked the hands away before her face crumpled. "I don't know. He came home. He was happy. I heard him singing as he entered the house. He and his associates went to his study for a drink, and then he became ghastly ill." Eugenia hunched her shoulders as she daubed tears. "And now I'm in here to rot until I die."

Faith watched the older woman pace back and forth agitatedly. A mosquito hummed next to her ear, making her wave her arm to deny it a meal. Flies came in through the door grate to dine on residual food left on a plate stacked in a corner. She longed to leave and go out into the fresh outside air, but waited. Her mother-in-law no longer had that privilege and if nothing were done, would never see the open sky until she walked to her execution. Faith waited and tried to ignore the itch of sweaty skin beneath her chemise.

Eugenia stopped pacing and settled back into her chair, clutching the Bible like a talisman. Faith looked at it, noticing for the first time how old and worn it looked. It's dark leather cover creased with use.

"I've never seen that before," she commented, watching Eugenia.

"It belonged to Ezra," the other woman replied, stroking the cover. The edges were worn and dark with use. "He kept it in his office. Although he didn't spout the gospel, I often saw him turning and reading these pages. It's all I have left of him."

Faith walked over to the one chair where Eugenia sat. "May I look at it?" she asked gently.

Eugenia handed it over with obvious reluctance. "Don't damage it."

It was surprisingly heavy for its size. Faith supported the Bible in one hand while using the other to turn the pages. She moved to where the light from the door grate shone the brightest so that she could see it better. Many of the pages were dog-eared. Others were marked with scraps of paper. Faith slowly turned the pages until she reached one of the marked sections. Looking closely, she saw some words were underlined while someone had written on the edge of a page. Despite squinting, she could not make out the words. It was far too dim in the cell to really read anything. Defeated, she closed the book.

Eugenia watched her quietly. "There is something in it, isn't there?"

Faith nodded. "I think he may have used it as a means to send messages. I need to examine it further to confirm that." Noting the other woman began to sputter, Faith added. "It may be the only clue as to who poisoned him."

Eugenia huffed. "Very well, but take care you don't damage it."

Faith smiled. "Don't worry. I intend to take very good care of this." She had a certain Patriot spy she intended to share it with. Jeremy Butler might be the only one able to reveal its secrets.

Chapter Seventeen

Will McKay straightened up, closing his eyes briefly to rest them. It had taken him over half the morning, but he had succeeded in setting a page of type for the *Virginia Gazette's* next edition. He hated the current weakness of his body and cursed the poison that had nearly killed him and left him an invalid. Despite Athena's reassurances, he feared he would never be free of the aches and ailments that plagued his body.

A mosquito buzzed by his neck. Will waved it away before checking that the type was held tightly in place with the wooden furniture blocks. Georgia's son, Marcus wielded the handles of a pair of ink bulbs, their leather pads covered in ink. It was messy work, leaving the young man with ink splatters on his apron, hands, and even in his light brown hair. Will smiled and rubbed a smudge of ink from his cheek. Having done the job, he was well aware of the consequences.

"Thanks," the young man said as he began gently patting the ink onto the type, the ink balls making a steady drumming on the metal. Marcus's fair skin was already flushed with the rising heat. As June approached, work inside the shop became less tolerable. The windows were open for air but also allowed mosquitos and gnats to enter in to feast on exposed skin.

Will nodded, waiting until he was done before pulling the lever that imprinted the paper with the image of the typed letter. It took some muscle to run the press. Sweat ran down his face as he held it tight. Across the room, Paul watched with thinly veiled concern from where he had been hanging sheets of paper to dry. He had offered to trade jobs, but Will refused.

Weakness terrified him. Most of his life had been spent doing tasks that required strength and agility. It had enabled him to survive the brutality of his childhood and the trip across the ocean. In his experience, the weak succumbed to their ailments all too quickly. Will refused to do so.

Releasing the lever, he looked at the page that lay covered with the damp sticky ink. He nodded and let Paul remove it to dry. Given his current clumsiness, he was afraid of smearing the page. Instead, he moved away to examine the pages currently drying on the line that stretched across the room.

The door rattled as people entered the store, shoe heels clattering across the bare wooden floor. Will pasted a smile on his face and moved to greet them. He tried to ignore his coworker's eyes upon him as he walked slowly across the floor, refusing the cane that leaned against the back of the press.

Across the room, Mistress Georgia Clements assisted a couple of ladies in the purchase of stationary. The soft sound of their chatter reminded him of birds. Her face grew animated as she chatted with them about the latest ball, clothing styles, and the suffering of people in Boston whose harbor remained closed by the British still angry about the incident with tea. Her northern relations kept her well informed on the situation. Georgia had published some of the letters she received. With each missive that was set to type, she stirred the pot toward rebellion even deeper.

Will smiled patiently at the petite middle-aged woman who had entered the print shop, accompanied by a taller enslaved woman who looked vaguely familiar. "How may I help you fine ladies," he said, bowing before them with just a faint flourish.

A girlish giggle escaped the smaller woman dressed in mourning. Will took in the starched black cap with its black satin bow, the black dress, lightened by a pure white neck handkerchief edged in delicate lace. Her lower sleeves were white as well, accenting her delicate complexion. Given the quality of her clothes and that she was in mourning, Will suspected her to be a member of the Moore family. Will regretted missing the funeral even though he knew he had been too ill to attend. Ezra deserved all the accolades he had likely received. The loss of his friend and mentor haunted him on nights when the aches in his body kept him from the sleep he sorely needed. His eyes swept the woman standing just inside the shop; she didn't look like she had been losing much sleep.

"I wish to place an advertisement for the next issue of the Gazette." Her voice was lower than Will had expected, given the giggle. Her dark eyes still held amusement as she continued. "My husband is taking over his late father's business concerns, we want his customers to know that Ezra Moore will now become Ezra Moore and Sons Trading, and we will honor all contracts and are open for business."

Will took an already sharpened quill and dipped it in the nearby inkwell. "Very well, Mistress?" He raised his eyebrows in query.

"Mistress Martha Moore, wife of Daniel, eldest son, and heir to his father's business."

Will dutifully took down the information pausing only to dip his quill into the nearby ink well. "I was not aware that Master Moore's will had been read, especially given his wife's current circumstances."

Mistress Moore's servant looked at Will before her eyes slid away. He wondered what she was thinking, given the expression that had briefly covered her face before she controlled it.

Martha Moore's tone turned chilly. "Our family's business is not open for spurious gossip. My husband has worked with his father for years. Of course, he will take over the business and the house."

Will paused in his writing. "I just want to make sure before we print it. Our readers expect the truth on our pages. Given that Master Moore had a wife and more than one child, he might have chosen to divide his worldly goods among them-wouldn't you think?"

The woman's tone sharpened. "Perhaps I should take my business elsewhere." She snatched the piece of parchment from under Daniel's pen, uttering an exclamation as the still damp ink-stained a snow-white sleeve. "Now look what you have caused."

Will stepped back. "No offense intended Madam." He offered her a clean handkerchief. Not that it would do any good. He knew good and well that iron gall ink came out of nothing it touched. His clothing was peppered

134

with it.

"This lace came from Belgium, it is ruined." The paper lay crumpled in the floor as she fussed over her sleeves. "Beatrice, help me."

Her servant grabbed the stained handkerchief. "This only smears the ink. Once we return home, I will use cold water and mustard to lift the stain. We need to hurry home before it sets. If you keep that arm down no one on the street will notice."

Martha Moore sniffed. "Very well. It appears I will have to make calls later." She spoke stiffly to Will. "Make sure the advertisement is placed in next week's gazette. You can charge it to my father-in-law's account." With that, she swept out the door, accompanied by Beatrice, who shook her head, out of sight of the woman she was forced to serve.

Georgia spoke behind him. "She seems quite certain that her husband will inherit everything."

"Yes, she does," Will replied, watching her walk down the street. "I wonder why."

Georgia shrugged. "I will charge her the standard rate. Can you get the type placed? There is room in the next page."

"You're going to run it?" Will looked over at her in surprise. Georgia checked a few sheets of paper hanging from the line, examining the quality of the work. Satisfied, she gave a nod to the lanky young man beside her.

"Paul, I believe these may be dry."

Paul moved behind her, his long arms easily reaching the line to remove the papers and stack them with the others. She checked the progress of printing, nodding as Marcus took the balls to ink type for another page to be printed. A smile of satisfaction softened her features. "Your father would be so proud of how quickly you are progressing."

Marcus flushed with pleasure but kept working.

Georgia turned to Will. "The Moores have always paid in a timely manner. She says her husband is continuing his father's businesses and we have no reason to doubt her." Her voice dropped as she moved closer to Will. "Although I doubt anything is settled. Only time will tell."

The door opened as a man came in with letters to post. Will took care of him while the other two men ran the press. Georgia Clements glided over to the long wooden counter to assist a woman in purchasing a book.

Later that evening, Jeremy Butler dropped by, slipping in the back out of sight of the public area. He came in just as they were sitting down to eat in Georgia's small dining room that faced the garden in the rear. Athena came within a few moments, popping a plate and tankard in front of him.

Butler raised the tankard and took a long drink. "You have the best short beer in this town," he said as he set the tankard down. "Far better than the fermented slop most of the taverns serve."

"Thanks," Georgia said. "My husband's mother came from Bavaria. She taught him how to brew beer among other things."

"Pity more of them aren't brewing rather than taking King George's pay to fight," Will commented as he took another roll from the basket nearby. He sighed with pleasure as he broke it in two, glad that he could once again enjoy a good meal.

Jeremy paused to wipe a trace of foam from his mouth, before setting his tankard down on the sturdy wooden table. "Not all the Germans in this country are here to fight. Some want the same freedoms as the rest of us. The Moravians just want to farm their land. As for the Hessian mercenaries, I've seen them in New York. They're well-trained professionals. They won't be easy to defeat."

Will sat down his drink as he looked at the shorter man. Dark shadows lined his eyes. He looked tired. "Do you believe it will come to that?"

Butler cut into a slice of ham before spearing and chewing it. The silence became heavy with waiting as he swallowed. "I can see no other outcome. There is too much acrimony between those who favor the king and those who demand independence. Even as we speak, men from all the colonies have gathered in Philadelphia to put resolutions on paper that will determine our fate. Only God knows what the end result will be."

He sighed as he continued to eat. "No one cooks like Athena. I hope she made a cake."

"You know I did," Athena's voice carried from the back porch as she entered. "Tonight, we have plum cake, fresh from the oven."

Jeremy sighed with pleasure. "Your cakes are worth more than all King George's gold."

Will was tempted to agree as the room filled with the scent of warm cake, redolent with the scent of cinnamon and cloves. He looked out at the table lit by candles as the evening shadows lengthened and knew the soul-satisfying contentment of being surrounded by good friends.

Chapter Eighteen

The elegant houses of the well-to-do circled the long rectangle of grass known as the Palace Green. A few boys rolled hoops down its length at the opposite end from where she stood enjoying a brief moment of peace before returning to the tavern with her news. Lushly leaved trees framed the edges of the space, with the exception of the end where the governor's palace lay.

The sun gleamed off its ornate metal gate, oddly bereft of the soldiers that normally stood at the entrance. Jeremy Butler strode toward them, walking at an unhurried pace toward his objective. Governor Dunmore would be in his office downstairs dealing with the various issues that came across his desk concerning the Virginia Colony. Despite his earlier excursion, he did not feel as if he had exhausted every possibility at the governor's opulent palace. It was possible the Governor knew something. He intended to find out even if it meant a less than cordial conversation. Butler was done with subtlety.

Between the columns of red brick, Butler paused as a sense of unease washed over him. The steady clops of horse's hooves on the road behind him carried from Duke of Gloucester Street just below the Palace Green. A boy's voice rose as he offered copies of the Virginia Gazette before it sank underneath the murmur of voices of other people hawking their wares at the market. There was nothing untoward to be seen.

He stepped through the open gate and onto the short walkway leading to the steps to the front door of the palace. No one hailed him. Butler heard the movement of people around back near the stables. He briefly considered slipping around and speaking to the servants tending the stock, but his business was with the Governor himself.

Butler had dressed for the part carefully, mindful that the governor might have remembered their previous brief encounter. His fawn silk weave breeches stretched snugly over his thighs down to where they buttoned at the knee with a row of polished brass buttons. White silk stockings clung to his muscled calves down to his black leather shoes that he had assiduously polished the night before. His buckles were fine pewter and gleamed softly in the early summer sun. His jacket and vest of silk weave identified him as gentry, as did the jabot of fine lace at his throat.

Athena loved the suit and had kept it in immaculate condition since he had it made from a French tailor in Philadelphia last spring. Butler felt constricted by the snug fit of the suit and the ruffles that ran down from the cuffs of each of his sleeves, which also hid a knife should he need it. Few people realized he was ambidextrous which meant he could hide weapons for use with either hand. It was a fact that had helped keep him alive more than once.

He removed his tricorn from his head gently so as not to disturb the simple but elegant wig that rested on his head. Tucking his hat under an arm, he raised a gloved hand to knock on the elegant white door. To his surprise, it opened, sliding soundlessly across the tiled floor. Stepping inside he looked about the main hall taking in the heavily paneled white painted walls decorated with weapons. After the bright sun outside, the interior felt dim although some light reflected off the steel of the swords amassed on the walls. He eyed the drawn shutters with concern. At this time the house should be bustling with activity, light streaming in from windows recently shined. Instead, the entryway felt abandoned and forlorn.

Shutting the door behind him, Butler called out. "Hello?" His voice echoed in the room. The adjacent parlor stood empty as well as unchanged from his previous visit. The sound of footsteps in the pantry on the other side of the entry hall alerted him that he was not entirely alone. Whirling around, Butler ran across the marble floor to the room directly across. "You there. Stop!" he commanded.

A man dropped the sack he was carrying with a cry. Glass shattered as it hit the hardwood floor. "I wasn't taking anything. I swear!" The servant was in his shirtsleeves, his livery nowhere to be seen.

Butler speared him with a glance. "I don't give a damn what you're taking. I want to know where the governor is."

The man looked longingly at the doorway behind Butler as the sharp tang of wine permeated the air. From the dark stains seeping from the sack on the floor, some of the Governor's wine had been destroyed.

Butler eyed the man with disgust. "I have little patience this morning so I will repeat my question only once more. Where is…"

"He's gone!"

Butler raised an eyebrow. "Gone? Gone where?"

"I don't know. I swear," he cried as Butler came closer. "They left out the back before dawn. Him, his wife, and all the children. The stable boy saw them slip out the back through the garden.

Butler swore.

The man backed away, raising his arms to ward off potential attack.

Butler strode past him back into the main entry. He'd lost his opportunity to confront Dunmore, but he could search for the Madeira kept in the house. He tromped through the hall not bothering to mask his presence. Entering the room where Dunmore conducted his business, Butler looked about. Paper lay scattered over the desk. Some anchored by books. Where did the man keep his liquor? Nothing obvious jumped out at him. On previous visits he had noted that the Governor had been careful with his best vintages, only getting it out for close friends or people he wished to impress.

Frustrated, Butler backtracked to the pantry, hoping that all the wine had not been stolen. The thief he had confronted had long since fled, leaving the front door open. Butler sighed in disgust. A good burglar never left signs of his presence. "Amateur," he muttered. He brushed against a chest set next to the wall and heard a suspicious clink. Opening the drawers, he found bottles lined up in the bottom; French, Italian vintages, followed by one bottle of Spanish Madeira. Tucking it under his arm, he walked quietly out the back and into the elaborate gardens, empty except for birds sweeping overhead.

The house would not be empty long. Word would get out. He only hoped it would not be looted. The residence was a jewel of beauty and refinement. He hoped it remained so.

The emptiness of the place unnerved him. It should be full of servants bustling about. But then, considering the enslavement of most of them, the Governor's absence had likely provided a unique opportunity to escape. He hoped they succeeded. Stepping back into the main hall, he headed to the enormous wooden stairway and up the stairs. A board creaked in protest as he strode over the landing and into the first bedroom. It lay in disarray, the bedclothes tossed on the floor, items scattered about without care. He wondered if Dunmore's family had left it this way in their hurry to leave or if the staff had laid waste to the furnishings in hopes of finding something valuable to pawn. At this point, it did not matter.

In one room, the printed bed curtains lay in a heap on the floor, as were the other bed coverings. From the brushes and feminine touches, he reckoned it belonged to Lady Dunmore. The mattress had been ripped apart; gouged as if someone were stabbing it to death. Butler stopped when light caught something sparkling in the tangle of cloth and stuffing.

Reaching carefully, he found the object and held it in his hand before walking over to the window for a better look. It was a diamond, small enough to grace a ring. Unset, it would travel easily in a pocket or concealed space. Despite careful searching, he found no more gems hiding in the bed. Pocketing it, he silently saluted the governor's wife for her cleverness. Moving quietly, in case he was not the only one exploring the enormous house, he headed back down and to the Governor's office. It looked as if it had been ransacked.

Remnants of fire smoldered in the fire grate. Taking a poker, he investigated the ashes, curious about what had been burned. Only fragments of paper remained, indications that someone was not leaving information for his enemies to read. He spotted a hand sized fragment against the back of the grate and managed to fish it out. A few sentences complained about the lack of protection for the governor, who had signed it. Butler pocketed it. It might be useful. He would send it with the next courier up to Philadelphia, where he knew Washington and the other leaders of the rebellion were.

Carefully placing his hat back on his head, he tucked the bottle under one arm and circled the garden on one of the many well-maintained pathways. Again, he heard the whisper of voices. Peeking over a hedge, he saw a few servants standing together talking. Their world had shifted. There was no one to pay their wages. He imagined the enslaved staff had fled once they realized their owner had gone. He hoped they managed to get far away before anyone noticed.

He continued back to the Palace Green, staying within the shadows of the tall trees that lined the expanse. Athena knew a lot about poison; he hoped she could determine if this bottle had been tampered with as well. That would tell him if someone had tried to kill the governor or if Ezra had really been the intended victim.

Not many were about at this hour which is why he had chosen it. As he gazed out, he spotted a woman paused on the edge of the green, her head bowed. It was Faith Clarke.

Puzzled by her presence as well as her demeanor, he strode up to intercept her.

"Faith?" He called softly, trying to get her attention without startling her. She didn't appear to notice until he brushed her arm. She startled at the touch. Her eyes rose to meet his as he took in her pale face and haunted features.

"It's happened again," She paused for a breath, looking out at the tranquil scene before her. "Daniel Moore collapsed while we were gathered discussing what Ezra's final wishes might be. Only time will time whether he lives or dies."

Butler stared at her, his face expressionless. "Who was there?"

"Everyone. All of Ezra's children, Louis, Eugenia, some of the staff."

"Eugenia? How did she get free?"

"Not free, let out on bail until the trial begins. George Wythe wrote a letter on her behalf that convinced the judge to send word to release her to her home." She added quietly, "Martha called for the Sheriff to be summoned before she told me to leave."

As she spoke some of the fog left her eyes. Faith blinked before taking in both Butler's presence and his elegant suit. "Why are you here?"

"I was going to speak with him regarding Ezra and see if he knew anything. Regrettably, he fled in the night, along with his family."

"Why would he do that?" Faith asked quietly. Only a few people strolled the green at this hour. A trio of laughing children ran down its expanse, trailed by a mischievous dog. They went past the long length of the green, past the stands of trees that lined the road, and off into a nearby field that stretched out behind one of the houses surrounding the green.

Butler let out a breath. "His support has been crumbling since he took the powder away. Even those not ready to join the rebel cause disagreed with him. He's been fearing an attack. Given that armed engagements have already commenced up north, it's only a matter of time before it spreads. The war for our independence has already begun."

Silence fell over the green as the children playing at the other end ran off into the trees.

Her voice was quiet. "What do you know about what's happening up north?"

He shrugged. "Not much. A group of patriots seized Fort Ticonderoga from the British a few weeks ago." Butler saw her puzzled look and added, "It's on the western frontier of the New York Colony."

"Patriots seized a fort from the British military?"

Her disbelieving tone made Butler smile without humor. "Yes, they did. Whether you accept it or not, American militias have been preparing for this outcome for some time. Even as we speak, representatives of all the colonies are meeting in Philadelphia to discuss their next move."

"I thought they were trying to negotiate with the king."

Butler sighed impatiently. "It's pretty clear that King George has little interest in listening. The only message he will notice will come at the end of a gun and there are too many hot-blooded people who are willing to point them in his direction or to his representatives. We need men of reason to take us through this crisis or there will be no end to the carnage. That's why Ezra's loss is such a blow. He understood the road to independence needed to be well thought out."

"Now he is gone, and the governor has fled."

"It won't be long before patriots come to ransack the palace and you don't want to be here when that happens."

"Is that why you're here?"

Butler shook his head. Sunlight picked out strands of his pale hair, haloing around his head and where it stuck out from his tricorn. "I wanted to ask him about the Madeira. Even though I doubted he personally poisoned him, he might have some thoughts on the issue."

"Surely he heard about Ezra's death," Faith's tone was incredulous. "Ezra Moore is a prominent figure in Williamsburg." She paused before correcting herself. "He was a very important man." Dunmore had not attended the funeral. Eugenia had been insulted although he had sent his condolences with a formal note.

Butler's voice was soft. "Yes, he was. But Dunmore has been distracted with fears of patriots attacking for some time now. He's been more concerned with the preservation of his own hide."

"What will you do?"

Butler shrugged as he stared past her at the recently deserted residence of the governor. "I have people to see if I'm to ensure Williamsburg doesn't descend into lawless chaos." He ran restless fingers over his wig, causing a few strands of his actual hair to escape from their confinement underneath.

His voice was bleak as he looked over the town as if imagining what could happen. "The strongest voices of the Patriot cause are in Philadelphia, planning a united response to the king. There aren't many here who could talk down a mob. "

No traffic came in or out of the Governor's palace. Dunmore's slaves had scattered, no doubt taking the opportunity to flee toward freedom. The elegant brick building stood isolated in its position at the head of the enormous swath of grass that formed the Palace Green. It stood bereft of the normal guard of British troops, though toward Duke of Gloucester Street horses and wagons still went about their business.

"No one knows where Ezra kept his will."

Butler's tone was dry. "Apparently it is the day for surprises."

Faith shivered. "I don't know what to think. His lawyer said Ezra had been revising his will. But no copies have been found. The house has been searched several times. The family had gathered to discuss what to do when Daniel collapsed and cried out he was poisoned."

Faith looked out over the green, her expression elsewhere. "He was so ill. I've never seen anything like it. Everyone was in a panic. Zachary sent us out of the parlor, but we could hear him retching." She paused to take a breath. Her hands shook as she rubbed them together as if trying to ward off cold.

"What did Eugenia do?" Butler asked quietly.

"Eugenia?" Faith paused. "She looked shocked as she backed away." Faith looked as if she might become ill herself. "He thrashed about like a tormented animal. I've never seen anything like it."

Butler nodded. He'd seen some pretty vicious deaths during the French and Indian War although they hadn't peppered his dreams in years. He took her arm intending to take her where she could recover, but Faith shook his arm off.

"No one will believe her innocent now."

"Not likely," Butler admitted. "Her presence at a second poisoning is pretty damning. If he was poisoned."

"You think not?" She looked at him sharply.

"I think it's too early to say. The physician may have another thought."

Faith snorted. "The physicians thought Ezra had cholera in case you do not remember. He died insisting he had been poisoned. It was only later someone discovered arsenic on that bottle of Madeira."

"Is that what everyone was drinking?" Butler was surprised. "I would think it a bit early for that."

Faith shook her head. "I don't think so. It was mid-morning. The maid brought in a light wine. It was pale in color and sweet."

"Sounds like some of that German vintage that Ezra had gotten in. He was quite fond of it."

Faith shrugged. "It's possible. I'm not familiar with what he kept on hand.

Anyhow, everyone gathered in the parlor. The disagreements began almost immediately. Daniel and Eugenia were at odds regarding the house, among other things." She shook her head. "Oh God, what a mess!" She swayed a moment before catching herself.

"Let's go to Mistress Clements. It's only a short walk from here. You need to recover before you head home."

"Olivia will not be pleased. Dinner has the largest number to feed."

"She would like it even less if you fainted on the Palace Green."

The safe harbor of shade she stood in was edging back with the ascendance of the sun, bringing its burning heat with it. Her head began to swim, adding to the pounding throb that had begun right after breakfast. This time she didn't shrug Butler's hand away.

Dust blew up from the road, coating the bottom edge of her skirt. As soon as possible, they moved to the walkway composed of brick bats, thereby avoiding most of the dirt and animal droppings that covered the mile of roadway constantly trafficked by both wagons and horses.

An open wagon jolted past, its back holding two children, a dog, and boxes covered with a blanket. It was followed by a carriage heading west toward Bruton Parish Church and Nassau Street. A horse snorted before taking an aromatic dump outside of Greenhow's store.

They walked in silence until they reached the print shop. Butler opened the gate to take them into the back beyond the view of prying eyes. Out of habit, his eyes swept the enclosed yard, checking for potential threats. Rather than housing neatly clipped hedges that surrounded orderly flowers and herbs, Georgia Clements' garden spread out in a profusion of green growth. Nasturtiums grew near a trellis of green beans, while cucumbers snaked across the rich dark earth that had been stripped of weedy intruders. A flock of hens clucked softly as they trotted down the rows looking for insects to eat.

Athena looked up from where she sat on a bench outside the kitchen shelling peas. Her dark eyes took in both of them. She rose and went into the kitchen to set down her bowl. When she emerged, she led them toward the back porch. "You," she pointed to Jeremy. "Go change out of that suit before you ruin it. I'll take care of Mistress Clarke."

He started to protest, but her glance quelled him much as it had when he had been a lad under her care. Bowing briefly, he trotted up to her rooms where he knew his everyday clothes remained from earlier that morning.

When he returned, Faith was cautiously drinking what smelled like rum, while Athena sat nearby letting the other woman settle. Will walked in and sat down by Faith, taking her hand in his, chafing it gently between his calloused palms. Faith lay her other hand over it as if hoping to draw warmth from him.

Butler sat down across from them stretching out his legs. "Is Georgia joining us?"

Athena shook her head. "She has a newspaper to run. Someone wants to place an advertisement for their new business. "Cooper," she added by way of explanation. "I'll talk to her later."

Butler nodded. "Very well." He began by sharing about Dunmore's disappearance before turning to Faith, who shared her story briefly.

She still looked pale but was far more composed than she had been.

Will's gaze sharpened as he looked at her. "It could have been you this time."

Faith shook her head. "I don't think so. I'm no threat to anyone. The poison, assuming it is poison," she added, with a look at Butler, "was administered to Daniel Moore. The question is why?"

"I think the question is who?" Will interjected. "Who benefits from this? It's clear who was there both times."

"Eugenia," Faith breathed. "That's hard to believe. I've seen her behave in a variety of ways through the years, but this is something I would normally never have imagined her doing."

Faith contemplated what had happened. The brutal scene playing in her mind was one she doubted she would ever forget. Speaking of it made bile rise up her throat. She picked up her glass and took another sip, the liquor running down her throat like liquid fire. The heat steadied her for a moment, long enough to complete her words.

Will whistled. "No will, that doesn't sound like Ezra. The man planned for everything."

Butler looked at his glass contemplatively. "No one likes to consider his own end. He may have not been ready to admit death was coming, even as it drained him of life."

Faith shook her head. "Everyone agrees he had one and that he was revising it. He was so weak it must have been difficult, even if he dictated it."

"He must have hidden it somewhere safe," Athena said.

Faith nodded. "I would have thought so, but the house has been searched over and over. If it's been found, no one has said so." Glancing over at Butler, she said, "I have something that might interest you."

Butler raised an eyebrow.

Faith continued. "Ezra's Bible is marked in some odd places. I may be wrong, but I think he used it as a key for his messages."

"Where is it? Do you have it with you?"

Faith shook her head. "No, I don't. It's at the tavern." She had placed it in the bottom of her clothes chest among the winter woolens, where no one would be likely to look.

Butler rose. "I need to see that Bible. I have messages sent to him by sources I normally don't have dealings with. He used a code of his own devising for that, one I'm not familiar with. I'll walk you home and you can get it for me."

Chapter Nineteen

They left the print shop in silence, their footsteps in tandem down the wooden steps and through the garden gate that led to the alley connecting to the Duke of Gloucester Street. Faith cast a glance back down toward the road where Ezra Moore's house lay.

"There is nothing you can do there and you wouldn't be welcome." His tone was laced with impatience. "Focus on what you can do."

Faith nodded and turned back east where Clarke Tavern lay just past the Capitol. The sun has risen to its zenith in the sky. Its heat burned through her hat and pounded on her head. Sweat beaded on her brow as she worked to keep up with Butler. Despite being a few inches shorter, he moved swiftly through the other pedestrians going up and down the street. She was huffing by the time they reached the oak trees surrounding the tavern. Dappled shade spread over the yard as she opened the gate and strode up the steps and through the front door, Butler at her heels.

Titus looked up from where he tended the bar in the main room. He looked at her and Butler before putting down the cloth he was using to wipe down the counter. "Is everything all right?" he asked in a low voice as Faith stepped into the taproom.

Faith's eyes met his as she shook her head. "I'll explain later. Can you get Master Butler a drink while I fetch something?" With that she left the two of them, stepping across the hall to the small pocket of privacy she had and shut the door behind her.

A knot rose in her throat. She desperately wanted to cry but there was no time for grief or the anger and shock that accompanied it. As she took a breath, something sharp jabbed her chest, reaching down, she ran her hands down her jacket until she located the offending pin that had worked its way inside, over the top of her stays, and through her chemise to prick her flesh. She pulled it back where it would quit stabbing her breast, thankful that the dark colors she wore would conceal any blood from the prick.

With the sun's movement overhead, light no longer streamed into her bedroom, leaving it somewhat shadowed. The lack of light didn't matter, she knew every corner of this space by heart, from the tile stove which lay quiet in the summer heat, to the rope bed she had once shared with a man she had believed she would love forever, to the small wooden clothes trunk, given to her by her father, built by his careful hands, at the farm outside Philadelphia where she had been born and raised.

Faith choked up as she ran her hands over its leather hinges which had darkened over time as had the wood. The lid rose smoothly in her hands, just as it had when her father had presented it to her when she had turned sixteen, telling her she was old enough to have something of her own. It was all she had of him, beyond a few letters, carefully kept within the trunk and she treasured each item. Within the sturdy wooden box were her clothes and a few personal items; an ivory comb from her grandmother, a woolen shawl knit with yarn she had spun herself over a long winter, and down underneath her winter petticoats, her hands touched leather.

The Bible was not large, it was meant for personal reading, not to embellish an altar. Some of the pages were faintly worn. It smelled faintly of pipe tobacco, bringing up an image of Ezra that brought tears to her eyes.

"I wish you were here," she whispered, acknowledging the pain that would not be denied. Faith swallowed hard. There was no time to mourn, not now and not anytime soon. She rose with the Bible in her hands. Pausing a few moments before the washstand and the mirror above, she wiped her face to hide the evidence of grief before going out to the public area, where eyes always watched.

Jeremy Butler stood near the bar, his body appearing at ease while his eyes assessed everything going on about him.

A few men played cards at a table not far from where light came in through a window not shaded by a tree. Another man sat near the center, the *Virginia Gazette* held up for reading. His lips moved slowly as he went through each column. In the corner, a couple of men sipped on tankards of ale, taking a break from the day's work. Titus returned to the bar from refreshing their drinks. The keys to the liquor cabinet clinked together from where they hung from a cord that dangled from the open collar of his shirt. His hair was pulled smoothly from his face in a tightly braided queue held together with a dark leather strap.

Faith walked in quietly, going to the counter surrounding the liquor supply, purposely ignoring Butler for a moment. This was her tavern and her home. Within these walls, he was a visitor. "How has the day gone?"

"Well enough." Titus continued running the cloth over the already shining surface. His expression softened when he looked at her. "How about you?"

"It was not what I expected," she said. "Eugenia came."

Titus' dusting paused. "I imagine the Moore children were not pleased."

Faith let out a breath. "It was ugly." She set the Bible down on the counter.

Butler reached over for it. Faith speared a glance at him. "I want it back when you're done with it. It's all I have to remember him by."

"It's all I have of him as well," Butler responded. "And it could hold vital information to our cause, a cause Ezra sacrificed a great deal for."

"Such as his life?" Faith couldn't keep the bitterness in. "He died far too soon."

Butler nodded. "Both he and his eldest son may well be victims of the enemies of the rebellion."

Titus startled. "His son?"

Butler's glance reminded him they were in a public place.

"Daniel Moore has fallen ill of what appears to be the same malady that took Ezra," he explained in a soft voice. "Eugenia is no doubt already heading back to the gaol since she was present."

He slanted a glance at Faith. "Once again, Madam, you are embroiled in a murder."

Faith shot him a look not wanting to be reminded of the events of the previous summer. She shivered and hoped she never had to see another

151

corpse. A small pewter cup appeared by her elbow.

"You could use a drink," Titus said as he capped the blue glass demijohn, before setting it back on the shelf behind him.

Faith downed the drink feeling the burn of the alcohol. "I normally don't drink rum, but thank you. I'd better change so I can help serve dinner." She turned to go to her quarters when a shout rang out in the street.

"The governor's fled!"

Further shouts filled the street, followed by the thud of feet on floorboards as men exited the tavern to hear the news.

Butler's eyes met Titus. "I hope they don't burn the place down."

Titus shrugged. "I would think the patriots would want to keep it for the next governor."

"I don't think King George will be in any hurry to send another one here."

Titus shook his head. "That's not what I meant. The next governor will be a patriot, appointed by those folks meeting up north."

Butler looked at him a moment, before raising a glass. "Here's to the new governor, whoever that may be."

Titus clinked a glass with him. "May he be a man who believes in freedom for all people."

Butler set the glass down. "May it be so."

Chapter Twenty

Faith stared at the gaol, pausing before entering the gate. In the past year, she had cause to be here a few times and it had never been a pleasure. On her arm was a basket filled with comforts for Eugenia, who she knew had been placed back inside, waiting trial for the murder of her husband.

Behind her, she heard the steady clop of horses' hooves as travelers continued into town, along with the rattle of wagon wheels. At this time of year, the market would be full of goods brought by nearby farmers intent on making what profit they could. She had already heard rumors that militias on both sides had taken to raiding farms for the food they needed. She was thankful to be in town. A brief breeze tugged at her hat, bringing with it the scent of hay and manure from the street. A handkerchief doused with lavender oil lay tucked into her bosom. It was faint defense against the scents she knew would greet her within the cells. Faith could not imagine how her proud mother-in-law was handling the confinement. She doubted Martha had supplied her with the comforts of her previous incarceration.

Going to the side door, near to the bolted door to the cells, Faith knocked, and then waited before knocking again. The door was opened by a dark-skinned man of medium height. He was unremarkable except for his eyes which were hazel and set with lustrous dark lashes. His clothing marked him as a household servant.

"May I help you, Mistress?" He stood blocking the door. Behind him, children's voices could be heard faintly, along with a woman's voice speaking to them.

"I've come to visit Eugenia Moore," Faith said. She gestured to her basket, "I've brought her a few comforts."

The man gestured for her to enter. "Wait here. I will ask the mistress about this."

Faith nodded and stood inside the small white-walled room. A glass-paned window let in the late afternoon sun creating a pattern on the plain wooden floor. She had chosen her time carefully after dinner so as not to leave her tavern shorthanded. It also allowed her to pack up a good meal for Eugenia, along with a shawl and a few other comforts. She wasn't sure what her mother-in-law might want or need and in truth, did not have the means to supply the things that the Moores could.

The man returned, followed by a woman Faith assumed to be Mistress Pelham. She wore a pale blue striped skirt over which she had a block-printed jacket of blue flowers and vines. Her cap and sleeves were edged in white, as was the shift that showed at the neckline and sleeves. Her dark brown hair was pulled back neatly under her cap. A child wailed in the background, as she smiled tiredly at Faith.

"My husband is at the church practicing on the organ, how may I help you, Mistress?"

"Forgive my intrusion, Mistress Pelham. I'm Faith Clarke. I own the Clarke Tavern here in town. My mother-in-law, Eugenia Moore has been incarcerated here. I am hoping to see her. I have brought a few items for her comfort."

Mistress Pelham nodded. "Mistress Moore is upstairs in the women's quarters. I brought her breakfast earlier today. I can have one of my sons take you there."

"May I look at your basket? My husband will expect me to know what has been given to each prisoner.' She looked apologetic.

Faith set the basket down on a small table next to one of the wooden chairs that lined the wall and gestured. "You may examine it if you wish."

Mistress Pelham's hands were well kept with short, neat nails and even cuticles. They were not the smooth hands of a lady, but of a woman who knew how to work. She pulled back the cloth cover and carefully checked the items inside, before recovering it. "You are kind to look after your mother-in-law in such a time as this."

Faith nodded without answering. Eugenia and she had never really had a comfortable relationship. Jon's sudden death had made it bitter, but maybe now enough time had passed that they could be at peace with each other. While Jon's death had stricken both of them, there were happy memories they could share with Andrew, his son.

Faith followed a teenaged boy up the narrow dark stairs to the ladies' cells. Down below she could hear men as they found ways to pass the time. Court would be convening soon. The cells were becoming increasingly crowded with people awaiting trial.

It was not a huge surprise to find that Eugenia was sharing a cell with another woman. From her revealing attire and heavily rouged cheeks, Faith could guess what charge had landed her in gaol. When Faith entered the cell, the woman cackled revealing missing teeth.

"Genie, you have a visitor! I hope she brought something good to eat. Those oats this morning were barely fit for a horse."

"Be grateful we feed you at all," the boy muttered as he shut the door. "My mother takes care of you ladies, unlike the men below."

"Oh, oh. Don't criticize his mam. Come in one night, little boy, and Sally will make a man of you! She laughed as the boy flushed red before turning and walking swiftly away and down the steps. His footsteps clattered loudly against the hardwood as he hurried down. Sally laughed before turning her gaze back to Faith.

"So Lovey, who are you?"

"Faith Clarke, proprietress of Clarke Tavern and daughter-in-law to Mistress Moore."

Sally's eyes widened. She had one blue and one brown eye which was startling at first. "You're that tavern keeper of that place where Phineas Bullard was chopped up."

Faith winced. Some stories never died. "He died there. I had nothing to do with it."

Sally nodded. "Sometimes you never know when a body's going to drop.

He was a cheap toff anyhows. He never wanted to pay the going rate for services rendered, if you catch my meaning."

Faith wished she didn't. Deciding to move on, she focused on Eugenia. "I brought you a few things to help make you more comfortable."

Eugenia's face was pale and drawn. "I didn't poison Daniel," she whispered. "I know no one believes me, but it's God's truth." Despair laced her tone. "Everyone has abandoned me and left me to rot."

"The truth will come out," Faith said. She started to take the basket over to a set of steps but was repelled by the strong scent of urine.

"That be the privy," Sally said, answering a suspicion.

Faith reversed course and chose to set the basket on the floor near Eugenia. "I brought you some ham and biscuits since I wasn't sure what you were getting here. Olivia also sent a jam tart along with a fruit cordial."

"Hallelujah." Sally chortled. "That's much better than the beer we've been drinking. Surely, you brought enough for poor old Sally as well." She came closer. Faith stood and stared at the other woman. As she approached, Faith caught the scent of musk and sweat. Her hair still held the elements of an elaborate updo, but strands straggled out until it looked like a windblown haystack.

Eugenia turned her head away from the other women. "Why should I eat if I'm going to die," she wailed as she placed her face in her hands, sobbing.

Exasperated, Faith held the basket away from Sally as she spoke to Eugenia. "If you give up now, the judge will convict you and hand you over to be executed. If you want to be exonerated, you need to tell me all you know. The judge could arrive any day now."

Eugenia uncovered her face and sniffled before taking a handkerchief out of a pocket and gently patting her face. "You know what happened, you were there."

Faith pulled out a trencher and offered the other woman a slice of ham and a biscuit, she did likewise for Eugenia's cellmate, who stuffed her cheeks as she walked back to the other corner.

"Thank you," she said. "I like jam tarts, too, by the way."

Faith shook her head before turning back to Eugenia. "I doubt I saw everything, and I don't know what happened before I arrived. When did you return home?"

Eugenia sat quietly for a few moments. Despite being in a cell, she still looked mostly tidy; her hair pinned into a knot high on her head. Although by now, her curls traveled limply down her back rather than curling around her shoulders. Her mouth tightened as she thought. Automatically her fingers rose to smooth out the crease that formed between her eyes. After a few minutes, her eyes met Faith's.

"I returned home late the previous evening. They were not expecting me." She sniffed. "Martha was most unsettled, although she bid me welcome. She would have placed me in a guest room," Eugenia snorted. "I set her right there and went to my and Ezra's room, which she had already been changing, no doubt intending to make it her own.

My maid, Lydia, attended me and helped remove the taint of the cells from my body and hair. Given the late hour, I took a tray in my room before retiring. The next morning, I rose early for the reading of the will. You arrived a few hours later."

Faith nodded. She had arrived after serving breakfast for her guests. The attorney had arrived just before her and had been taken to the parlor where Ezra had lain in state over a week ago. She had taken a hard-backed chair near the door behind Ezra's gathered sons. Their wives and the daughters sat in a semicircle near the windows. Eugenia's presence had been a surprise, sitting front and center, close to the middle-aged man, dressed in a formal suit of dark blue with a lighter blue embroidered vest underneath. His stock and cuffs were white with only a minute amount of lace. A dark brown wig completed his uniform.

Refusing the offer of a drink from Daniel Moore, the man sat down and began to speak of Ezra and the many conversations they had shared before his death. He paused before saying, "Ezra was busy writing his will the last time we spoke, and unfortunately he chose not to share it until he had completed it."

Daniel leaned forward. "So, where is it? I assume it is in your hands."

The attorney shook his head. "Regretfully not. I have notes of his thoughts, but he would not consent to leave a draft in my hands. Ezra Moore burned his old will in my presence. His will, or at least what he had written of his wishes is in this house."

"That's impossible," Daniel said. "His room has been cleaned thoroughly since his death. Any papers would have been found."

The attorney shrugged. "I do not know what to tell you. I have lists of his investments, titles to various properties. Some things he had already shared with members of his family. He set aside small sums for a few long-serving members of the staff."

Silence fell over the room, heavy enough that the cries of a few birds could be heard outside. Faith would have preferred to be out in Ezra's beloved gardens rather than in this crowded room, rife with tension. Ezra's wife and children sat stiffly as they realized the magnitude of the problem before them.

"The court may have to intervene," he continued.

"My father's legacy will not be carved up by a judge," Daniel's voice was grim. "This is for his family to decide. My brothers and sisters and I will work this out as my father would have wished."

Eugenia interrupted. "He was my husband for over fourteen years. I knew him better than anyone. I know what he would have wanted."

"You know what you want," he shot back. "You've always been clear about that since the day my father brought you home."

Eugenia's eyes sparked with anger, but she didn't raise her voice. "You speak ill of a well-respected man. No one made him do anything he didn't wish, not me and not any of his children. He knew better than to invest in ventures based on sentiment."

"What did my father discuss with you?" Daniel asked the attorney. His voice was remarkably calm considering the outrage on his face. Zachary stood beside him, his face intent. His strong, square hands drummed restlessly on the sideboard where glasses and bottles had been placed by a servant who stood silently nearby.

The baiting continued as they argued over all components of Ezra's legacy. Her father-in-law would have been greatly disappointed in all of them. An aching sense of loss consumed her, muting the voices around her. She closed her eyes as they began to sting and took a few breaths, as deeply as she could given the constraints of her corset. She mentally cursed Olivia for pulling it tighter to fit into her more formal dress. She was startled into awareness by a strangled cry.

Daniel dropped his glass on the floor as he doubled over. It shattered, leaving sharp pieces all over the floor. His face contorted as he cried out, before staggering over to a nearby spittoon to retch. "I am poisoned," he cried as he dropped to his knees, then to the floor.

Martha rushed over to her husband along with Zachary. She called to one of the servants, "Get Doctor Galt. Take a horse from the stable. Hurry!"

Zachary's wife, Beatrice stood still by the table where glasses of wine still sat, watching events unfold. Looking back, Faith remembered her stillness, as if she were waiting for the next act in a play.

"What were you two arguing about when he collapsed?" Faith asked. Noting Sally creeping closer, she picked up the basket and slipped it in between Eugenia and herself.

"I like cake," Sally said wistfully. "You don't get much sweets in here."

Faith sighed and picked up the basket. She looked over at Eugenia who was giving Sally an evil look. "Would you prefer apple cake or jam tart?"

Eugenia looked in the basket. "They're both mine, aren't they?"

Faith nodded.

Sally called out. "Don't forget who killed that rat last night. It doesn't pay to be selfish."

"Cake, please," Eugenia said, picking it up with a glare at her cellmate.

Faith lifted up the rejected tart and started to offer it to Sally. It was snatched out of her hand with the speed of a lightning stroke. Sally went back to her straw mattress in the corner. Despite her boldness, she ate the treat in tiny, neat bites before wiping her hands on what had once been a pretty floral apron over her ruby red dress. Faith wondered what her story was and how she had ended up here.

She took a few moments to gather her thoughts as the other women ate.

She was surprised as Eugenia shared the bottle of wine with Sally. Within the gaol, the constraints of class and money had disappeared, leaving two women both facing a grim future. Eugenia took the cloth that had wrapped the cake and wiped her fingers before tossing it back into the basket. Although dark shadows remained under her eyes, her eyes were clearer as she looked back at Faith. "I wanted my house and what was rightfully mine. I don't know who poisoned Daniel," she paused, and her tone turned shaky. "I don't know who would have wanted to harm Ezra either." She wrapped her arms about herself. "I would not have harmed a hair on his head. He was everything to me. Everything."

"Who handled the liquor in your household?"

"Mordecai," Eugenia answered. "He's been with us for years. He is completely reliable. Ezra was arranging his emancipation. I cannot imagine him wanting to harm anyone."

Faith nodded. She knew the elderly man. She had seen him serving at the table at the Moore household many times. "Nonetheless, I need to speak to him. He may have noticed something."

Eugenia sniffed. "Talk to whom you wish. That is my house and my servants, no matter what those other Moore women may say."

Faith nodded. She had been there for the eruption following the attorney's statement. "What was Daniel drinking?"

"What we all drank," Eugenia said, "A light wine Ezra had imported from Germany. No one else became ill." Her face paled as realization hit. "Someone poisoned him there, didn't they? Why? And who? All gathered were family."

"Just family?"

Eugenia shook her head. "No. There are always servants, ours and those his children brought with them."

"Who released you from the gaol?"

Eugenia sighed. "Master Pelham. He'd received a message from Master Wythe's associate guaranteeing my bond. I had enough time to go home and repair my toilette before he came to read the will. It was most tiring." Her mouth tightened. "I would rather burn it to the ground than to let Martha get her claws in my house. She had no right to come in and change things. And to think I treated her like a daughter."

Faith ignored the jab. She knew how easy it could be to earn Eugenia's ire. Both Eugenia and Martha enjoyed the finer things in life. Both liked being in control. "So you saw nothing odd?"

Eugenia shook her head. "If I had, do you think I would be here? I would have shouted it from the rooftops. Instead, here I am, caged like an animal waiting for slaughter."

Faith rose and gathered her basket. "I need to go and talk to your servants."

Eugenia looked at her. "What makes you think you will be allowed in?"

Faith smiled grimly. "What makes you think I will wait for permission?" She went toward the doorway, her steps soft on the floorboards.

"Faith," Eugenia said.

Faith turned to see Eugenia looking down at her own hands. "I realize now it wasn't your fault."

"I had nothing to do with either poisoning."

"That's not what I mean," Eugenia paused, looking subdued. "I was referring to Jon. I don't think anyone could have saved him. He fell ill so quickly," Her voice trembled. "I should have been there, by his side. It's not your fault."

Faith didn't know what to say, not after so many months of rancor. She sighed. She was too tired to take it in. She looked over at Eugenia and wondered if she had heard her correctly. "No one knew Jon was going to fall ill." She paused as painful memories she preferred to suppress rose to the surface. It had been months since her last nightmare replayed her husband's final days. "He took ill and died swiftly, too swiftly for you to return from the country. I'm glad your memories of him are those of him hale and hearty." She did not add that her memories were much darker.

Her mother-in-law nodded. "You don't have my skill with herbs, nor did you have the advantage of raising him to read that he was unwell. Most of the physicians here have limited skills."

Faith stiffened at her words, then decided to let it go. Eugenia would never see past her veil of self-importance. At least she had found a way to accept her middle son's death. Faith picked up the empty basket and knocked on the door, stepping back as one of Pelham's sons unlocked it and swung it open to let her out.

"Either I or Olivia will check on you in a day or two," she called over her shoulder.

"Don't forget to bring more food," Sally called out from the depths of the cell.

Pelham's son snorted as he led Faith down the steep winding steps to the main floor of his home"Keep an eye when you're around that one, your pockets will be light before you know it."

Faith nodded as she followed him down the hall and to the outer door which he shut firmly behind her.

The afternoon sun beat warmly down on her head and shoulders, dispelling the chilled feeling the gaol always instilled within her. Despite the distance, Faith walked down the road toward town and Bruton Parish Church. She had not stopped by the graveyard in a long time.

Dust blew up from the road coating her stockings and skirt. She chose to ignore it. A little dirt would not disturb those she was visiting.

Next to the graceful brick building where Williamsburg's finest families worshipped, lay a quiet yard of neatly clipped grass broken by tidy rows of headstones. Jonathan Elijah Clarke lay buried near his father on the outer edges of the cemetery with the more recent dead. Grass had grown over the grave in the past year, covering what had been a bare mound of soil, now almost level with the surrounding ground. She looked at the neatly engraved stone Eugenia had placed to mark Jon's remains. It looked almost identical to what she remembered of his father's marker in the previous row.

"You were too young to go," Faith said softly. "I'm sorry you suffered, that you don't get to see our son grow to manhood. I think you would be proud of him." Birds called in the trees near the church. In the distance, wheels rumbled down the dirt road into town and people spoke, carrying on their business, while within the resting place for the dead, time stood still, continuing only as memories, sinking ever deeper into the past.

The sound of footsteps caught her attention. She was no longer alone.

Not far from where she stood, a man placed a posy of white flowers against a headstone. As he rose and stood, she recognized her brother-in-law, Louis. Curious, she joined him at his father's headstone. She had never known Abram Clarke; he and his eldest son had died long before her marriage to Jon, during the previous war with the French and Indian allies. Louis has been a small child.

He glanced over at her. "Visiting my brother?" he said. "How is Jon?"

"At peace, I hope," she replied. She was in no mood to share memories with anyone. "Have you come to pay your respects?"

Louis was silent so long, she had ceased expecting an answer, then he said. "I was only eight when my father died. I don't have many memories of him. I remember that he had a laugh like a braying donkey that embarrassed my mother. That he liked to take me and my brothers when he went to the horse races. My mother cried for days after hearing he and my brother had been killed in the fighting. An elderly enslaved woman, Deborah, tended me back then. She tended all of us for days while my mother carried on. She died when I turned twelve." He shook his head as if dispelling a bad thought. "I don't know where she's buried."

Light hit the top of his head, accenting the lighter tones of his dark hair and revealing how it was thinning around his temples. For once, he was dressed soberly in plain tan breeches with a dark blue coat and vest with only a faint amount of embroidery at the cuffs and collar. He nodded at the stone. "I often wonder what life would have been had he not decided to join the fray."

Faith shrugged. "It's hard to say."

"Indeed. I imagine you wonder how life would have been if you had not been widowed so young."

"Not as much as I did," she admitted.

"Do you think my mother will be convicted?" Louis looked at his father's grave as he spoke, revealing a somber profile.

"I don't know what evidence they have," Faith answered.

"That's not a comforting response, Faith," he turned towards her, his smile not touching the sadness in his eyes. "She's all the family I have left. Once she goes, I have no one." He sighed. "I never thought life would be like this. That everyone near and dear would die so soon."

Faith reached for his hand. "Don't give up hope. We still have time to find out what happened to Ezra. The truth will be revealed."

"The judge arrived just after dinner," Louis said. "He's taken rooms with Mistress Vobe. He plans to convene court starting tomorrow."

Shock washed over her. "Eugenia comes to trial tomorrow?"

Louis shook his head. "He'll deal with the easy cases first. I imagine murder will be at the end, but it won't take him long. If you hope to prove her innocent, you need to act now. Do you have anything that points to who did this?"

Faith shook her head. "Nothing definite. All I know is someone tampered with a bottle of Madeira Ezra received from Governor Dunmore. But it's hard to say who had access to it. Now Daniel has fallen ill as well, it cannot be an accident."

"Daniel's been going through his father's wine cellar, he could have found the bottle and unknowingly imbibed."

Faith shook her head. "No, the Madeira was no longer in the house when Daniel took ill. The poison had to have been administered another way." She looked at Louis. "I need to speak to the servants and see if they know anything."

Louis looked startled. "You suspect the staff tried to snuff Daniel. His wife has been wielding authority with a heavy hand. I suppose someone could have reacted badly."

Faith looked at him. "Can you get me into the house?"

Louis grinned. "Martha will not be pleased. By all means, come by. Tomorrow will work well. Since dear Daniel appears to be recovering, she's planning a trip to the milliners to ensure she and her daughters have adequate mourning clothes. I will tell the doorman, George, that you have business in the house. Now I must return to work before one of those nosy clerks claims I'm shirking my responsibilities." Bowing slightly, he turned and walked toward Duke of Gloucester Street, placing a tricorn firmly on his head before he left the cemetery.

Faith stared after him before turning back to her husband's stone. "I never thought I would see him here," she said to the empty air. She shivered as shadows from the trees began to reach over the grave. The emptiness no longer seemed soothing, but eerie as the sun continued its journey down to the horizon. She wanted to be home with her son and her people about her, the bustle of the tavern occupying her mind and body. Faith looked once more at the plot with its formal headstone. "You're not here," she whispered at last. "You are gone, and I must move forward past you and what will never be."

The wind sighed as if acknowledging her words. Without hesitation or regret, she left the land of the dead and the regret she had unconsciously harbored. There would be no need to return, for no one waited for her on this wide grassy space. Memories were all that remained deep within the recesses of her heart.

Chapter Twenty-One

Although she had been to the Moore home many times, Faith still felt nervous as she walked down the neat cobblestones to the front door. She jumped as the gate hit the post behind her disturbing the quiet morning light reflected off the windows, obscuring who or what might be lying behind them.

Despite Louis' assurances regarding Martha's absence, a flicker of unease ran down her spine as she stood on the top of the semicircular steps that surrounded the front door. Shadows from the balcony above cast the rich red of the roof into shadow, removing metallic shine from the knob.

Rustling from the bushes compelled her to twirl about. A pair of birds shot out of the trees, shooting across the lawn in a cacophony of wild cries. Catching her breath, she continued up the walk toward the semicircular steps that led to the front door.

Her thoughts turned to Will, who would be working in Georgia Cléments' printing shop, setting type for the next issue of the gazette. Even as she struggled to come to grips with Ezra's death, life continued. Will would not be free from his indenture for four more years, but she didn't care. Faith felt no need to hurry into a relationship. She was content to be without a partner.

The door opened before she touched the knocker. Surprised, she stared at the familiar face of George, longtime footman of the Moore household.

"Mistress Clarke," he bowed before allowing her to enter. "I will tell Mistress Beatrice you are here."

Faith nodded as if that had been the plan all along. Beatrice was Zachary's wife. She vaguely recalled the wedding over the Christmas holidays seven years ago. They had moved immediately to land along the James River owned by her family. Her main impression had been of the bride's incredible paleness. Her hair was nearly white-blonde, which made her eyelashes and brows nearly invisible. Her skin was almost as pale as her hair. Faith's first impression had been that it was hard to tell if she was alive or a statue.

When Beatrice entered the receiving room, Faith saw that little had changed. Beatrice's hair was arranged high on top with elaborate curls cascading down the back. Her maid had talent. A starched white cap rested on top of her head embellished by a solid black bow. It coordinated with the black striped silk dress she wore. Although still ivory pale, somehow, she had found a way to add a little color to her cheeks and lips. It wasn't obvious, but Faith remembered how colorless she had once been.

Beatrice said nothing as she surveyed Faith. "Why are you here?" she asked finally. "This is a house of mourning and pain. It's neither the time nor place for socializing."

"How is Daniel?"

"Sleeping. The physicians are done with their purges and bloodletting. Hopefully, he will recover, and this business will be done."

"Not if his poisoner still roams free."

Beatrice blinked. "Eugenia resides in the gaol until her trial. Surely that is the end of this sordid tale."

"Are you certain Eugenia did this?" Faith watched her sister-in-law as she contemplated the implication.

Her lips tightened briefly before her expression cleared. "What are you suggesting?"

"That before our mother-in-law is condemned, we should be certain she is the guilty party and not someone with an agenda as yet unseen. Eugenia had nothing to gain from Ezra's death and everything to lose. Nor do I believe she poisoned Daniel in a fit of rage. I was there with you when Daniel collapsed. Eugenia seemed as shocked as the rest of us."

"A subterfuge," Beatrice replied, although her tone was uncertain.

"Have you ever seen her being subtle in all the time you've known her?"

Faith pointed out in exasperation.

Beatrice shot her a look that was almost amused. "Not that I can recall."

A servant entered the room with cups and a pot. Beatrice motioned to a chair. "Join me for coffee and explain what you intend to do."

Faith took the hot cup and added sugar and milk. She hadn't sat down for more than a minute before now. It felt good to take a moment to catch her breath.

"First I want to examine the wine bottles to see if anything has been tampered with."

Beatrice shook her head. "The sheriff's men took all our liquor this morning. Zachary has been out all day arranging for more. The servants expect their drams regardless of life's events."

"You have no alcohol at all?" Faith was startled. Every household relied on a steady supply of beer, ale, wine, and other liquors. Given that even well water could cause illness, everyone relied on distilled beverages to drink.

"Not even the short beer you provided Ezra last month. They took every last drop. There has been nothing worth drinking beyond the few bottles Zachary bought from the Raleigh Tavern a short while ago. We will have to purchase additional beer and liquor to accommodate the staff. It has been most inconvenient."

"I see." This was a problem Faith had not foreseen. She wasn't sure the sheriff would talk to her. She paused to sip her coffee, buying time before she replied.

Beatrice offered her a tray of cakes and small sandwiches, of which she accepted a small cake. "Thank you."

Beatrice nodded before pouring her own cup, which she drank without any amendments.

"May I speak to Mordecai?" Faith asked.

"The old man?" Beatrice shrugged. "He's been despondent since his master's death. After Daniel's collapse, I dismissed him from serving the family. Edith has had him polishing the silver and sorting vegetables in the cellar, checking for rot. You can speak with him if you wish."

After a few inane remarks regarding weather and popular colors of ribbon for the summer, Beatrice rose saying she had a letter to complete.

Faith rose as well, brushing any stray crumbs from her good gray dress. "I can find my own way to the kitchen." She said to Beatrice's retreating back.

She waited a moment before walking down the hallway past the dining room to the back door. The separate kitchen was a large building well away from the main house. A dense cloud of smoke rose from the chimney indicating that someone was at work preparing the midday meal. As she walked down the steps, she marveled at the size of the garden and the many outbuildings that surrounded it. This was far more than a simple home; it was an estate, where the Moores' and their enslaved servants lived out their lives. Faith watched a pair of children exit the garden and go to the kitchen, skipping as they carried vegetables to the cook. Servants moved back and forth as she walked down the gravel path to the kitchen. No one met her eyes. Seeing them busy working made Faith contemplate the reality of their lives, held in constant bondage, never knowing when they might be sold and forced to leave. Ezra's death must have been terrifying for all it could mean for them.

Edith stood at a long table inside the kitchen, chopping vegetables with a steady rocking motion of her knife. She didn't pause when Faith entered the room but remained focused on her task. Behind her, a few low flames danced over the logs keeping a steady heat under the dark kettle bubbling over it. Bowls lined up on one end held a variety of foodstuffs.

"Can I help you, Mistress?" Edith's voice contained no inflection as she worked. Off to the side, a girl of perhaps twelve, was scrubbing new potatoes in a large wooden bowl. Underneath her plain yellow skirt, bare toes peeped out, dusty from being outside. Her nose wrinkled in concentration as her hands, red from work, rubbed a cloth over the small potato.

Faith smiled at the girl who ignored her before walking to where she stood across from the busy cook. "You look well, Edith. I haven't seen you since Ezra invited me to see the bloom of the tulips he had planted last fall. He stopped to ask you about strawberries."

The enslaved woman shrugged. "That may be so. I don't recall."

Faith waited as Edith moved her chopped squash to a bowl and took a large onion from a bowl and laid it on a board on top of the table.

"You've been here a long time. I bet there's not much that goes on around here that you don't see."

"I don't know about that. I spend most of my days here, fixing meals for people. It doesn't leave much time for checking up on other folk." Edith chopped off the root end of the onion and began removing the skin.

Faith's eyes began to burn and sting. She raised a hand to wipe her eyes. Edith appeared unaffected by the noxious fumes of the vegetable. Faith sniffed as her nose tickled. "I mean you no harm," she wheezed. "I'm trying to find out what happened here."

Edith snorted. "You want to find a way to get Eugenia out of trouble."

Faith paused to wipe her eyes. She sniffled as her nose filled with liquid as well. Edith finished the onion and picked up another, methodically chopping without so much as a blink. A light breeze danced in through the open window and door, clearing the air as it provided some relief from the relentless assault of onions.

Faith inhaled the fresh air grateful for relief. Her head cleared allowing her to focus on the matter at hand. "Someone poisoned Ezra as well as others in this household. Don't you want to know who?"

Edith paused to put the last of the onions in a bowl before grasping a carrot. "Master Ezra was good to us. He always said he would arrange for us to be free one day, though he didn't act on it." She paused in her chopping. "I liked Theodore, everyone did. He died first. One of the maids found him collapsed on the floor by his bed."

"Theodore?" Faith asked, trying to think of who that could be.

" Master Ezra's valet. He'd served him for years, long before he came to Williamsburg and married Mistress Eugenia. They sickened within hours of each other. But while doctors were called for the master, Theodore died alone in his room." Edith's voice dropped. "He was a good man."

Faith spoke softly "I had heard his valet had passed. I'm truly sorry. His life matters just as much as Ezra's. I never meant to imply otherwise."

Edith stared at her, her face unreadable. A few moments passed before she picked up her knife again. "No one pays much attention to a slave until something goes wrong."

The carrot fell into small pieces. She swept them into her hand and placed them into a bowl. Her wrist flexed with the rhythmic up and down of the knife making a sound as it connected with the board covering the table.

Faith watched her work, chopping her way through a small mountain of vegetables that thankfully did not include any more onions. Edith avoided her gaze as she worked, pausing only when the girl rose from the floor to hand her the newly cleaned potatoes.

Edith took the bowl and inspected them. "Very nice, Grace, Now go find me a nice batch of lettuce in the garden." She smiled and offered her a large wooden bowl. The girl took it and skipped out the door, her braids flying behind her.

"Where will I find Mordecai?" Faith asked as they both watched the girl head into the garden, sunlight catching loose strands of hair as she passed a few women hoeing beside a trellis of cucumbers.

Edith shot her a look as she added her chopped vegetables to the iron pot over the fire. A small piece dropped out and hit the fire, hissing as it blackened and curled.

"Ezra's death devastated him," She picked up an enormous wooden spoon and stuck it into the pot. "He's been with Ezra since he was a boy. He's lost without him and consumed with guilt. He's haunted that he poured that Madeira for Ezra and the others." Edith sighed as she cleaned off the table in preparation for another task.

"Mordecai devoted his life to Ezra after he lost his wife. He was the closest thing to family he had. That woman said he couldn't handle the wines anymore, put him to polishing silver, scraping plates, menial work for a man of his years. Ezra put him in charge of the wine to make things easier for him. He's too old for anything else."

"So where is he now?" Faith said. Outside, voices from the yard drifted in, casual chatter about the number of new calves in the pen near the stable out back.

Edith shot her a look from underneath her lashes. "I'm not sure, mistress. There's always a lot of work to be done around here. I need to get back to fixing dinner or the mistresses won't be pleased."

"I'm sure there is always much work to be done," Faith said as she gazed about the kitchen. A few boys drifted in to take dishes to wash, while a young woman dropped off a bowl of green beans. Outside, the steady chopping of an axe informed her that more wood was being chopped for the constantly burning kitchen fire. Sweat dripped down her back as she looked at the other woman considering what to say.

She had no way of knowing what her relationship with Ezra's daughters-in-law might be and she didn't want to cause any trouble that could come back on the enslaved woman. "I need his help," she said at last. "He oversaw the wine. I'm hoping he saw something that could reveal who is doing this. I don't believe he or Eugenia poisoned anyone, but someone did."

Edith began checking through the beans, picking out stray stems and a few bugs. For a moment Faith thought she intended to ignore her, then she spoke. "He gets real tired midday. Sometimes he takes a brief rest in the sheep barn before helping serve the evening meal. None of us care if he takes a nap, he's got a lot of years on him."

Faith nodded. "Thank you." She turned and walked out of the pressing heat put out by the fire and into the yard. She took a moment to enjoy the cooler air before walking down past the garden to where she knew the sheep barn lay. Since it was past shearing season, the building was virtually empty. Ezra's sheep had been sent outside of town to a farm where he kept the majority of his stock. A pen at the back kept a few head who grazed lazily on the rich grass, the lambs napping in the shade of an elm out of the warm summer sun.

The door stood slightly open allowing air to come inside. The door leading to the pen stood ajar undoubtedly for the same reason. Faith knocked on the wooden door frame as she stepped inside. She didn't want to startle the old man.

"Mordecai?" she called as she walked deeper into the dim exterior. "I'm Faith Clarke, Ezra's daughter-in-law. I wanted to speak to you." She waited for her eyes to adjust. The barn was silent except for the faint rustle of some creature in the back recesses. She paused to look about the unfamiliar building. There had been no reason for her to visit Ezra's sheep. Light seeped in through cracks in boards shrunken from the ceaseless heat of Virginia summers. It provided enough light to see a few wisps of straw scattered on the packed dirt floor. Cobwebs dangled from the corners, still in the airless room. The room smelled musky from all the raw wool.

A tremor of unease ran down her spine. It was too quiet. "Mordecai!" she shouted. "Where are you?"

No one answered her, nor was there any indication of anyone's presence beyond hers. Faith regretted not snatching a candle from the kitchen before coming out here. Nonetheless, she intended to discover what Ezra's trusted sommelier knew. Time was running out before Eugenia's trial began.

"Mordecai," she called again and walked further into the room. There were few places to hide. Her eyes swept the room, taking in the bales of wool waiting to be combed and spun. A washtub for scrubbing the grease and dirt from the raw locks stood at the ready. Both combs and cards lay in a basket by a sturdy upright chair. In one corner, the bales stood tall enough to obscure the back wall. As Faith approached, a board squeaked underfoot, causing her to startle.

"Silly goose," she muttered as her heart settled back into a regular rhythm. "One would think you expected a ghost." No one responded to her muttering. No one else was in the shed with her. Not even an old man could sleep through all the noise she had caused.

Nonetheless, she continued to the corner almost completely obscured by the wool bales. As she moved closer, the animal smell intensified along with something she could not readily identify. Rounding the bales, she spotted the end of a blanket on the floor, the end covering an oblong object.

She stopped as she realized the blanket was covering a foot as well as the attached leg. Mordecai lay behind the wool bales, partially covered by the other blanket despite the heat of the room. He looked as if he had gone to sleep, lying on the simple cot on the packed earth floor. He lay on his back with his arms crossed above his belly. His head was turned to one side as if the man had drifted into a deep sleep.

Despite the shadows, Faith knew he must be dead. No one living lay so still. Nonetheless, she cautiously checked for any signs of breathing. His chest remained still without the characteristic rise and fall of someone alive. She hesitated and reached out a hand to check his neck for a pulse. The skin was cool and dry. With sudden clarity, Faith identified the odd odor in the room, it was death.

Rising from her crouch, Faith backed away, turning to run as she got further away. Her memory recalled when she had smelled the arrival of death before, over a year ago when fate had made her a widow. With a soft cry, she fled across the yard away from death and the memories it drew forth. There were some ghosts she had no desire to encounter, regardless of the reason.

Chapter Twenty-Two

Jeremy Butler stared down at the book of scripture in frustration. He had spent most of the day examining Ezra's notes and marks on various pages trying to decipher what code the deceased man had used to communicate with his contacts. None of it made sense to him.

He dearly wanted to swear, but felt constrained by a childhood filled with stern-faced nuns and priests, first in Ireland and then as an indentured servant compelled to attend mass with the rest of the staff. Along the way, he had memorized a lot of Latin phrases, but had never had to deal with an English Bible. It stunned him that Ezra had written notes on the margins as if it were a schoolbook. Butler smiled grimly. Ezra had never been switched by an ornery nun for smearing ink on a parchment.

Setting down the volume yet again, he rubbed his eyes to dispel the tiredness. A drum-like throbbing continued in his head with muted military precision. He wanted nothing so much as to toss it down and go out to clear his head with a lengthy walk and a long drink, but he needed answers. With Ezra's murder, came a break in the chain of spies that kept him and the Sons of Liberty apprised of goings-on in Virginia. It allowed Butler to operate in different areas of the colonies while remaining informed. Now he felt blind, and it made him uneasy. He'd never delved into who Ezra had recruited to keep tabs on the town's prominent Tories and Ezra had strict orders never to reveal Butler. It kept them all safe. It had never occurred to him that someone would kill the mild-mannered businessman.

Rising from the small table that served as a desk, he paced back and forth as his mind went through possible ciphers, all of which he had tried and failed to unlock the book's secrets.

Giving up for the moment, he trotted downstairs. A light breeze stirred the trees into a gentle dance. He lifted his head to take it in. Even after all these years, he took pleasure in having the freedom to enjoy a summer breeze and not have to answer to anyone.

The morning haze had cleared away, leaving rich deep cobalt skies stretching on into infinity. Butler took in a deep breath, taking in the scents of the city. Athena was frying bacon. His mouth watered as his stomach growled. It reminded him that it had been some hours since his last meal.

A mockingbird took charge of a fence post. Its bright eyes glinted at Butler as it announced to his kindred Butler's presence.

Butler's eyes crinkled in amusement at the bird's boldness. "I'm no threat to you, my friend. Your kind has saved my life more than I can count." It was true. Startled birds had warned him of nearby enemies more than once. Turning on a heel, Butler headed toward Athena's kitchen, intent on satisfying the needs of his belly.

She was bent over an iron skillet resting on a spider over the muted flames of the ever-present fire. Sizzling fat filled the room with sound. Athena wrapped a thick cloth around the handle and moved the pan from the fire to the edge of the stone hearth. Without turning she said, "It's about time you came down. You missed dinner."

"I smelled bacon. Are there biscuits to go with it?" Butler's tone was wistful. Many times she had filled a hungry Irish boy's belly while fixing dinner for their master in the big white farmhouse in Maryland.

"Sit down," she said as she reached for a plate from the stack on a shelf nearby. "I'm sure I can find something." Within moments, she had a plate loaded with crispy bacon, biscuits, stewed apples, cornmeal mush, and a mixture of green beans and squash. From a barrel in the corner, she drew a generous draft of home-brewed beer to wash it all down.

Butler sighed contentedly. "No one cooks like you." He grasped his fork and began eating.

Athena watched him for a minute. "I haven't seen much of you today. What keeps you upstairs? You're not hiding again, are you?'

Butler shook his head and paused to swallow before taking a drink of his beer. "No trouble. I've been trying to decipher a Bible."

Athena cut a glance his way. "Men have been endeavoring to do that for hundreds of years." She paused a moment. "I didn't think you were much of a Bible reader."

Butler frowned at her. "I've nothing against the Bible. I just happen to prefer to hear a priest read it in Latin. I don't understand the need to put it in common language."

Athena shot him an exasperated look. "How many people do you know who speak Latin, much less read it?"

"That's not the point," Butler said stubbornly. "A proper mass is given in Latin. Besides, this is Ezra Moore's Bible. It's in English."

"I thought you could read English." Athena cleared his plate and stacked it with others to be washed by one of the boys who helped in the kitchen.

"I thought I smelled pie," Butler shot her a wistful look. "You used to make the most amazing blueberry pie."

"Amazing," Athena repeated, a smile of pleasure raising a dimple in her cheek. "I remember a boy who could eat amazing amounts of food." She looked over at him. "Not much has changed except you've gotten taller." She pulled a cut pie from the cabinet where she had placed it to keep insects away. After cutting a generous slice and placing it in a bowl, she put the pie away.

Butler waited for her to set it down in front of him with a spoon. "Thank you," he said softly before digging in. "I can read the words; I just don't know how Ezra is using them to communicate with his network."

Athena's gaze turned thoughtful as she watched him down the pie. Butler knew there was little she could do to help him. He had tried teaching her to read as had others. He had seen her laboriously write letters when she thought no one was looking and struggle to see the words. When Athena copied words, letters turned backwards or transposed, no matter how hard she tried.

"You need to talk to Gowan," she said abruptly, before turning to stir a pot on the stove. "I cannot think of anyone more knowledgeable of God's word."

"Who is Gowan?" Butler said as he rose to stack his bowl with the others waiting to be washed by either Paul or Silas.

Athena fussed over the hearth, moving over a few logs and shifting a covered Dutch oven to a warmer section of the fire. The girl who helped her came in with a basket from the garden. Backing away from the fire, she turned to inspect the basket. It contained green beans, onions, and parsley. Athena removed the onions and herbs and placed them on the table in front of her.

"I'll take care of the onions and parsley while you snap the beans," Athena said as she picked up a large wooden bowl from a shelf. "You can work on the bench outside." The girl nodded as she hooked the basket handle under one arm, took the bowl, and headed back out to the bench.

"It's cooler out there," she noted, wiping away beads of sweat that had accumulated on her forehead. She paused to organize her workspace, lining up her knives and stacking bowls and platters for the serving of food. Picking up a soapy cloth from a bucket under the table, she wiped it down before picking up a pan that had been resting just outside the fire. Dark brown coffee beans rattled as she shook them into a bowl, before turning to retrieve a large stone mortar and pestle. The beans gave off a rich aroma that tickled Butler's nose.

"Do you make coffee now?" Butler asked curiously.

Athena chuckled. "This is a patriot household. No one is drinking the king's tea." She shook her head. "That herbal stuff, Mistress Georgia puts together doesn't have much kick to it. I convinced her to give this a try. Now we go through a couple pots every day."

Butler nodded. He drank coffee on occasion but had never seen Athena prepare it. His mind returned to more pressing matters. "Who is Gowan?"

Beans rattled as she poured them into the bowl of the pestle. "Gowan Pamphlet is pastor of the church I attend on Nassau Street. He's a very knowledgeable man." The beans crunched under the application of the mortar. She eyed him carefully, weighing her words.

She rarely did this with him, and it irritated her that after all these years, she still hesitated to tell him some things. Butler waited. While he considered

Athena a second mother, he recognized that he would never see the world as an enslaved or formerly enslaved person did. He had seen her whipped when her master had sold her only daughter and been helpless to stop it. He could not begin to comprehend the scars she carried from her previous life. His were nothing in comparison.

"We meet in an old carriage house, both enslaved and free to worship God in our own way," she said in a soft tone. "No one causes any trouble. We sing and listen to the scripture just like anyone else." Her eyes, when they met his, were fierce.

"I would never assume otherwise," Butler said surprised by her passion. "Why do you think Gowan Pamphlet can help me decipher this Bible?"

"No one knows scripture like he does. He reads it every day. That man can explain words and phrases I never understood before."

Butler nodded. "So he knows the Bible." His tone was patient which made Athena's head snap up.

"I'll wager he knows more than you or a lot of the other pastors in town."

Butler raised a placating hand. "I meant no offense, Athena. I'm just not sure how a preacher could figure out secret code."

"Maybe you need someone who understands the word of God," she snapped.

Butler shrugged. He had failed in his own attempts to understand Ezra's notes; maybe Athena's preacher might spot something. "Where would I find him? Nassau Street?"

Athena shook her head. "He's enslaved to Mistress Jane Vobe, who owns The King's Arms Tavern. It's down Duke of Gloucester Street, along near the Raleigh Tavern and a few others.

Butler nodded. He'd passed it before on his way to other places. When he wasn't checking in with his sources in the small Clarke Tavern behind the capitol, he would catch a drink and a meal at the Raleigh. Many favorable to the patriot cause came in, including members of the dismissed house of Burgesses. Rising, he headed for the door.

"How does Mistress Vobe feel about this?"

Athena shrugged. "I've never met her. Gowan doesn't speak of her, but he doesn't seem concerned."

Butler took his leave, trotting back upstairs for the Bible before walking briskly down Duke of Gloucester Street. As usual for midday, the streets were filled with horses, wagons, and carriages all going about their business. The cobblestones echoed with the steady clopping of hooves. On a street corner, a man called out the latest news to be had, his well-modulated voice carried over the sounds of animals and the clatter of wagons. He already knew that important men from all the colonies had gathered in Philadelphia. It didn't sound like the crier's news was more current than his sources.

He continued down the road, dodging other people out and about their business. He muttered an apology when he bumped into a man carrying a barrel out from the cooper. The man shrugged and heaved it into the waiting wagon.

Within moments, he stood at the white walls of the King's Arms. Inside, business appeared brisk. A well-dressed woman of middle years stood near the heavy rail of the staircase, greeting her guests. Butler was glad he'd taken time to don his dark blue jacket with the matching braid over his buff breeches. She smiled as her eyes met his, her eyes sizing him up as he crossed the room to greet her.

"Milady," he bowed over her hand, noting the rings on her hand were well-wrought and set with fine red stones.

"Welcome to the King's Arms," Mistress Vobe responded in a cordial tone. "I don't recall seeing you here before, Master?"

"Butler," he responded. "Jeremy Butler, milady. I'm in town attending to a few items of business and have heard much of your fine establishment."

"Then, come and enjoy a fine meal." She looked across the room. "Irma, please find a table for Master Butler." Vobe smiled. "Enjoy your visit to the capital."

Butler followed the woman to a small square table against the wall. The room was full of the murmur of voices. He settled in as the woman soon reappeared with a tankard of ale. He took a careful sip, unsure of the quality of her brews. He shouldn't have worried; Mistress Vobe's reputation was deserved. The liquor was smooth on his tongue and slid like silk down his throat. It was very welcome after being out in the summer heat.

A plump African American gentleman came towards him. "What can we get for you today, sir? We have a succulent beef stew, freshly fried fish with new potatoes, rabbit, fresh berry pie, and spice cake. What would you like?"

Butler looked up at the man and smiled. "That depends, are you Gowan Pamphlet?"

Dark eyes studied him thoughtfully for a beat before answering. "I'm called Gowan, sir. I don't believe we've met. Now, how can I serve you?"

Butler indicated the red stoneware tankard. "I'm fine with drink and some conversation at your convenience. Athena Wise suggested I discuss the Bible with you."

Pamphlet's expression revealed nothing. After a moment, he flicked a glance around the room. "My time is my mistress's, Master Butler. I will be busy here for some hours."

"When do you suggest I return? Butler didn't like to wait, but he recognized that an enslaved man had few choices. His fingers tapped a restless beat on the wooden table almost inaudible over the noise of people and crockery within the room.

"Once the tavern closes for the night, I help sweep and clean for the next day. It will be quite late when I leave." He paused. "Mistress has given me tomorrow morning to prepare for Sunday. I can meet you at our church. Athena can direct you."

Butler released a breath. "So be it."

A voice called for more drink from across the room. Pamphlet raised a hand in acknowledgment before heading away to tend his mistress's patrons.

Butler sat alone at his table, sipping fine ale, pondering the best way to use the time now on his hands.

Chapter Twenty-Three

Faith eyed the dress she wore in the mirror anxiously. The pearl gray skirt swung gently from her hips to the floor. The neckline dipped into a deep U that revealed the tops of her breasts, lifted up by boned stays. Ivory lace lined the rim, emphasizing her pale skin. It highlighted the white pattern of leaves and flowers printed on the fabric.

"You need to wear your lace gloves to hide the calluses on your hands," Olivia said as she eyed Faith and adjusted the overskirt over a matching petticoat. "You also need to quit frowning; you'll get wrinkles doing that."

Faith looked at her. "I'll get wrinkles anyway as I get old."

"Crinkling your nose like that will make it worse and that pale skin of yours shows everything. Even freckles," She handed a powder puff over to Faith, who daubed it on her nose while trying not to sneeze. "The Mistresses Moore have invited you to supper. You need to dress the part."

Faith grimaced. "I know." The invitation had taken her totally by surprise. "This is not a social occasion. They want something." Though she couldn't figure out what that might be.

"All the better to be prepared for whatever might happen," Olivia noted. "Jeremy asked me to give this to you." She handed the other woman a small pistol. "It should fit in one of your pockets."

Faith looked at the small weapon with its beautifully carved handle and deadly small barrel. "Why would I need a pistol for a dinner party? I've never used a pistol. I'm not putting something in my pocket that could go off and kill someone."

Olivia listened for a moment before responding. "I can teach you how to use it. You need to be able to protect yourself if needed. These are dangerous times and you have become a valuable member of the patriot cause. That alone could make someone want to harm you should it be discovered. Men have been coming into the capital from all over, both patriot and Tory. Fights have broken out in the taverns and in the street. You may never use it, but if you encounter a lawless thug when you're out, you may need it."

Faith eyed the weapon cautiously. She had noticed the rising numbers of men in the streets, some shouting their allegiance. It made her uneasy, but she could not afford to hide at home. She was a businesswoman, and the same men who crowded the street might take a room at her tavern. She couldn't afford to be picky.

"Very well, show me how this works and it can go in my reticule." She eyed Olivia. "I didn't know you could shoot a pistol."

Olivia met her gaze. "These are dangerous times for everyone. I don't fancy being attacked on my way from the market." She checked the pistol. "It's not loaded, but we can fix that. It loads like the rifles you've used for hunting."

Faith eyed the weapon. "I'm not taking it until I've practiced with it. There are too many things that could go wrong toting a weapon I do not know." She patted the starched white cap with its solemn black ribbon. "I'm as ready as I can be." Eugenia had arranged for the dress. It had arrived in the arms of her maid before the invitation, showing that even in the gaol she knew what happened in her house.

Surprisingly, it had taken little alteration. Aided by the nimble hands of Ellen, the new maid, it looked like it had been made for her.

Olivia set the small gun down on the table. "We'll take time to practice tomorrow. I assume you know how to load a gun."

Faith rolled her eyes. "Yes, I do. I started hunting with my father when I was twelve. He taught all his children to hunt and shoot. We all worked to put food on the table."

"Then this shouldn't take much time to master." The front door opened. Titus' voice carried through the door.

"She should be out shortly, Master George. My wife is helping her with her toilette."

Faith brushed her hands down her dress and checked to make sure her cap was straight before taking her reticule and heading out the door. She felt odd walking down the steps allowing a young footman to hand her up into the carriage the Moores had sent for her.

As they bumped down the main road that was Duke of Gloucester Street, she peered out. The streets seemed busier. Small groups of men gathered outside taverns, voicing their displeasure with the king. Olivia had told her that the local militia had started drilling almost daily, which explained the sound of gunfire off in the distance early in the morning. Now that the governor had fled, it was likely that patriots would take advantage of his absence. Outside of Shield's Tavern, a group of men stood about as if they had nothing better to do. It worried her. Residents of the town still had businesses to run and families to raise. They didn't need the added burden of dealing with restless men decrying the British and causing trouble.

Within moments, the carriage had turned onto Frances Street and rolled to a stop at the entry to Ezra's house. Faith stepped out and down to the step that the footman had moved into place. As her feet touched the ground, she looked up to see Martha along with Beatrice and Zachary Moore waiting to greet her. She nodded to the group, a cautious smile on her face.

"Welcome Faith, we're so glad you could join us." Martha was dressed in an elegant gown of black with touches of white lace at the elbow and neckline. A band of large luminescent pearls encircled her throat emphasizing her delicate complexion. Martha's smile appeared sincere as she took Faith's hand to lead her into the house.

Faith allowed herself to be swept in, nodding agreeably as her sister-in-law chatted about the weather, the difficulty in getting goods from Europe, and the challenges of training a staff unfamiliar with her ways of doing things. They stopped at the parlor.

"We're not entertaining out of respect for dear Ezra's passing," Martha explained. "But we are having a simple supper as a family to celebrate his life and plan for the future." With that ominous message, she gestured for Faith to sit. "Could we offer you some wine? It's a French vintage we recently acquired."

Faith shook her head as Martha looked at the glasses and scolded, "Not the pewter, wine goes in the glasses with the rounded bottom."

The man bowed and took the offending pewter away.

Martha shook her head. "It is regrettable that Mordecai passed in his sleep. That man knew what glass to serve with a beverage every time. It will take me an age to train someone to be half as knowledgeable."

"He died in his sleep?" Faith interrupted, earning a stare from both sisters-in-law.

After a brief pause, Marth huffed slightly. "I had forgotten you discovered the old man. You're developing an uncomfortable habit of discovering death, Faith. People may begin to talk. Mordecai was very old. Our butler assures me that all signs indicate he died very peacefully in his sleep. He has already been buried and his room cleared for other members of the staff."

"You didn't ask a doctor to examine him, after what all has occurred here?" Faith was astounded.

Martha's tone turned chilly. "He was a longtime servant in this house. No one had any reason to harm him. He was old. You would be wise to quit looking for trouble that is not there. My husband is not joining us because his condition is still delicate after that woman attempted to poison him. I know you have been visiting her, but you may not ruin dinner by discussing her."

More questions bubbled to the surface of her mind, but Faith contained them. Within moments, dinner was ready. Zachary offered her his arm as they walked into the dining room. Louis escorted Martha, while other family members fell in behind them.

Sconces lit the room, casting shadows on the brilliant green walls. White wainscoting covered the walls from hip height to the floor. Faith was seated midway down the long rectangular table in between Louis and one of Ezra's sons-in-law. His name escaped her memory.

Once they were seated, the serving of courses began. A servant with close shorn hair and white gloves served a creamy asparagus soup lightly sprinkled with fresh parsley. Steam rose in wispy strands from the white bisque bowl. In spite of her nerves, hunger rose once the aroma hit her nose. Faith lifted her spoon and started eating. Conversation was muted as bowls were emptied. Within moments, bowls were taken away and plates of poached fish were set down along with a savory meat pudding. Faith looked about her down the length of the seats to those gathered about. Not a single table in her establishment had a third of the length of this one that went from end to end of the sumptuous room. Eugenia and Ezra had spared no expense in the decorating of this residence. From the elaborately plastered ceiling to the brightly colored walls that contrasted with the brilliant white wainscoting.

A servant passed by on silent feet, carrying a bottle wrapped in a white linen cloth. As he went about, he filled stemware glasses with white wine. As he poured into Faith's glass, her nose tickled from the scent of fermented grapes with a hint of lemon and apple.

She raised the glass and took a careful sip, taking time to enjoy the pleasure of an excellent vintage. While she stocked a few good-quality bottles for her more discerning customers, her inn couldn't afford the types of wines Ezra Moore could with his landholdings and trade. Faith sighed. He should be here at the head of the table, teasing Eugenia and holding forth on topics he found of interest from music to politics. Instead, here they were, his children by blood and by choice, eating in grim silence with nothing but the creaks of chairs accompanied by the faint clink of china and utensils.

A fly buzzed past Faith's cheek. She waved her hand to shoo it away and was greeted by stares from the other diners. Embarrassed, she placed her hand back in her lap. Once the first course was taken away, a middle-aged man came in with the second course of chicken pie along with a ragout of cucumbers and a pie that spilled a rich flow of berries from in-between layers of flaky crust.

By the time the third course of desserts came about, Faith felt stuffed from the largesse. The crowded room felt stuffy and contributed to the waves of drowsiness that threatened to engulf her. She bit her tongue hoping the pain would keep her eyelids from drooping.

Finally, Martha nodded to the server. "We will take brandy in the parlor and discuss Ezra's holdings. My husband will join us. Daniel has been recovering slowly and tires easily. Nonetheless, he insists on being present. We need to settle Ezra's estate and move forward. It is what he would have wanted."

She led the others over to the parlor. Faith moved slowly behind the others. The only time she had been in that room had been when Ezra had been laid out before his funeral. As she moved over the threshold, she thought she detected the faint scent of lavender still trying to mask the lingering remnants of sorrow and decay.

Daniel sat near the empty fireplace, swaddled in a blanket. His skin looked yellowish in the afternoon light. Martha drew a plain wooden chair up close to him and took his hand in hers.

The others sat in chairs around the room forming a loose semicircle. A servant entered the room carrying a tray with glasses that sparkled when the man crossed in front of a window where the sun streamed through.

"I've taken the liberty of opening a bottle of French brandy for this occasion. Ezra had been saving it for the right occasion. I believe he would approve of us opening it now." Martha signaled to the server who began offering glasses to those assembled.

Faith set her glass down on the table. Although the liquid gleamed with amber fire that tempted her, she knew she needed her head clear. She looked at those around her, wondering what was going through their minds.

Louis broke the silence as he cradled the bowl of the glass in his hands. "While I respect that you wish to settle your father's affairs, I must point out that his beloved wife, Eugenia is not here." He raised a hand. " Let me finish please, we are, after all, family. I'm sure dear Ezra would want us to be just. There is no evidence she had anything to do with these tragic events. Indeed, they lived happily as man and wife for many years. While I do not know what happened to his will, I do believe he would wish she was provided for."

Daniel started to rise, only Martha's restraining hand kept him seated. "That woman killed my father and nearly killed me. He was revising his will before he died, he wrote and told me so. I can only believe that someone took it to avoid it being enacted, which leaves us, his true family, to take care of his earthly concerns."

Faith stilled when she heard the words "true family." Jon had told her that the children from Ezra's first marriage had struggled to accept Eugenia and her children, but she had realized that those feelings had lingered. She expected nothing from Ezra's estate, not after all he had already done, which left her puzzled as to why she had been invited to this meeting.

Martha reached over and stroked his arm. Daniel reached a hand to cover hers. "My brother Zachary will lead this discussion on what we consider to be an equitable arrangement."

Zachary rose to stand next to his brother's chair. "As the eldest children of my father, we feel that it has fallen on us to execute his wishes as we best understand them. I acknowledge that should Eugenia be proven innocent of the charges placed on her some provision should be made for her care. We will leave that discussion for later. For now, we will focus on my father's business interests." He went on to discuss ships Ezra owned interest in, along with the husband of one of his daughters, as well as a farm on the James River that Zachary managed along with property of his wife's family, that would go to him. Faith's attention drifted until she heard him state. "My father also invested in a small tavern run by Mistress Clarke. Since Daniel has business interests here, he will manage that."

Faith interrupted. "Your father very generously helped me clear a debt on my tavern. He in no way claimed ownership of it. That is my property."

Both brothers stared at her. "Can you prove this was a gift and not a loan? It was a substantial sum of money."

"I have a clear deed," she replied stubbornly. "He told me he expected no repayment, and I signed no note to him for the amount."

"So there is no written document of this gift?"

"No," Faith gritted her teeth. "You have nothing indicating it was anything else."

Zachary shrugged. "Our attorney believes we have a legitimate claim on your business, so unless you can prove otherwise…"

"I thought you planned to carry out his wishes, not mar his legacy with greed." Faith rose to her feet. "I will not let you take my inn. Ezra took care of his family, including us. He was an honorable man who looked after us after the death of my husband. Your behavior is a despicable mark on his memory."

Martha's voice cut through the tension. "No one intends to take your home, Faith. We all know how hard you have worked since Jon's passing. But Ezra's investment must be accounted for in some way."

"I've heard enough," Faith said. "I wonder what is really happening here. First Ezra dies, then his wife is conveniently imprisoned while his children plan how to use his wealth since his will has vanished. Too many people have died in this house under suspicious circumstances, and I believe the answer lies somewhere in this house."

"Are you suggesting one of us poisoned our father, and then Daniel?" Zachary asked.

Faith was too angry to back down. "Everyone here has a motive. Maybe we need to look at who, besides Eugenia, had access to poison and chose to use it."

A choking cry broke off the conversation. Louis grasped his stomach as he heaved and dropped to the floor moaning.

"Not again," Martha cried as she backed away.

Faith went toward her brother-in-law, only to stop as he began violently vomiting on the rug. She looked at the shocked family members. "Get a physician," she hissed. "Hurry!"

Louis's eyes rolled back in his head. "I'm dying," he cried as his body contorted over the rug, narrowly missing where he had been ill. He whimpered as he curled up on the rug, rising on an elbow to empty his stomach again.

Faith heard Martha calling servants to help Daniel to his room. Beatrice's voice could also be heard sending staff out for help. The parlor cleared except for Faith and Louis.

"Louis," Faith whispered urgently. "Did you see anyone touch your drink?"

Louis's eyes were closed. She thought he shook his head but wasn't sure if it was a negation or reaction to whatever poison he had been given.

He moaned loudly, clutching his stomach. "Forgive me, sister, for any sins

189

I may have committed. I want to go to heaven with a clear conscience."

Faith checked her exasperation at his dramatics. "I'm not sure you're dying, Louis. Let's see what the physician says." Louis rose halfway. Faith backed away in case he became ill again. A servant entered with a blanket.

"I heard Master Louis fell ill," he said.

Faith nodded. "Yes, he is."

"I'm Jude, I'm his valet." He looked down at Louis. "I help out when he becomes indisposed."

Faith noted his noncommittal face. "Does that happen often?"

Jude shrugged. "We all have our moments." He knelt down by Louis. "Master Louis, can you hear me?"

Louis nodded.

"Let's get you upstairs to your room so I can tend you."

Louis moaned again. "I'm dying."

Jude took him under the arms and helped him up. Louis heaved but was not ill. "One step at a time, sir. One step at a time." They left together, the servant supporting Louis out of the room.

Faith followed, eager to leave the foul-smelling parlor. Two maids went in with a pail and cleaning rags. She found the others in the entryway with the exception of Martha and Daniel. They looked as shocked as she felt.

"Is everyone else alright?" she asked.

Zachary answered her. "No one else has collapsed."

Beatrice looked over at her. "Trouble seems to happen when you appear Faith. Didn't you have someone die in your tavern?"

"Not by my hand," Faith retorted.

"As you noted, someone in the house is causing death. You were a frequent visitor of my father and you have been present when Daniel and now Louis fell ill just as you felt threatened."

Faith stared at her. "What are you implying?"

"That you probably have as much knowledge of poison as Eugenia and far more to lose. For all we know Ezra was calling in your loan and you decided to pay him back in a different manner."

"Really?" Faith said. "That's what you think? You're stupider than I gave you credit for, Beatrice. Ezra supported me and offered advice to run my inn. He was my dearest friend. As for the rest of you, why would I want to harm you? I barely know any of you." Her heart pounded in her chest, echoing in her ears. The injustice of the accusation infuriated her. "Ezra treated me as one of his own. You dishonor his memory with such behavior."

No one remained sitting. Faith noticed how quickly the men put the women behind them as if expecting an attack. Zachary's hair stood up in tufts, the short ends separating from the long strands pulled behind his head. He clasped his hands awkwardly, as he began to speak. "My wife spoke out of turn. I know Ezra regarded you fondly. But with all these poisonings, there has to be an answer. Someone is guilty of a crime."

Faith stared at him in disbelief. "Obviously, someone connected with this family is poisoning people. The question is why? We need to look for a reason someone would want all these people dead."

Martha spoke from behind Daniel. "The sheriff must be called."

"Yes," Faith said. "And we all need to stay here while he searches the house."

"For what?" Daniel said. Sweat beaded along his forehead emphasizing the waxiness of his complexion. The poisoning had left him haggard, but his eyes were alert as they met Faith's.

She shot him a grim look. "Poison. Whoever is doing this has easy access to poison. These attacks occur at a moment's notice, but someone has planned for them. Since we do not know who is behind this, we need to stay here and wait."

Beatrice stepped out from behind Zachary, pushing aside his restraining hand. "It could be in a pocket or tucked in a sleeve. We need to search each other."

Daniel's eyes bulged. "That's ridiculous. I won't be treated like a common criminal."

"Would you prefer to be poisoned again?" Faith's tone was dry. She was ready to act. All this arguing wasted time. "The ladies can search each other while the gentlemen do the same."

Martha emerged to stand with Beatrice. "Do not forget the servants."

"All of them?" Beatrice raised an eyebrow.

"Don't be ridiculous," Martha snapped. "We need only look at the servers who were with us when Louis took ill. Although I cannot imagine why anyone would want to poison him."

"Perhaps he annoyed the wrong person," Beatrice suggested.

Martha snorted. "That could include half the town. He's a poor gambler I'm told."

Faith let the women talk. She was not an intimate of this household and it helped to listen to how they engaged with each other. Even now as they awkwardly checked each other's pockets for signs of poison, Faith could see that the two older brothers and their wives were very comfortable with each other. They went off with their brothers-in-law. Ezra's daughters' Rachel and Eliza joined the women as they took turns, checking pockets, shaking folds of skirts and the folds of neckerchiefs.

Martha chuckled as her cap fell off. Eliza pounced on it and turned it inside out in her enthusiasm. "If you can hide something in your hat and keep it from falling out, I want to know your secret."

Faith turned about slowly as Beatrice went through her pockets and checked her sleeves. No fold went untouched. By the time the sheriff arrived, they had turned to the servants, Martha checking the serving woman and Zachary the enslaved man who had poured the wine. They found nothing.

As she straightened her skirts, Faith listened to the sheriff as he directed his men to search the property, in particular the still room. Two of his men went out to examine the kitchen. Faith wondered if Edith would decide to chop more of her powerful onions.

Once the physician arrived, he was directed immediately upstairs to attend the ailing Louis. The house was quiet except for the rise and fall of voices. It was time for her to leave and get back to her tavern. She missed the regular rhythm of the day, with the coming and going of souls needing food and/or a room. This house with its imposing formality left her feeling out of place. It wasn't her world, and she would have it no other way. Finding Martha in the small room Ezra used as an office, Faith made her excuses and headed toward the door. There was nothing to be gained by staying and she needed to prepare for the possibility that Ezra's sons would try to take the tavern from her. Zachary's words frightened her. She had worked too hard to keep her tavern running; she refused to surrender it without a fight.

Faith walked slowly toward the Duke of Gloucester Street, not only to keep the road dust off her dress but to marshal her thoughts as well. Ezra had paid her outstanding debt on Clarke Tavern with the understanding he could use it for the horses he kept for messengers to go back and forth but also to ensure he was not easily connected to the patriot cause. She doubted there was any documentation of their agreement. He had given her the note he'd retrieved from her original loan holder, Phineas Bullard, who had been killed himself a little over a year ago.

She was relieved to spot a familiar wooden gate before her. She opened it and entered the narrow green yard beside Georgia Clements' home and business. The front, which housed her print shop, fronted Duke of Gloucester Street. Faith chose to go to the door on the side, hoping to attract less attention.

Her light tap on the door was answered by Georgia Clements, who took in Faith's fine dress with a faintly surprised look before inviting her inside.

"What brings you here, Mistress Clarke?" she asked after leading her to the small room that served as office and parlor.

Faith shrugged, offering a small smile. "A little peace, and perhaps some wisdom, if you have the time."

"Well, I don't know about wisdom, but I am willing to listen to what you have to share," Georgia settled into an upholstered chair before offering Faith one across from her, a low table in-between.

Faith looked at her. Georgia Clements was older than her, her son was nearly a man. She had learned from Will that she had two older daughters who were married and had homes of their own in other colonies. But they were both women operating businesses in a world that favored men. She had no doubt that sometimes Georgia had faced tough choices to avoid losing everything she had. Drawing in a breath, Faith said. "As a fellow woman in trade, I was hoping you might have some insight on how to deal with a problem." Before she changed her mind, she plunged into the events of the past two hours ending with Zachary's threat to take her tavern.

Georgia said nothing for a moment, before rising to pour drinks for both of them. "Quite a lot happened in the past few hours. Which concerns you more, the attack on another family member or the threat to your livelihood?"

Faith paused before answering bluntly, "My business."

The other woman nodded. "That makes sense. The tavern provides you both food and shelter. I wonder if they want it or if they're trying to intimidate you?"

"Intimidate me. Why would they want that?"

"It's about control, dear. They can't reign you in when you own an independent business. You have no husband for someone to appeal to. They want to make sure you are manageable." She switched topics. "Do you have any papers from your father-in-law regarding the debt he paid for you?"

"He gave me the note that my husband signed for Phineas Bullard." She kept that in a safe place. Sometimes it didn't feel real, being out of debt. Ezra's stunning act of generosity had overwhelmed her. That paid note had given her a sense of security she had never had.

Georgia looked thoughtful. "My attorney, Mr. Jeffers, has helped me since my husband passed. I will contact him and ask him if he has time to discuss your situation with you. No one should be able to take your tavern away from you."

Faith sighed in relief. If an attorney could solve her problem, all the better. She had enough challenges as a woman running a business. She had no desire to try to survive under the thumbs of Ezra's sons.

The door leading to the shop opened, revealing Will McKay. He walked into the room with the slow, careful gait that he used since recovering from the arsenic he had accidentally ingested. His eyes were clear, but Faith thought the lines that creased the corners of his eyes and the sides of his mouth more pronounced. Surprise crossed his face at the sight of her sitting with the woman who owned his indenture.

His eyes swept up and down taking in her carefully upswept hair and dress. Will's mouth tightened as he took a seat on a nearby bench that rested against the wall.

"What brings you here?"

Faith blinked at his abruptness. "I came to speak to Georgia regarding a personal matter."

Will brushed a few stray strands of hair from his head and leaned forward. He closed his eyes briefly and took in a deep breath before letting it out slowly. "I didn't mean to show you the rough side of my tongue, Faith. It's been a long day and I've just finished with a gentleman with a less than charming disposition. Forgive me."

Faith nodded. "It's time I went home. I've chores to attend to before the sun sets." A basket of mending had been sitting by a chair next to the window in her room for days. It was not going to disappear on its own. Every moment she spent away from her tavern was another task left undone. It was time to go home.

Will smiled at her. "If my mistress permits, I will escort you home."

Georgia chuckled. "I believe I can manage for an hour or two."

Will's smile widened. "My lady is generous."

"I know better than to stand in the way of love."

Chapter Twenty-Four

The afternoon sun gilded the edges of leaves along the street as they walked together. Faith let her eyes gaze over Will as he walked beside her on the cobbled walkway. This time of day few people were on the street, having conducted their business earlier in the day. Most people were either home or rapidly headed that way. A carriage creaked down Duke of Gloucester Street, heading east toward the Palace Green.

She was glad to see that Will appeared to be recovering from the arsenic that had almost taken his life. Light filtered through the trees and dappled the ground around them. Before long, Will steered them down a side street where the rattle of wagons and movement of late travelers trickled away to almost nothing. Faith looked over at him. "Is there a place you need to stop?"

"Yes," Will said before he pulled her under an enormous oak tree. Underneath the privacy of its deep shadows, he kissed her long and deep. His lips were warm and gentle like the caress of velvet on her skin.

She startled at first, then relaxed as he wrapped an arm gently around her waist. His hold was easy, designed to show affection but not to trap. Within a few moments, he released her and stepped back.

"I've been wanting to do that for a while," he confessed. "But I wasn't sure whether you would accept it or slap me silly."

"Mmm," Faith pretended to think about it. "You were pretty forward with me. Do you think I should act properly and tap you with my glove?"

"No," he reached over and kissed her again. "I think you should take more long walks with the man who loves you and enjoy the beauty of a summer day."

Faith laughed. "I still have a tavern to run, you know." She took a moment to brush imaginary dust from her skirt and straighten her kerchief. Her cheeks burned with the blush covering them.

Will offered her his hand. "Then let me escort you home although I am sure Olivia has everything well in hand."

"She always does."

Together they stepped onto the dusty road, leaving the cobblestones behind as they moved beyond the bustling business area near the center of the city. Faith was sure Will knew where he was going, but the increasing solitude of the route made her uneasy. Although a few people were busy in the yards surrounding houses, few trod the street. Will turned off onto a narrow alley that ran parallel to Duke of Gloucester Street. Before long, they crossed the back area of one of the taverns. A voice broke out in a raucous song as someone exited out the back of what Faith realized was the Kings Arms.

Will released her hand and placed himself in between her and the yard that enclosed the tavern. His eyes scanned the yard. "Let's step a little quicker, shall we?" he said softly.

Faith complied, lifting her skirts so her feet would not step on them. Within moments they were past the tavern and the singing faded into the afternoon. They were back to the singing of birds and low of a few cattle behind a fence.

"Once we pass behind Shields Tavern, we'll be back on the main road," Will said. "It won't be long now."

Faith nodded. Her heart pounded in her chest as she continued to walk swiftly in her fine dress and shoes. Looking over at Will she realized he was falling behind so she slowed her pace to stay with him.

His face was flushed as he marched forward. "What are you looking at," he growled. "Keep walking." His left foot slid out under some loose stones causing him to stumble. For a moment she feared he would fall. She reached out a hand to help him before drawing it back quickly when he glared at it as he used a fence rail to steady himself before returning to walking.

Faith bit back a reply as she turned away. She didn't know what was wrong with him. First, he was tender and loving and now he was snapping at her. Hurt by his behavior, she picked up the pace leaving him behind.

Ahead lay a thick cluster of trees. Their branches arched over the path, leaving it in deep shadow. Past it she could see a road. To the left voices from the nearby tavern cut through the silence. A door slammed and the path grew silent again.

Eager to be home, Faith hurried onward, focused on the road that would take her back to the safe, secure world of Clarke Tavern. Already her mind turned to tasks needing to be done while the sun remained in the sky. She stopped short when a man stepped out of the woods to block her path.

"Where are you hurrying off to my pretty?" the man asked as his eyes ran up and down her body in a sly fashion. "Surely such a well-dressed lady has a few coins to spare a man down on his luck."

"I do not," Faith said. Her heart raced as she looked at him. Strands of dark greasy hair had escaped from its tie at the back. His stocky shape indicated he was familiar with physical labor as did his calloused hands.

"That's a shame," he said. "Nosy women should always be prepared to pay a price for their prying. You should stay home and mind your own business Faith Clarke, now I have to teach you a lesson."

Faith recoiled when his hand reached out, barely missing being grabbed.

"Leave her be," Will shouted as he closed the distance. His breath huffed loudly as he approached. The grim set of his mouth indicated he had heard every word.

"Oh, it must be lover boy, no wonder you are out wandering in the woods so late in the day." He looked at the sturdy stick Will had picked up. "Do you think you will beat me like a stray cur?" He grinned evilly, displaying yellowed teeth with gaps where some were missing. "You know, some people never recover from arsenic poisoning. They exist as shadows of what they once were, sickly and weak, dependent on others to the last of their days. You'd've been better off to have died when she could remember you as the strong, young buck you once were."

"Go away," Faith said. "You have no business with us."

The man laughed. "You are my business little tavern wench. Someone wants you to learn your lesson and quit asking questions."

"Who?" she asked hoarsely; "Who paid you to accost me?"

"Well, now," he said. "That would be telling. I'm many things but I'm no snitch." This time she failed to dance out of reach. He dragged her forward. Off balance, she staggered into a tree, the hard wood smacking the side of her face and shoulder. She almost fell.

Behind her, Will growled. She heard the stick smack into flesh. Her captor cursed as he released her, turning to face his attacker.

Faith turned to see Will stagger back, blood streaming down his face from a fist to the nose. He fell to the ground half-sitting looking dazed.

The man turned, as he reached for Faith, she clawed his arm as she kicked his leg, regretting she wasn't wearing boots instead of fancy shoes. He slapped her across the face causing her to gasp as stinging pain enveloped her. She screamed as he reached for her again.

A shot rang out above both their heads dropping a leafy tree limb on top of them. Her attacker cried out and grabbed his shoulder as he cursed.

The scent of smoke burned Faith's nose as she turned to look at the new threat.

Jeremy Butler stood a short distance away. A smoking pistol lay at his feet; a short sword was grasped in his left hand. He moved with lethal swiftness to the man.

"Who in hell are you?" the man cried out, backing away.

"A friend of the lady," Butler answered. "Now answer me, who hired you?"

The man picked up a branch, swinging it until it whistled in the wind. "This is no concern of yours."

Butler smiled grimly. "I say it is. You can talk to me and save your skin, or I can cut you to pieces for threatening these people. The choice is yours."

The man whipped the limb at Butler who leapt to the side with the grace of a cat before bringing the sword up to strike, this time slicing into the man's thigh. Blood ran down his leg, spilling onto the ground. Throwing his branch down the man turned and ran into the forest, Butler at his heels. Within minutes a scream rang out, followed by a dull thud.

Butler returned a few minutes later looking grim. His sword was tucked back into a sheath at his belt.

"Is he dead?" Faith asked as she knelt to check on Will.

"He fell over a log and broke his neck," Butler said bleakly. "I was hoping to question him." He joined her by Will who was struggling to sit up. "How bad are you hurt McKay?"

Will groaned. "I'll be alright. It was a lucky shot." He used a sleeve to try to stem the blood.

Butler handed him a handkerchief before leaning in for a closer look. "It's not broken, you're fortunate although I'll wager you'll feel it for a while." He rose and offered Will a hand. His glance swept over Faith. "What about you Mistress Clarke, are you hurt?"

Faith shook her head, regretting the action as her face ached in reaction. "Nothing too bad." She looked at Butler. "How did you know I would be attacked?"

"I didn't," Butler admitted. "I had some time to pass so I was in the tavern enjoying a meal when I saw him slip out. I didn't like the look of him, so I followed. I had no idea you were his target."

He studied both of them in the waning afternoon light. "We're not far from your tavern. Let's get you home and see if we can discover whose feathers you have ruffled this time."

Faith resented the implication that all this was her fault. She huffed as she stood up. "I have done nothing wrong."

Butler raised an eyebrow. "I didn't say you did. I believe you did something to unnerve our poisoner. A frightened criminal will make mistakes and I am counting on him to make one that will reveal himself to me."

Will looked at him. "You never believed it was Mistress Moore, did you?"

Butler shook his head as he handed the long stick back to Will. "Use this to support yourself. There are some tree roots that are easy to trip over." He returned to Will's question. "I wondered at first, but her poisoning Ezra made little sense. The man adored her and gave her everything she wanted. She didn't care about his politics as long as he kept her in silk and lace." He paused. "I saw no reason for her to poison the son either. He's an arrogant piece of work but she knew he'd be back to his estate on the James River before long. Whoever did this, had a reason. I just don't know what."

They trudged along in silence, shoes crunching on the gravel and branches lying along the path. Faith felt relieved when they left the shadows of the forest for the sunlit road. Only a few people hung about the outer gates of the Capitol for which Faith was relieved. She caught the stares at her torn dress and Will's bloody face and wished she were anywhere else.

Once they passed the gates of the Capitol, Butler took them down an alley that turned and twisted alongside houses and tenements until they arrived at the gate of Faith's tavern. Butler opened the gate and let them in.

Titus must have seen them from the window because he met them alongside the house within seconds. "What happened?" he said as he slid an arm around Will and led him around back. Will didn't object this time. He appeared dazed and would have fallen if not for Titus' support.

Olivia met them in a room at the back of the inn, just off the rear porch. Her eyes widened as she beheld Faith and Will. With a few sentences, Butler told them of the attack. She looked at Titus. "It's a good thing it's not supper time yet. Joshua and Dorcas can keep an eye on things while we tend these two." She gestured at Titus, "Can you tend Will while I take care of her," she gestured to Faith.

"I'm not hurt," Faith protested.

"Your face says otherwise," Olivia said. "We need to get a compress on that before the bruising gets worse. Come along, I doubt you want to undress out here."

Mutely, Faith followed Olivia to her own bedroom. Olivia shut the door and began the process of removing layers of clothing. She sighed over the dirt. "I'll have this delivered to the laundress, maybe she has a way to remove these stains." Once she had Faith stripped to her shift, she began checking for injuries, making a mental list of the herbs she intended to use. "I have some black oak bark I've been soaking. It will ease the swelling. I'll make some sage tea for both of you for headache."

Faith nodded numbly. Now that the shock had worn off, her face hurt fiercely along with her body. She was willing to take anything Olivia offered as long as she didn't have to face anyone. But she still had an inn to run.

"What about supper?" she asked tiredly. "You'll need my help…"

"Not tonight," Olivia said. "Tonight, you rest. There's not that many people here so it shouldn't be too busy. If it picks up, I'll put Jeremy to work clearing tables; it won't hurt him."

"Jeremy?' Faith asked.

"Jeremy Butler. Our conduit to the Sons of Liberty," Olivia replied. She went out and spoke to someone in a low voice. Moments later Dorcas brought in a basin and a basket of herbs, along with a cup of a blackish-brown liquid.

Olivia began her ministrations. "Jeremy is taking Will home, then he's going back to examine the body before he has someone 'discover' it in the woods. I told him to suggest to Mistress Clements that Will take it easy tomorrow. He's too stubborn to admit he's hurt and needs time to heal."

Stubborn was a good description of Will McKay. Too stubborn to admit weakness and too proud to accept any perceived sympathy. She was still angry with him about his behavior. She didn't care if he needed to walk more slowly. He'd nearly died.

Olivia offered her a warm cup of chamomile tea sweetened with honey. "Get some rest Faith. You will need it tomorrow." Faith lay back on the bed, watching the sun's light fade from the sky through the window. She didn't want to think about tomorrow, there were too many things unresolved today that left her confused. She fell asleep troubled by restless dreams in which she wandered lost and afraid, unable to find what she sought.

Chapter Twenty-Five

Jeremy Butler's boots crunched down the dirt road that was Nassau Street feeling the cool morning air brush across his ears under the tricorn placed firmly on his head. He had headed out early after downing a large mug of Athena's powerful coffee along with the ham, biscuits, and cornmeal mush she had plopped down in front of him as he blew on the mug in hopes of avoiding scalding his tongue. He looked up at her as the plate clunked on the table before him in her kitchen.

"You need more than coffee to fill your belly," she noted before turning to fill a tray with similar items to go into the house just a short walk away.

"Thank you," Butler said. He hadn't asked for breakfast, but Athena had a mind of her own. It had gotten her into trouble when she had been enslaved. As a free woman and his frequent associate in spying for the patriot cause, he was grateful for it. She had saved him from himself after his wife and child's sudden death from fever many years ago. She was one of the very few people whose judgment he trusted absolutely, even if he didn't always agree with her. It was the main reason he had left the coziness of her kitchen and taken off to consult with Gowan Pamphlet.

Nassau Street bustled with activity even this early in the morning. Despite the faint mist rising from the ground, wagons bumped down the dirt road heading to the market in the heart of town. Riders from various places also clopped along heading north toward Duke of Gloucester Street. Butler wondered about the Governor's mansion, abandoned by the King's royally appointed leader, some days ago. He'd sent word to his contacts at the Continental Congress. He doubted it would be long before someone staked a claim on it.

Butler continued down the road, not sure what he was looking for. The grass along the road was damp with early morning dew. Pamphlet had told him they met in a carriage house, but Butler couldn't wrap his head around how a glorified stable could be turned into a church. His Irish childhood produced images of sturdy stone structures with high steeples that cut into the sky. While logic told him that no such structures existed in Williamsburg, his imagination could not let go of it.

After walking the length of the street twice, he finally started paying attention to the people moving up and down the street and around the surrounding buildings. At first, nothing caught his attention. Then his eyes caught a small but steady stream of African Americans going in the same direction. Butler hung back but kept them in his line of sight until finally, he came to a relatively small building painted white. Inside voices sang praises to God. He waited outside for a moment before cracking open the door and stepping inside. To his surprise, it was standing room only. A few men near the door stared at him. Embarrassed, Butler doffed his hat and shuffled to a back corner. It had been a long time since he had been to anything resembling a worship service. Nonetheless, he copied the actions of those around him, bowing when they bowed and singing along when he recognized the words. Further down the wall he saw one of Athena's boys standing near a pretty girl he had seen before at the Wythe house.

After a number of songs, Pamphlet stood at the front and read from the Bible. Butler stayed for the entire service hoping to catch the reverend after it concluded. After another round of singing, Gowan Pamphlet dismissed his flock, who then proceeded out the door in an orderly fashion. Butler heard bits of laughter and a buzz of voices. All of which fell silent as people drew close to him. Butler didn't blame them. There were a multitude of reasons to distrust a white man if you were a person of color. The Reverend showed no surprise at his presence.

Welcome to the house of the Lord," Pamphlet said. His deep voice resonated off the walls of the building.

Rich and deep like maple syrup, a voice like that could draw a crowd and keep them enthralled for hours. Butler shook off the disturbing thought. He hadn't given much thought to God since his wife's death many years ago. It was a subject he preferred to avoid. "Have you had any success with the book?"

Pamphlet looked at him. His eyes were so dark the pupils were not discernable. They said a great deal that he did not. "Let's go back to the room I use for studying. We can talk there."

Butler fell in behind him. As they walked his eyes took in the interior of the church. Despite its humble beginnings, care had been taken to turn it into a house of worship. It had been painted white throughout which reflected light from the small windows. Spotless and clean, not a single cobweb resided in the corners or arches of the ceiling.

He followed Pamphlet to a small room in the back that was furnished simply with a couple of wooden chairs and a small table that served as a desk. Ezra's Bible lay on top of it.

Pamphlet sat down and gestured for Butler to join him. "I've been admiring your friend's copy of the scriptures. It's of excellent quality, bound together in leather, hand-stitched, and kept in excellent condition.

Butler nodded impatiently. "I know I've examined it myself. But I believe it is more than what it appears."

Pamphlet chuckled. "That can be said of a lot of God's creation." His broad hands opened the Bible and began gently thumbing through it. "You told me you thought your friend used this as a codebook. After looking through it myself, I believe you are correct." Gowan flipped toward the back. Here, in the book of James, he has marked this verse. "But be ye doers of the word, and not hearers only, deceiving your own selves."

Jeremy frowned. "What does that mean?"

"Exactly what it says. Each of his men had a like book of scriptures. Master Moore's instructions would come in the form of a verse. That's how he managed his apostles."

Butler's glance speared the other man. "You knew this already, didn't you? Are you one of Ezra's men?"

Pamphlet shook his head. "I serve one earthly mistress until she sees fit to free me. Otherwise, I'm a simple man of God and that is where my allegiance lies."

Butler leaned forward to demand more but backed down when Pamphlet lifted a hand.

"People tell me many things that I hold in confidence. Being an enslaved person is dangerous even with the most generous master. Your life is not your own and circumstances can change in a heartbeat. I will show you what this Bible revealed to me and hope it helps you."

His hands lightly pulled the cover backward toward the spine. "Interesting thing about this Bible, it has two covers. Between the two was a pocket large enough to hide a few things. "First of all, there is this note about four men he called Matthew, Mark, Luke, and John. I believe this is a rough map of regular meeting places where he had contact with them."

Butler looked at the roughly penciled shapes. As he squinted at them, his mind began to fill in the images. He recognized the long sweep of Duke of Gloucester Street. It was the other images that took a moment to identify. He silently blessed General Washington for introducing him to the craft of surveying many years ago when an adolescent indentured Jeremy Butler had been forced to march with his master along with the Virginia Militia. Washington noted his steady hands and eye for detail and recommended he be apprenticed to a surveyor, which was how Jeremy had ended up at an enormous farm in Maryland under the tutelage of its owner and the care of the woman now known as Athena Wise.

All the training benefited him now. Once he recognized a few of the buildings he had a good idea who Luke and John were. It was a start. He sat back from the table. "Thanks for your help Reverend Pamphlet," he said.

The other man smiled. "Call me Gowan. I've only been ordained by the hand of God, not by any seminary. It is only by his grace that my master allowed me to be educated well enough to read his word." He moved his hand to another document folded small. "I found this hidden in his Bible as well. It's a bit crumbled, like it was hidden quickly."

Butler unfolded it slowly, wincing as the paper crackled in protest. The words were in Ezra's own hand. His eyes widened as he realized what he held. "Many thanks, Gowan. This paper holds the answers to many things Ezra wished to have done. I will make sure it gets into the proper hands."

Pamphlet nodded. "I thought it was important. Do what you believe best with it. Just don't mention my part in any of this. These are dangerous times for all of us and I have no desire to be dragged into any conflict."

Butler nodded. "I will not mention your assistance to anyone." He stood and paused at the doorway. "If I have any other questions regarding the scriptures, may I call on you?"

Gowan Pamphlet smiled. "Yes, Master Butler. I'm always happy to help anyone seeking God."

Chapter Twenty-Six

Faith Clarke stood in the yard behind her tavern, watching Titus measure powder into the flintlock pistol that Jeremy Butler had sent her. Once he had tapped the amount he wanted into the barrel, he rammed down a patch to hold it in. He added ammunition, did a few more things, and pronounced it ready.

Titus held the gun with both hands as he aimed it at the unsplit log in front of him. It went off with a loud bang and a puff of acrid smoke.

Faith wrinkled her nose at the acrid scent arising from the discharge. She had held the gun briefly, enough to be startled by its weight.

Olivia's comment had been, "You want it heavy enough to knock someone in the head should you miss your shot. Once you've fired, you need to use the butt to strike."

Faith had felt the pistol's weight before. For a small weapon, it had respectable heft to it. Although she had used her father's brown Bess to hunt before her marriage and relocation to Williamsburg, she wasn't comfortable with the pistol. She had not intended to do anything with it before the attack in the alley. Her face still felt sore although the bruising was less than she had feared thanks to Olivia's ministrations.

The gun roared and belched out wisps of white smoke as the bullet smacked into the log. Titus blew smoke away before setting it down on the bench by the kitchen. "It's a nice piece, Miss Faith. With a little practice, it will serve you well."

"If you say so," Faith said. She eyed it cautiously before reaching to pick it up.

"The barrel will be hot," Titus warned. "You need to be sure of your shot when you use it. It's one chance only."

Faith nodded as she picked it up by its stout wooden end. "I've fired guns before Titus, just nothing this small." She blew on the barrel to help cool it, before loading it again under his direction.

"You only need about 30 grains of powder," he reminded.

She nodded and carefully loaded the pistol with powder, packing, and the single bullet before fully cocking the weapon. Using both hands she sighted down the barrel and fired it at the log. The roar deafened her for a moment. Smoke burned her nose as the weapon discharged.

"Not bad," Jeremy Butler said as he came into view from around the side of the inn. "Keep it where you can get to it easily should the need arise."

Faith looked over at him as she laid the pistol back down. "Why are you here?"

He smiled, ignoring her abruptness. "I've come to see your companion." He looked over at Titus. "Luke, I presume?"

Titus acted like he didn't hear. He bent over to examine the log. "You have good aim, Mistress. Maybe I should let you do the hunting."

Faith shook her head with a laugh. "I'm more than happy to leave that to you. I hate the skinning and cleaning."

Butler stepped forward, determined to continue the conversation.

"I believe you want to speak to me," Olivia said. She had emerged from her kitchen from where she had been chopping vegetables. A large knife was still in her hand.

Jeremy raised an eyebrow. "Olivia?"

She stood her ground, an implacable expression on her face. "Did you think only a man has ears? Ezra Moore valued talent over gender and skin color. He called me Luke because Luke was a healer and I know how to take care of people."

Jeremy nodded. "I meant no offense. In the time I've known you I never had a clue you gathered information for the Sons of Liberty."

Olivia gestured him into her kitchen. "You would be wise not to mention that name in public. This town is full of Tories." She went back to chopping squash. "There is plenty to be heard in the market and other places." The knife went in and out with a rapid staccato of precision. "Did you not think my people would have an interest in liberty?"

Butler flushed. "I have no use for slavery, Olivia. I'm sorry if you think otherwise. I'm trying to unearth Ezra's sources so I can continue the network. The patriot cause needs you and the others. Do you know who else worked with Ezra?"

Olivia shook her head. "He didn't speak of them, although I knew there were others. He referred to them as his apostles."

Jeremy nodded. He wouldn't have shared that information either. "I need you to continue doing what you have."

"Who do I send information to now?" she asked. "You're not in town often."

Jeremy frowned. That was another problem he had to address, finding a replacement for Ezra Moore as local spymaster. "I'll let you know. Right now, you can speak to me. I can drop by for a meal or a drink while I'm here. I'm sure Mistress Clarke will keep an account for me."

Olivia snorted. "I will let you discuss that with her. She turned to add vegetables to a pot over the fire. A slice escaped and hit a log with a hiss. She danced back a step, checking for sparks that may have jumped out.

Jeremy spoke to her back. "I will check with you later this evening. I have other business to attend." He walked out the door and into the back yard. Titus was chopping wood for the fire. The steady thump of his axe precluded conversation. Faith Clarke was not in sight, so he went up the back steps and into the tavern where he felt certain she was.

Faith Clarke stood in the main room of her tavern checking on her liquor supplies. A key hung from a cord around her neck, undoubtedly to the cabinet that housed bottles and small kegs. She stood when she heard him approach and locked it before turning to greet him.

"What do you want with Olivia and Titus?" Her hands rested on her hips as she stared down at him making use of her slight advantage of height.

Butler shrugged. "I had a question or two for one of them to answer. I'm not overly familiar with this town."

CHAPTER TWENTY-SIX

"Really?" Doubt filled her expression.

"I need to talk with you as well. Where can we speak privately?"

Faith took a turkey feather and began dusting the nearby mantel. "I do have a business to run. I can't step out every time someone demands a meeting with me."

"This concerns Ezra," Butler's tone was abrupt. "And does not need to be shared with everyone. His eyes swept the room, which was nearly deserted mid-morning. A man dozed in a corner kept company by a tankard. Another man read a newspaper near a sunny window.

"Very well," she said. Faith spotted Titus' teenage son sweeping the floor. "Joshua, please keep an eye on our patrons while I speak with Master Butler."

Joshua nodded and put down his broom. His lively dark eyes took in the nearly deserted room. He came to stand by the liquor cabinet.

Faith lifted the key from around her neck and handed it to him. "Until I return, you're in charge." She flicked a glance at Butler. "Follow me."

They went across the hall to her office. Her account book covered a section of her desk along with an inkwell, a feather, and a small knife for sharpening the quill. She shut the account book and moved it over out of sight. "What is so important? Do you know who killed him?"

"I wish I did," he said softly, unable to keep the anger from his tone. "I know what I would like to do to that individual once he or she is unmasked." One hand fisted unconsciously in frustration. He exhaled and withdrew a small, folded sheet of parchment from a pocket in his jacket. "I think you may find this of use."

Faith took the sheet with a puzzled look. As she unfolded it, her expression became intent. Walking over to a window, she held it to the light. The sun added highlights to hair not covered by her modest cap. A few tendrils curled loosely around her ears and temple as she read. Her lips moved slowly as she poured over the words.

As she read, a man walked in through the front door of the tavern. Faith ignored him. Butler gestured the man towards the main room. Shrugging, he followed his suggestion and headed in. His voice could be heard asking for cider to take the road's dust from his throat.

At last, Faith looked up. "Have you read it?" she asked. There was a husky note in her voice as if she were holding back strong emotion.

Butler nodded. "I have. Ezra considered you another of his children. It doesn't surprise me he would think of you and Andrew in his final moments.

Faith rubbed her eyes with her sleeve. "This needs to go to his attorney, immediately." She folded it and placed it inside one of the pockets inside the slit in the side of her gown.

"I'm escorting you," Butler said firmly. "I'm not taking any chances."

Faith nodded. "Thank you."

Chapter Twenty-Seven

They walked swiftly down Duke of Gloucester Street until they reached the attorney's home just off the Palace Green. Although Faith knew it was at least a mile, it felt like they arrived within mere moments. The doorman eyed them with caution when he opened the door.

"The service entrance is around back," he said in a voice almost as deep as Butlers. "I will inform the butler of your presence."

Butler prevented him shutting the door by pushing it open with a booted foot and a strong arm. The man fell back, panic on his face. "Fear not, my good man. Our business with your master will be brief and hopefully, beneficial to all."

As they entered the hall, the attorney stood in the doorway of an inner room. His wigless bald head gleamed in the light streaming in from the open door. He showed no surprise at the intrusion.

He nodded at his servant. "Shut the door, Thomas. We will take tea in my study." He gestured at the two of them. "Come in."

Faith wasted no time once they had entered the sanctity of the office. "Take this," she urged as she handed over the parchment.

The man paused to don a pair of spectacles with small circular frames. He unfolded the document carefully, his expression becoming intent as he focused upon it.

"This is Ezra Moore's handwriting. I've seen it many times." He looked up at them. "This appears to be his will. Where did you find it?" Minutes passed as he read the text, pausing from time to time to reread a section. Ezra's cramped hand filled two pages. The writing became sloppier as it ended, the last two paragraphs and the signature far more jagged than the rest.

Butler answered. "He hid it in his Bible. I found it today with the help of a pastor."

The attorney looked at them. "This pastor will swear to this, in court if necessary?"

"He would," Butler said, "Except that the court does not accept the testimony of the enslaved."

The attorney paused. "You're referring to Gowan Pamphlet. A number of my staff attend his church. By all accounts, he is an honorable man. Nonetheless, you are correct. Our court system does not accept the testimony of any person of color. It is regrettable." He tapped a finger on his desk. "So, all I have is your word."

Butler nodded. "And I would prefer to be kept out of this business."

"That may be difficult. His sons will want to know how it came to be found."

Faith spoke. "Could you not tell them it was found in his Bible? Surely they will recognize it."

Butler reached into his pocket and removed the volume. The leather was looser than it had been although the stitching still held the pages of the text together. He handed it over to the attorney, who looked at it dubiously.

"I will send word that a will has been found. Some of the directives in here will cause discord within the house."

"Maybe it will settle things as well," Faith said. "Too many people have died in that house. I cannot help but believe that greed may be at the heart of it rather than political leanings."

Butler glanced over at her. "I think you're right." He turned to the attorney. "When can you be ready to call on the Moore Family?"

"Give me a moment to prepare and we will be on our way."

The moments it took for the attorney to don his wig and button his coat seemed to last forever. By the time he declared himself ready, his driver had pulled around to the front of the house. As he handed Faith up into the carriage, he said. "I sent a messenger to the house; hopefully the family is ready to receive us.

Faith doubted anyone was going to be ready. As the carriage jolted forward, she reached to catch herself on a side wall.

Jeremy Butler sat across from her. He glanced over at her as they sped toward Ezra Moore's home. Despite the rain that had fallen overnight, the wagon traveled smoothly over the roads until it reached its destination.

Faith was grateful for the chance to avoid getting mud on her dress. Her hem was already damp from walking over the grass in her own yard. She was careful to wipe her shoes before proceeding down the walk to the front door.

The Moore children were waiting inside. Daniel rose to meet the attorney. He ignored Faith. Martha indicated a seat beside her which Faith gratefully accepted. Butler had disappeared although she felt certain that wherever he was, it was where he would hear everything.

The attorney cleared his throat. "What I believe to be Ezra Moore's will, has been given to me. I would like to share its contents with you."

Daniel spoke from the upright chair to which he had settled opposite from his wife. "How do we know it is my father's actual will?"

"I recognize his writing," the attorney began. "I can also see handwritten notes I had put in the margin the last time he and I met regarding his affairs. It falls in line with what we discussed that day. Without any evidence to the contrary and given it was hidden within his personal Bible, I believe this is his."

"Very well," Daniel said. "Let's hear what it says."

The attorney rose and began to read. After a few seconds, Faith no longer heard the attorney, but Ezra's voice as she remembered it, before he fell ill.

"I leave my shipping interests to my eldest son Daniel who has always enjoyed commerce. My estate on the James, comprising some 300 acres to my son Zachary, who resides on an adjoining property with his wife and children along with the slaves, livestock, and indentured persons to make use of as he sees fit. To my daughters, Rachel and Eliza, I leave each an equal property that once belonged to their mother to be divided on either side of the stream that runs the length of it. To my current wife Eugenia, I give the house in Williamsburg, all the servants, and livestock, and an annual percentage of the profits from my trade here in town to keep her provided for. To Faith Clarke, who I regard as another daughter, I leave clear title to her establishment known as Clarke Tavern and enough money to provide for the education of her son Andrew in a profession of his and his mother's choosing."

The bequests continued on to pensions for elderly servants, requests for manumission for a few others. It ended with an abrupt statement. "I leave Louis Clarke, son of Eugenia, the clothes in his wardrobe, and my prayers that God forgive him for all his transgressions."

The attorney stopped speaking. "That is all that is written. I'm afraid I have no explanation."

"I do," Jeremy Butler strode into the room. "Does anyone know why Louis would have a bottle of ipecac in his room?"

Faith was startled. "Ipecac? That's a purgative. There's no reason to take it unless…"

"You wanted to fake an illness?" Butler's silky tone did not mask the icy rage underneath. "Where is he?"

Martha looked shocked. "He rose today for the first time since he fell ill. He said he was planning to call on Louisa Paget. She has sent notes and baskets of treats made by her cook in order to help him recover."

Beatrice snorted from her place near the mantel. "The widow Paget is nearly Eugenia's age. The only reason he would be courting her is financial. Her late husband left her very well endowed, and her sons are in London completing their education."

Faith rose. "I know where she lives. I will take you there."

Together they left the house. Butler walked so swiftly Faith broke into a trot to keep up. He leaped aboard the lawyer's carriage, causing the driver to squawk. Faith followed suit, grabbing up her skirts to make the leap up to the seat. "Tell your master, we will return his conveyance shortly," he said before pushing the other man to the ground and putting the horses into a brisk trot."

Faith grabbed the side of the carriage as it jolted forward. "Do you know what you are doing?" she called out.

"Confronting a killer," he returned. "Now where are we going?"

"She lives down the road from me, close to Christiana Campbell's tavern."

Butler snapped the whip lightly over the horses' heads. They began to run down Duke of Gloucester Street. Faith held tightly to the side as they began to weave around the slower wagons in the street. She watched a man leap out of the way and into a puddle. He raised a fist and began shouting curses at the speeding carriage.

"I would prefer to arrive in one piece," she called up at him.

"You will," he said. "There's not much traffic now. We should be able to make good time. If we're lucky, we catch him before he's finished his tea."

Butler slowed once they passed the Capitol, taking the horses back down to a trot before stopping in front of Faith's tavern. "We'll walk from here," he said. "The carriage will draw too much attention." He handed her down and handed the reins to a startled Titus. "Walk them a little before you put them in the barn. They've had a run and would benefit from a gentle hand."

Titus nodded. "We'll take good care of them."

Butler took Faith's arm. "Take me to Mistress Paget."

In truth, the house was a stone's throw away down Waller Street. Faith had never had cause to enter the immaculate white house, but she had admired it in passing.

Butler studied the simple brick walkway before guiding Faith around back to the servant's entrance. He watched as a dark-skinned woman exited the door with a tray, entering what was likely the outdoor kitchen. "Stay quiet," he ordered as they went up the steps and into the house.

Faith stayed behind him as he followed the sound of voices to the parlor. As they entered, Faith saw an older woman with immaculately curled hair pouring tea for her brother-in-law. Louis smiled at them although his eyes remained watchful.

"Sister Faith," he greeted. "What a surprise. I had no idea you and Louisa were friends. I'm afraid you're a bit late for tea, we've already started."

Louisa Paget didn't look pleased. "I didn't hear my footman announce guests."

Butler blocked the door. "Don't worry madam. It will be a short visit. I desire a word with young Louis."

Louis raised an eyebrow. "Who are you? I've seen you lurking about Faith's little inn. I meant to inquire." He looked over at Faith. "A woman should be careful of her reputation. Rumors can start so easily."

Faith looked at him. "Ezra's will has been found. He left you nothing."

Louis didn't look surprised. "Ezra always was careful with his money, unless it involved Mother. Now, she understood that everyone needs a little pocket money."

" Was that why you killed him?" Butler said. "Because he wouldn't pay your bills?"

Louis blinked. "That's a terrible thing to say. Do you have any proof for your accusation?" He set his teacup down gently on the table and rose to his feet.

He wore an elaborately powdered wig tied with a dark blue ribbon. His dark blue suit featured scarlet and yellow flowers up the sides and along his cuffs. His vest strained around his belly. Huge white embroidered birds flew up towards his stock just making it over the curve. Faith could not begin to contemplate the expense.

"You've been stealing from him for a while, haven't you?" she said. "Daniel caught you, but I bet Ezra did too. That's why he cut you off."

"You are upsetting my intended," Louis said softly. "Louisa and I will make a lovely life together far from this provincial hole known as Williamsburg. Already we've been planning to sail to London to the home she owns there and you two will be forgotten along with all the other dogs barking revolution." He pulled his left hand out from behind his coat revealing an elegant but deadly dueling pistol. As they watched, he completely cocked it, pointing it at Butler. "Louisa's husband was a collector of many fine things. She gifted me with this set of pistols just before you arrived." He gestured to a carved wooden box on the floor that Faith had not noticed.

"You've only got one shot," Butler said as he watched Louis.

"That's all I need, dear man." Louis smiled revealing a dimple on one cheek. "Precious Louisa, please go out and send someone for the sheriff.

We can't have people break into your home and threaten you. It's rude and uncivilized."

Louisa rose and slowly circled around out of range of the gun. Her face under its façade of powder had turned pale. As she left the room, her shoes clattered as she hurried away.

Louis looked disappointed. "I've been courting the old woman for weeks now." His head turned, following the sound of running feet as they went down the hall and out the door, slamming it behind them.

Butler tackled Louis, knocking him to a chair as the gun went off filling the room with a deafening sound as it fired. Acrid smoke caused Faith's eyes to tear as she tried to see what was happening. Two men wrestled on the floor, knocking over furniture.

The tea set crashed to the floor smashing the delicate china. As Faith slipped away, she saw the wooden box the pistol came from. As the men rolled toward the mantel, she grabbed it and set it on an untouched side table. The other pistol lay inside. She lifted it out with care, wondering if she could club Louis with the wooden grip. As she lifted it, she smelled powder. The gun, like its twin, was loaded. "Idiot," she muttered. She cocked it and balanced it in both hands, not liking what she might have to do. "Stop," she shouted.

No one paid any attention to her. Someone pounded on the door behind her, trying to get in. Butler must have locked it to prevent Louis from escaping. Faith started toward the door. Louis rose and made for the window, which was open, to catch a breeze. Butler stood and headed toward him; Louis laughed, leaned down, and grabbed the edge of a rug, yanking it suddenly.

Butler fell back into Faith, knocking them both to the floor. The gun roared as it discharged. Through the haze of smoke, Faith heard Louis scream.

A dark stain spread over the arm of his suit. He threw himself out the window. Butler followed.

Faith unlocked the door, letting in the butler and a handful of servants wielding clubs, axes, and a rolling pin. She left them for the door, opening it to see if she could see either man.

Outside a misty rain had begun to fall, obscuring the view and turning the road to mud. Through the rising fog, Faith saw Louis at the gate before he opened it and ran into the street. Through the milky haze, a dark shape moved down Waller Street. The driver urged the animals forward through the mud slick road. She heard the shrill neigh of the animals as fright overwhelmed them. Amid the rearing and kicking of animals, Faith heard a faint cry before it was drowned out by the curses of the driver struggling to control the team. The wagon trundled halfway past the house before it rolled to a stop.

Faith hurried down the walkway, sliding on the wet cobbles. Before she had reached the gate, Butler was at the scene in the road. He knelt briefly before rising back on his feet revealing a crumpled heap in the mud. She paused before opening the gate.

The driver walked back after turning the wagon around on the deserted street. As Faith approached, she heard the man say, "I never saw him, poor fool."

Butler saw Faith approach. He moved swiftly to block her path. "You don't want to see this," he said. "He's dead, far beyond the justice of this world."

Rain-soaked her hair and skin, streaking down her cheeks to drip off her chin. She shivered but didn't feel cold. "Is it really over?" She asked.

Jeremy nodded. "I need to go. Tell the sheriff everything. He will handle the details." With that, he bowed to her and headed down the street. His presence soon obscured by the mist and rain.

Faith watched him go. There was nothing more she could do besides explain to the sheriff, who she saw walking in the rain toward the house.

Chapter Twenty-Eight

The next day brought no news until long past the midday meal. After speaking to the sheriff, Faith had gone home. The rain had cleared by midnight, having washed away all traces of what had occurred. Titus looked over at her. "He'll come see us when he has something to share."

Faith went back to minding the liquor. A few people had come in for drink or to share a game of dice. Her brother Seth cleared the tables of those who had left.

She was surprised to see Zachary Moore enter the tavern. "Welcome to Clarke Tavern," she said slowly. "Could I offer you a drink?"

Zachary shook his head. His eyes were shadowed as if he had slept very little. "Can we speak in private?"

Faith nodded and led him into her office. He stood and looked about the small room. "You like doing this?" he asked.

"I like having choices," she said. "This is my business and I make the decisions needed in running it."

He nodded. "My brother and I have decided to honor my father's wishes. We will not press a claim on this establishment." He paused for a moment. "He left you a small amount. Once things have settled, my brother and I will arrange for it to come to you." He looked around at her modest room. "I imagine there are many ways you could use the money."

Faith nodded, choosing to ignore his less than gracious assessment of her tavern.

"Is there anything else I should know?"

"Eugenia is home. My brother and I are looking at residences within the city." He paused before turning to go. "I have no hard feelings against you, but I have never considered you part of my family. I think it best we leave it at that. Farewell, Faith Clarke."

Faith watched him go, wondering if she would ever have cause to visit any of the Moores again. She hoped not. She had already received word of Eugenia's release from the gaol, so all of her obligations were complete.

She turned to go back into the taproom when she caught sight of a familiar fair-haired man. Jeremy Butler looked none the worse for wear. Faith paused to see if he would speak.

"Would you go with me to the kitchen?" he asked before walking down the hallway to the back door and exiting.

Puzzled, she did as he asked. For once, Faith had no sharp retort to remind him who was mistress of Clarke Tavern.

Olivia greeted him warmly and offered him a seat. "It's past dinner time, but I can fix you a plate if you like."

Butler shook his head. "I've eaten, but I wouldn't turn down some of your cider if you have some available."

Faith said, "I'll get it." She filled a tankard and set it on the table.

Butler lifted it up, "My thanks," he said before taking a long drink.

Faith waited for him to finish. She was in no hurry for whatever news he might bring.

Butler studied her with his pale gray eyes. They were unnerving in their intensity. "Ezra trusted you a great deal. I always considered him an excellent judge of character."

"Thank you," Faith said, surprised.

"That's why I wish you to continue his legacy."

"What do you mean?"

"Ezra managed information for the Sons of Liberty of Virginia. He kept me apprised of events. I want you to do the same."

"You already use my home as a listening post," she replied.

"I do, but you can do more. I need someone who lives here to manage Ezra's contacts and let me know anything of value."

Faith's heart hammered. "You wish me to be your spymaster."

"Not exactly," he smiled. "Although I believe you would make an excellent one. I wish you to check the dead drops I will show you and pass on anything of note. I need you to carry on with Ezra's cause since he no longer can."

"You can do it," Olivia said from her place near the fire. "Titus and I will help you."

"Why would you do this," Faith asked the question she had wondered for some time.

"Because liberty should be for all," Olivia replied. "And that's what I hope will come of this."

Faith looked at both of them. She already knew her decision. "Very well then, let's get to work."

Later, after going over some details with Jeremy Butler, Faith left the tavern in the capable hands of Olivia and Titus in order to share news with Will. She had not seen him since the altercation in the alley. She worried he had hidden injuries from the fight.

Duke of Gloucester Street bustled with business. Despite the burgeoning conflict with Great Britain, the town appeared as yet unscathed. She doubted that would last for much longer.

A bell on the door jangled as she went in. Georgia Clements smiled at her from where she checked to see if leaves of newsprint had dried. "Greetings, Mistress Clarke, it is a lovely day is it not?"

"A very lovely one indeed," she answered. The sun had dried up the streets and now shone down from a vivid cerulean sky. Outside the clear glass panes of the shop, a mockingbird sang its song perched in a large maple. Faith carried a market basket on one arm. She removed a few letters for mailing and handed them to the other woman. "Could you mail these for me?" she asked."

Mistress Clements took them from her and read the addresses. "Pennsylvania, I see."

Faith nodded. "I have family there." That was true, although these letters weren't for them. Changing the subject, she asked. "Where would I find Will?"

"He's out back. He's been working on repairing a table for me. One of the Randolph children fell on it and broke a leg."

Faith gestured to the back door. "Would you mind if I walked through?"

Mistress Clements smiled. "Not at all. I'm sure he will be happy to see you."

Faith found Will sitting on a bench smoothing what she presumed was a replacement leg for the table. "Hello," she said, sliding in beside him.

Will nodded. His expression remained intent on the wood before he placed it between them.

Faith reached for his hand. She barely touched his fingers before he flinched and moved it back to her side. "What is wrong?"

His expression turned sad. "I've been meaning to call on you." He waved a hand about the yard. "I have many responsibilities for my mistress that have kept me here."

Faith looked over at him. "I think she would have given you time to see me. I've been worried about you."

Will sighed. "Aye. We both took a tumbling the other night." His gaze turned reflective. "I should have been able to protect you. You needed me and I failed."

"You did not," Faith protested. "He was a large man and neither of us expected it."

"I should have. I know the dangers of working with Jeremy Butler."

"That had nothing to do with him," Faith said, worry creeping up her spine. Will wasn't acting right.

Will put down the wood and turned to look at her. His gaze was bleak. "I've wanted to speak to you in private. I'm not recovering quickly. No one knows when or if I will get better." He held up a hand to stop her from interrupting. "Let me finish, Faith. Please."

"Georgia will keep me on. She says I'm doing plenty enough to earn my keep although I doubt that." Will brushed a hand over his eyes. "I've thought a lot about us, what kind of future I could offer you like this. You deserve better. You deserve a whole man, not an invalid. I'm releasing you from your promise to wait, Faith. It's the only honorable choice left to me."

"No," Faith said. Shock jolted her heart into jerky rhythm. "You haven't given yourself enough time to recover."

His smile was sad. "It's been over two weeks and I'm not much stronger than when I was first able to rise from the bed. I don't sleep. I can barely eat. Setting type takes me half the day and that's with the help of Georgia's son and our journeyman. It's not enough." He rose from the bench and walked back toward the back entrance of the print shop. He moved slowly as if the weight of the world had settled on his shoulders.

"Go home, Faith Clarke. I'm letting you go." He opened the door before stepping inside and shutting the door in her face.

Faith stood staring at the merry blue paint before turning to stumble down the steps and back home, the aching in her heart a raw wound. Despite all her hopes and dreams, revolution was not only taking place in her home, but also her heart.

Numb, she turned toward home, down Duke of Gloucester Street, past the bustling businesses and crowds of people engaged in life. She breathed in and out, focusing on what she could control, pushing aside the chaotic emotions raging within. She couldn't think, couldn't allow her feelings to break through and tear her apart.

As she crested the brief rise at the end of the road that led to the Capitol, she stopped to stare at the imposing brick structure. It looked indestructible, although she knew it had been rebuilt from the ashes of fire many years ago. Now it stood, stronger than before as if the destruction it faced had motivated its designers to design it to weather whatever it might have to face.

Faith wiped her face, wishing she could wipe those last few moments of her life away as well. From the shade of one of the trees that reached over the walls surrounding the Capitol building, she took a moment to breathe out and in and again. It did little to ease the ache in her heart. She wanted to yell at Will for his hard-headedness and then weep at the despair on his face. Most of all she wanted to throw herself in bed and cry until no more tears came. But none of that was possible. She had responsibilities, obligations, and too many debts to pay. The best she could do was put one foot in front of another and pray that one day, the pieces of her world would come back together. "I will get through this," she said although she wasn't sure she believed it. Taking a deep breath, she turned and headed home, the only place she knew she belonged. Inside its doors lay peace and stability. It was her whole world and she would do anything to protect the family within.

As she approached, two familiar boys darted across the yard, fishing poles in hand. One tall and dark like his father, the other fair with curls that would not stay tame. Titus stood on the other side of fence surrounding the tavern, watching them before he saw her approach. Faith raised a hand in greeting. She wasn't ready to talk to him or anyone else. Instead, she walked past the gate on the far side, where a bench beckoned in the shade of the trees. Sitting down, she looked out at the place she now owned free and clear of debt, except the one she owed Ezra to continue his dream. She would aid his cause and keep her family safe, somehow. Tears streaked down her face as she let herself grieve over all the broken dreams shattered within the space of a moment. Tomorrow, she would rise and start anew, one day at a time until her heart was whole once more.

A Note from the Author

Some may wonder where I got my ideas and while I admit to a highly active imagination, some plot pieces are based in fact. History buffs may recall that George Wythe, Thomas Jefferson's mentor as well as a signer of the Declaration of Independence and the Constitution, was in his later years a victim of poisoning by an avaricious nephew. That event served as a loose inspiration. Other events such as the seizing of the contents of the Williamsburg arsenal and Governor Dunmore's exit are well documented historic facts.Gowan Prophet was a real person who was both a pastor and enslaved to Jane Vobe. I don't know if he aided in the revolution, but I do know he was an important member of the African American Community. The Baptist Church on Nassau Street appeared some years later after 1775. I moved it to Williamsburg a few years early so that Rev. Pamphlet would be available to help in solving the mystery.

Acknowledgements

Nothing is created in a vacuum and I am fortunate that I have both friends and family who are wonderfully tolerant of my interests. A special shout out to Aunt Barbara Esther for her eye for detail and thoughtful questions.

About the Author

Julie Bates grew up reading a little bit of everything, but when she discovered Agatha Christie, she knew what she wanted to write. Along the way, she has written a weekly column for the *Asheboro Courier-Tribune* (her local newspaper) for two years and published a few articles in magazines such as *Spin Off* and *Carolina Country*. She has blogged for Killer Nashville and the educational website Read.Learn.Write. She currently works as a public school teacher for special needs students. She is a member of Mystery Writers of America, Southeastern Writers of America (SEMWA), and The Historical Novel Society. When not busy plotting her next story, she enjoys doing crafts and spending time with her husband and son, as well as a number of dogs and cats who have shown up on her doorstep and never left.

SOCIAL MEDIA HANDLES:
  Facebook: Julie Bates, author
  Twitter: JulieLBates72
  LinkedIn: Julie L. Bates
  Instagram: juliebates73

AUTHOR WEBSITE:
https://juliebates.weebly.com

Also by Julie Bates

Cry of the Innocent

Writers Crushing Covid-19 (anthology)